molly jones and the little shoppe of horrors

Red Rock Ranch Mysteries #2

Morie Smith

Salt & Honey Publishing

*For my Mommom—
my Marge inspiration,
And my aunts Jean, Peg, and JoAnne—
my JoBeth inspirations.*

prologue

"HI! Did you find everything you were looking for?" Two college aged girls with matching blonde blow-outs and Lululemon tennis skirts bounce up to the marble check-out counter, each with a wicker basket full of merchandise. As I pull out candles, scarves, a coffee table book, and other assorted items, the two girls look at one another, and then around the shop again curiously. I've been watching them wander around for the better part of thirty minutes, like they are clearly looking for something in particular but aren't quite finding it on the large, round, display tables or hand carved wooden racks scattered around the open floor of the Shoppe. They've aimlessly picked up the most random assortment of items and dropped them in their baskets with unimpressed, blank looks, and I'm not sure if I should take their selections as insults or compliments at this point.

After a minute or so of awkward silence while I ring up their purchases, one finally leans close to me across the counter. "This... this is where they found that body, right?" She whispers, arching her eyebrows conspiratorially as a small smile spreads across her face. Her friend behind leans forward and wiggles her eyebrows, too, clearly interested in the answer.

I pause, holding a scarf in one hand and looking warily from the girls to my friend, Mandy, at the adjacent counter expertly poking lavender stems into a large summer floral arrangement. She rolls her eyes ever so discreetly as she turns to me and slides behind her arrangement so the counter customers can't see her face. "Um, yes, we had a bit of an incident a few weeks ago before we opened. All a big misunderstanding, and I can't really talk about it," I laugh nervously as I start stacking their purchases in a craft paper gift bag with our intertwined R Red Rock Shoppe logo embossed on the side. They both give me an expectant look, like they need more details, but I try to ignore them as I finish up their transaction. "Your total is $178.32. Will that be cash or card?"

They exchange another bothered look before one pulls a credit card from a small bag looped over her shoulder and around her torso. In my day, we called those fanny packs, but I've been told by my twelve-year-old daughter they've had a bit of a rebranding and renaissance, and are actually cool again, just not to wear on your actual fanny. She taps it on the card reader and scribbles a signature on the screen. Her receipt shoots up from the printer and I slip her copy in the bag as I give them a big smile and slide the bag across the counter to her.

"We came all the way from Dallas because we're huge true crime junkies. We thought it might be fun to shop where there is a mystery going on, you know? You can't tell us anything?" The other one pleads, shooting me large puppy dog eyes as her friend begrudgingly pulls her purchases off the counter with a sulky yank.

"You drove three hours to shop here because we found a body in the attic?" I ask, trying to temper what probably sounds like old lady judgment in my voice. I probably did some equally, if not dumber, things in my college days but sheesh, that's dumb. And gas was a lot cheaper back then, too.

"Well, yeah. We were listening to Trudy Grimes's podcast *Trudy Crimes* about wild unsolved mysteries in Texas and this was featured in the up and coming stories last week. We just wanted to see it in person. You can't tell us or show us anything?" Blondie #1 pouts out a bottom lip that looks like it has had more than just God's help to be as plump as it was, and frowns to her friend. Her friend gives her a frown in kind and they both stare back at me with their matching injection-fueled puppy dog pouts.

"I'm sorry, girls, but I can't talk about it and honestly, Trudy Grimes shouldn't be talking about it either, whoever that is. But I appreciate y'all shopping with us today. Come back and see us again," I shrug, giving them another apologetic smile and deciding to take their selections as a compliment while silently patting myself on the back that we might reach an even younger demographic than I planned. My goal was a "Kate Middleton meets vintage western" vibe, and I was banking on us hitting with the 30-50 crowd, but maybe that's an even cooler style than I thought it would be.

"Whatever, it's fine. At least I knocked out my grandma's birthday gift."

chapter
one

"Alright, tell me again when you first saw it?" There are two beads of sweat rolling quickly from his forehead down his temple like they are having a race, and I'm so distracted by whether the left or the right one is going to win, I nearly miss Sheriff Cooper's question. Before I can answer, he takes a bandana out of his back pocket and wipes from temple to temple across his forehead, and my interest is quelled. We've been standing in the tight upstairs hallway for a little over an hour, without air conditioning, because the electricity to the building hasn't been turned on yet. My plan had been for my husband Shep and me to take a look around inside quickly for planning purposes, and then head out to lunch at the Mexican food restaurant down the street. It's only late spring, but the tight space, plus no air circulation, and the sun beating through the high, old windows has us all sweating profusely, and no closer to any answers than when we started.

"Shep and I wanted to look in the attic, so we pulled the string, and it fell out like it was resting on the pull down door. It fell on the floor, and when we saw it, we went straight out and called y'all. You're up to speed, Coop. For the fourth time," I say, trying not to sound as exasperated as I feel. I crossed into hangry territory a while back, and I'm starting to wonder if keeping me from eating long enough to make me want to smack a goat is a prerequisite for law enforcement interrogations since that's been my primary experience every time.

"Alright, alright. And no idea who it might be?" he questions, not even looking up from scribbling on his palm-sized notepad for my answer. There is a touch of sarcasm in his voice like he doesn't truly believe I have no connection with this body. I stare at him silently until he finally stops and makes eye contact with me. He raises his eyebrows like he is expecting an answer, and I just throw a hand in the direction of the body with an emphatic snort.

"Sheriff, how am I supposed to know who that is? It doesn't have a face," I reply pointedly, my voice sounding a little shriekier than I want. There is a long, pregnant pause as we stare at one another– me defiantly, and him expectantly– without words. After a period of direct eye contact so long that it would make even a psychopath uncomfortable, we both look down to the person in question lying in a heap about three feet from us. Crime scene investigation officers are carefully laying out numbered tents and cordoning off the body and attic pull down door while Cooper and I have our staring contest. The body in question truly is a heap—all the arms and legs are sprawled at unnatural angles and it barely resembles a person at this point as it is mainly a skeleton held together by the tattered remains of its clothes. He finally concedes and returns to his notepad, furiously taking more notes.

It's at this moment that I look around and notice that my husband seems to have vanished into thin air. As I was telling my story to Sheriff Cooper this last time, he was lingering in the corner near the stained-glass door to the first floor, but that corner looks pretty empty now. "Coop, where did Shep go?"

Sheriff Cooper looks up from his scribbles and glances around too. "Oh, uh, I think he's down with the paramedics." He absently gestures toward the first floor before turning to a CSI officer. "Make sure you get pictures of the exact angle the body fell. We need to be able to gauge where and how the body was in the attic prior to the door opening. Molly, how long have you owned the building?" He turns back to me as I am halfway out the door to check on Shep. I stop short and check my watch.

"Um, about twenty-one hours, sir."

"I beg your pardon?"

"We closed yesterday afternoon; we've not owned it even a whole day."

"Did you look around before you closed?"

"Well, yeah, but not the attic. I'm not generally a fan of attics, so I didn't check it before now."

"What about your inspector?"

"I have no idea. I can get you a copy of the report, but I don't really remember if it said anything specific about the attic. Like I said, it wasn't high on my priority list to check, you know? I was more focused on making sure it said 'wiring won't kill you by burning the place down', and 'pipes aren't poised to burst any second and cost you a fortune'," I reply sarcastically, trying to peek through the door down the stairs to see if Shep is on the first floor.

"Well, maybe you should have looked a little harder for 'dead body in the attic', huh? Especially given your track record these days," he retorts, giving me another pointed look that wiggles his mustache slightly. I give him a short and pointed laugh in reply, along with a silent stare, and he returns the stare for another long moment before turning back to CSI to ask more questions. I take that opportunity to slip down the stairs and look for Shep, concerned about why he could be getting care from the paramedics.

"... I think that if you try the omeprazole once to twice a day, and you still have symptoms, it might be time for an EGD. But I can't really say for sure since I don't practice anymore, you know?" Shep is standing with a group of three EMTs near the front windows and one looks like he has cornered Shep to get free medical advice and answers on his GI ailments. You can take the physician out of the practice but sometimes the practice chases the physician down against his will.

"Hey, Shep? Can I speak to you over here, please?" I politely interrupt their impromptu clinic visit, and Shep's face washes with relief as he claps the EMT on the shoulder and quickly joins me over by the stairs.

"How's it going up there?" he asks, tugging at his Under Armor t-shirt a little to get some air flowing in it. A member of the Sheriff's Department opens the front door to slip in and we both enjoy a few seconds of breeze before it becomes stiflingly still again.

"Nothing new since they got here," I say, pausing before glancing around to make sure we are out of earshot from everyone. "Shep, who do you think that is?"

He looks at me wide-eyed and slightly panicked. "How should I know? I didn't get to finish taking attendance on all the ghosts that live in this haunted hole before that one interrupted! You don't have any ideas?"

"Not a clue. I don't even know if that's a man or woman. I'm guessing old either way because I feel like older people are on the smaller side, and that person is smaller. Don't people shrink as they age?" I feel like I am reasoning through utter nonsense, but I'm so shaken up, I can't think straight. "Do you think Asa knows about this?" I turn to Shep with sudden concern and try not to jump to conclusions. My question came out as a whisper, but one of those harried, scream whispers, and Shep jumps a little in surprise.

"Do you think Asa would sell us a building with a known dead body that could be easily tied back to him?" Shep asks in a hushed voice, looking to either side of us to confirm there is still no one within earshot.

Asa Shoemaker sold us the historic Russell building after he began downsizing all his assets following a murder attempt and estate scam by his ne'er-do-well niece (and my somewhat arch-enemy) Becki Lane, and his ranch foreman, True Walker. Becki and True had schemed together to take out Dick MacDougal, our neighbor across the road for his estate, and then take out Asa to inherit it all outright. Dick MacDougal had absolutely no friends or allies left in life, and with that, the sheriff's department was more than willing to let it roll and call it natural causes without another word, second, or sniff, but with my pushing and well, nosiness, we uncovered the full plot of murder, extortion, and elder abuse. The entire ordeal left Asa run down and ready to simplify, so he sold out his ranch land to a fellow rancher and good friend of ours, and sold his gorgeous two-story red brick stunner of an antique building to us to start a curated boutique featuring fresh beef from our ranch. His centuries old farm house was donated to the Crawford County historical society to become a ranching heritage museum, and he is now comfortably nestled in a one bedroom apartment at the Cinnamon Court retirement village playing bingo and drinking mocktails (with the occasional whisky snuck in). He is one of the kindest men I've had the privilege to know, and my gut tells me that there is absolutely no way he knows there is... was... has been... a dead body in the attic of this building for an indiscriminate amount of time.

"Well, no, that wouldn't make sense." Just then, we hear

the stairs creak heavily with footsteps as the Sheriff and several of his deputies descend from the second floor.

"Alright, Joneses, we are going to be taping off the second floor here until CSI can finish documenting the crime scene, and complete the removal for further testing. We will be keeping the entire building on lockdown until all that can happen, but you can have extremely limited access to the first floor if necessary with prior given permission. Since we have your sworn statements, you are free to go at this time, but please be available for further questioning in the immediate future. We will be needing a copy of your closing paperwork and your inspection report as quickly as possible, and we need the name of the seller," Sheriff Cooper drones off his list, and I briefly zone out when I hear that we're not allowed in without permission for an indeterminate amount of time. While I'm obviously sympathetic and all about the unidentified body that deserves justice currently in residence upstairs, this is really going to wreck my carefully crafted time table to getting my dream boutique open.

"Mrs. Jones? Molly?" Shep elbows me as Sheriff Cooper is looking to get my attention back from my daydreaming and mental schedule rearranging. "Uh, yes, we can do that," I say, not really knowing what I'm agreeing to since I wasn't listening, obviously.

"We've got all that paperwork in a file in Molly's car, Coop. We can follow you to the station to get copies made. We bought the building from Asa Shoemaker. Part of his liquidation prior to going into assisted living at Cinnamon Court," Shep answers for me, and I nod in agreement once I get up to speed on what we're talking about.

"We've actually got duplicates in the file, so you can have the extras. Any idea when the building might be released, sir?" I ask tentatively, trying to balance my curiosity with sensitivity. I realize that body is someone's... someone, but I'd love to get going on the Shoppe sooner rather than later. I've already hired some staff, and I hate the idea of letting them down for an indeterminate period of time, or worse, risking losing them to jobs they can actually work.

"My guess is CSI is going to move as quickly as possible in order to preserve as much as possible from the crime scene," he replies, tucking his notebook back into his vest and moving to the door. We follow behind him to grab the paperwork out of my Suburban, and I pause for a second as we move through the door.

"Wait—crime scene?"

Sheriff Cooper looks at me like I'm not the brightest suspect he's ever interviewed and nods slowly. "Yes, the crime scene. Upstairs." He points upward with his pudgy index finger, then moves out onto the porch.

"Yes, I realize where you are referring to, but I just meant, like a crime scene? Like you're positive a crime happened up there? That body is the victim of a crime, for sure?"

"As opposed to what, Molly?"

I hesitate for a second. "Like an accident? Don't you think that body could be there because of an accident, maybe?" I offer tentatively. I'm optimistically hopeful he will consider this, and maybe lean more toward this in an effort to wrap it all up quickly, especially considering that's what happened the last time.

"I could be wrong, of course, but generally speaking, if it's an accident, it doesn't take this long to find it. And we've got to be extra sure we're crossing all our t's and dotting all our i's this time. We've taken a bit of a public whomping the last few weeks about almost letting the MacDougal thing slip through, so we've got to get this one right." He pats me sympathetically on the shoulder and readjusts his straw Stetson. "We'll get it figured out as quickly as we can, and anything you can do to help will be appreciated." I give him a flattered smile, grateful that all my work and meddling might actually be respected and valued. "Well, of course, Sheriff, I'm happy to help in any way."

"Good deal. Probably the most helpful thing you can do right now is to cooperate when needed, don't gossip around town, and stay out of our way."

—

"Mia! Hayes! We brought you lunch!" Shep and I come through the side door to our kitchen a little later, weighed down with plastic takeout bags full of lunch for our twelve year old Mia, and ten year old Hayes, plus our twenty-something ranch hands Cooter and Roy, who feel like our two additional children a lot of the time.

I step through the kitchen into the family room to see Mia curled in an oversized navy gingham armchair reading a worn copy of *To Kill a Mockingbird* with headphones in. Hayes is in a loud and rowdy Mario Kart race with Cooter and Roy on the old school Nintendo unit hooked up to the large TV hung over the fireplace. It appears that Cooter's car containing Mario is slowly bumping along directly behind Roy's Luigi, and both of them are being handily beaten by Hayes as Donkey Kong.

"Coot, get off my butt, man!"

"It's called drafting; look it up!"

"I'm smoking both of you, who cares!"

Shep lets out a long, loud wolf whistle and the entire room grinds to a screeching halt. "Y'all want your lunch before it's soggier than it already is?" He holds up the two plastic sacks, he is farmer carrying for them to see, before setting them on the kitchen island behind him. Mia bookmarks her book nonchalantly and makes her way to the kitchen, pulling out a

Styrofoam box of chicken tenders and mac and cheese that she takes into the breakfast nook, about as far away from the noise of the living room as she can get.

Hayes makes it over the finish line a few seconds later and tosses his controller on the coffee table before heading into the kitchen to grab his lunch. Cooter and Roy putter to the finish line a few minutes later, essentially tying, but continuing to argue about the winner as they toss down controllers too, and come looking for their take out boxes. Shep and I stand in the kitchen, slightly dumbfounded, as we watch the four of them eat their food in near silence. We were a decent amount of time later than we had told them we would be, and yet, no one has hardly acknowledged our presence. We spent the morning with a dead body, and it would seem everyone hardly cares.

"Did y'all check on that group we moved to the northwest yesterday?" Shep asks Cooter and Roy as they are shoveling enchiladas and Spanish rice in their mouths like there is no tomorrow. I hand them both napkins and sit down for what feels like the first time all day as they look back and forth at one another to determine who is going to answer Shep.

"Uh, we did," Roy mumbles, keeping eye contact with his foil take out container. Shep raises his eyebrow in concern, but stays silent just to see if either of them will share any more information unprompted or if he needs to continue this specific line of questioning.

After a few long seconds, Cooter can't take the awkward silence anymore, and lets out a quiet, nervous laugh. "Sir, how many calves are supposed to be in that pasture again?"

Shep pulls out his phone and scrolls through our management software app to confirm. "There should be twenty five in that pasture."

"They were the group 12 ET calvers?" Cooter asks, finishing up his lunch and looking back to Roy like they are up to something.

"Was everyone there or not, guys?" I sigh as I get up to make myself an afternoon cup of coffee and try not to completely lose my patience with them beating around the bush.

"Well, we counted several times and we only came up with twenty four. Do you think one could have gotten caught up somewhere?"

Shep sighs, and I know this is the last thing we need in the middle of dead bodies and an indefinite postponing of the Shoppe opening. Things happen every year and we've never made it through a calving season without losing at least one calf. We've had some heartbreaks and some wild circumstances, but at the end of the day, sometimes nature just isn't kind. What's weird though is that these are already a few months old and were born to experienced moms, making it especially unusual for them to be potentially missing. That calf was an embryo transfer born using a recipient cow, meaning it would be in a group intended to be the best of the best of our genetics, and would theoretically be the worst of the worst to lose.

"Alright, let's finish up lunch and ride out there to double check. It could be lagging back over by the gate we moved them through, or maybe in that brush. We need to take inventory and see which one we're missing exactly. I'm gonna print that calving list and we'll head out in a few minutes." Shep moves through the kitchen into our office to print records as Cooter and Roy simultaneously stand and throw out their lunch trash before heading to the side door to get horses ready.

As I dump a few generous tablespoons of creamer in my coffee, Shep hurries back through the kitchen and gives me a kiss on his way out. "Y'all be careful!" I call after them and sit back down on a kitchen stool with my coffee. I feel like I've been awake since yesterday and it feels like I'm barely holding my head up at this point.

"Hey, Mom?" Hayes says after a few minutes as he walks past me to throw away his lunch trash.

"Yes, bud?"

"Mimi called while y'all were gone. She said to tell you someone needs to check on Great Marge."

"Did she say why?"

"No, just to call her when you get home and she'll tell you what's up." He shrugs, and heads up the back stairs to his room as I heave myself off my kitchen stool to grab the cordless land line. The combination of the lack of information from my pre-teen boy, and the endless possibilities of issues that could be arising from my mother and her mother have me worn out before I even dial the number.

Years ago, when my parents retired, they decided to be snowbirds-winters in Texas and summers in the sandhills of Nebraska where my dad grew up. It has worked well for them for the most part, but my grandmother, Margaret, has always been a pistol and sometimes needs additional supervision when they aren't in town. She was in her late forties' when I was born, and insisted she didn't want an "old" sounding grandmother name, so she suggested "Grand Margaret" at the time. Obviously that was too much of a mouthful for a small child, so it was gradually shortened to "Grand Marge". Since she is my kids' great grandmother, they adopted the name "Great Marge" for her, and she's given up any semblance of having a dignified grandmother name as this whole vain debacle has clearly backfired on her. She's currently in her late eighties, and is mostly with it, but has an eccentricity that seems to grow with age.

After three rings, my mom picks up the phone in what seems to be a rush. "I can't talk long because we're moving heifers right now, but I need you to go check on Marge. She called me in a panic this morning because something broke, I think? I just need to make sure she's physically fine, and then fix whatever is wrong. And if you can plug her Ring camera back in, that would help me a lot." I hear bellows at varying volumes and the steady hum of a UTV in the background, so I can tell she and my dad are out in the pasture on the move. They run their own commercial cattle between their ranch here and their property in Nebraska, as well as some of ours we are developing to be embryo transplant recipients.

"Why is her camera unplugged?" I ask absently, rummaging through the pantry to find something chocolate. Like any woman in her forties, I probably shouldn't have sugar, but some things are worth the consequences. I find a bag of chocolate sea salt caramels on the very top shelf that I must have pushed up there for such a time as this, and I take them back to the counter to bust into them.

"Because she's convinced the government uses them to spy on her. The joke's on her because it's not the government, that's exactly what I use them for. I try to hide them in places I don't think she'll find them, but when she does, she unplugs them and I can't see what's up with her. Plus, she usually causes a ruckus by unplugging it. That's probably why something broke. The one unplugged should be in her dining room facing the sitting room, so just hide it in the knick knacks somewhere and plug it back in, please."

"You got it," I warble through a mouthful of chocolate and caramel, trying to hear my detailed instructions through the cacophony of cattle noise.

"How is everything else there? Did you get your building squared away? Are you still thinking the opening will be in four weeks?" They had just taken off back to Nebraska before I found our neighbor a few weeks ago, so they missed our first murder debacle. It put them in quite the tizzy of worry not being here for it, so I hesitate whether to make them worry again by sharing the second one.

"Um, yes, it's sort of squared away. The opening may end

up being pushed out a little, though. We found something in the attic that needs to be taken care of before we can start working again, but I think we can fix it quickly."

"Oh, no. Is it mold? A news story popped up on my phone that mold is rampant this year because of all the early spring rain. It's incredibly expensive to eradicate mold. I had a friend one time that ended up having to demo his house because it was cheaper than eradicating the mold."

"No... no, it's not mold... it's, uh... anotherdeadbody," I say, running the last, least savory part all together quietly so maybe she won't understand it and we can just wrap it up and move on.

"Did you say a DEAD BODY?" She screeches out every separate word as I brace for impact. I should have known nothing gets past Mimi.

"Just like the skeleton of one," I offer timidly, hoping that makes it sound better.

"Go back to the house. I have to go back to Texas," I hear her shriek to my dad and the strained chug of the ATV trying to make a turn.

"Mom, you don't need to come back! Y'all have stuff going on up there and Dad needs your help. We're fine here. We have no idea who it was, so it's not like we're in the middle of it this time. The sheriff's department is handling everything, so we're fine. They just have our building plans on hold for a little bit until they figure it out. Promise me you won't come back right now."

I hear a snort in disagreement, but she doesn't say anything. I hear my dad tentatively ask what is going on, and she quickly tells him she'll explain it to him when they get back to the house. "Mom, seriously. There's not anything you can do here. For real, the authorities are handling it this time."

"They sure didn't last time! If it wasn't for you, a cold

blooded murderer would be building a cattle empire right now!"

"I mean, yes. But it's not like that this time. I don't know anything about the person they found, or anything going on. I'm just waiting for the go ahead to get back in the building to start the prep for the Shoppe opening."

After another very long pause, she seems to finally relent. "Okay, we'll stay put. For now. But if anything changes, we're coming back. And we'll be back in four weeks whether you are opening or not just to check on y'all."

"Okay, sounds good, Mom. Y'all be careful moving those heifers," I say, hoping to wrap this up.

"Alright, you be careful checking on Marge. She's the real one to worry about around here."

chapter
two

"MARGE? ARE YOU IN HERE?"

An hour or so later, Mia, Hayes, and I quietly slip in Marge's side door from her car port. Marge moved into one side of a duplex on the outskirts of Buffalo Creek several years ago, with her sister JoBeth moving into the other side. JoBeth is ten years younger, never married, and has no kids, so to an extent they take care of each other, insofar as two women in their seventies to eighties do. In reality, they both need supervision and mainly just keep one another company while getting themselves in and out of the kind of trouble women in their seventies to eighties are good at finding.

We are met with an odd smell, like something burnt, but also like something old and musty. Mia wrinkles her nose while Hayes quickly ducks his head under his shirt collar to hide his face up to his eyes. I smack him on the arm silently as we all glance around looking for Marge, who isn't in the living or dining room.

The three of us tentatively approach the swinging door to the kitchen and brace ourselves for what we might see on the other side. "Grand Marge? It's Molly," I say as I timidly push the door and peek around it, throwing out a hand to signal the kids to wait for me to see what is going on first.

I hear a small, quiet chuckle coming from the middle of the floor where my grandmother is sitting, covered in blobs of something dingy white and bright yellow. Her microwave door is slowly swinging open on her countertop, and the culprit of whatever is covering her and most of her kitchen seems to be steaming inside it.

"Molly! I'm so sorry it's such a mess in here!" she says when she sees me standing dumbstruck in the doorway. I am still trying to figure out what I'm looking at when the door swings again and smacks me in the behind as my kids come barreling on through to check it all out.

"Great Marge, what happened?" Hayes exclaims, tiptoeing through the mess right up to her, and picking a few blobs out of her backcombed white bob. Mia gingerly steps over to her other side, and together they pick her up off the floor and set her in a wooden chair at her kitchen table.

"Well, sugar, I don't think my eggs cooked like they were supposed to," she says quietly, wiping a time weathered hand across her forehead. I grab the roll of paper towels off the holder on the counter next to me and rip off a few to hand to her. She dabs her face, knocking off little chunks of cooked egg to the linoleum floor. Mia and Hayes dust off the other chairs at the table and take a seat with her.

"What do you mean, Marge? Were you trying to hard boil eggs in the microwave?" I ask, picking up what I think is a stray scrap of egg shell off the counter before I lean against it.

"We have a senior ladies' luncheon on Monday for our Bible study group and I just wanted to make a little dab of potato salad to take. But it's so bloomin' hot out, I didn't want to heat up my kitchen to hard boil my eggs. I've done them in the microwave plenty of times but they just blew right up on me today," she says with a little devious chuckle, and I try to stifle a laugh. My mother would come unglued on her mother if she were here right now, so Marge should probably be glad it's me and the kids.

"I'm glad you're okay, though... Are you sure you're okay?" I take a peek in the microwave and see there is an empty bowl with no water—the likely reason they exploded instead of cooked evenly—and then glance back to give her another discerning look up and down to make sure she is actually okay.

"Yes, yes, I'm fine. But what am I going to do about my potato salad? That was the last of my eggs and I can't make it without them." She seems legitimately distraught and I shake my head a little that this woman in her late eighties just evaded death by exploding eggs and is most concerned about the other old bitties at the church judging her for what she does or doesn't bring to their gossip laden get together.

"We'll figure something out, don't worry. I can make you something to take and give you a ride. Mom said you called her because something was broken. Is there something else that happened this morning?"

"Oh, I found another one of those blasted government cameras and when I pulled it out, one of my little snow angel babies broke. I left it in the dining room, but I need her to make sure we get rid of all those cameras."

"Okay, we can figure that out for you. Where's JoBeth?"

"She's at the library board meeting." Grand Marge waves a dismissive hand before turning back to the table and patting Mia and Hayes on their arms respectively. "Now, how are you two? I'm so glad you came to see me today. Mia, did you bring your embroidery with you?" she says with a genuine smile. My kids have been visiting Marge at least once a week since the day they were born, so her increasing eccentricity is nothing out of the ordinary to them. Marge has been teaching Mia simple embroidery since giving her a kit for Christmas, and they've been slowly supplying the family with pillowcases and small scenes with sayings I find a little cheeky for a twelve-year-old and eighty-eight-year-old.

"It's good to see you, too. Yes, I brought it if you want to work on it with me?" Mia replies, pointing to her quilted Vera Bradley tote bag at her feet. Marge nods and they move into the matching floral upholstered arm chairs in her sitting room while I continue working on cleaning up the spongy egg remnants all over the kitchen.

"Hey, Hayes?" I ask quietly as he gets up from the table to follow them into the sitting room. "You want to help me with a secret mission?"

He sidles up next to me to indicate his willingness and I lean over to give him discreet instructions. "Mimi says Marge has a Ring camera somewhere in her dining room facing the sitting room that she's unplugged. Can you find it and hide it somewhere new without her seeing what you're doing?"

"Do I just hide it in the breakable crap?"

"Hey, language, bud," I scold, stifling a laugh. "But, yeah. Hide it in the breakable crap and don't leave the cord out for her to find or trip over."

Later that afternoon, after relocating Marge's camera and cleaning up her priceless-to-her, but worthless-to-anyone-else figurine, I promise to cover her contribution for her ladies' luncheon, and the kids and I pack up to head home. As we pull in the driveway, I see Shep and the boys hauling bags of our weaning to yearling bull and heifer development feed out of the feed barn and stacking them on the driveway nearby. I pull up my Suburban to a point that I won't block their pathway and get out to see what's going on now.

"Is it a leak?" I ask tentatively as the kids head inside. So far today we've had a crack of dawn workout, a dead body in the attic, possible missing calves, exploding eggs, and now some sort of issue with feed storage to work out, so there's no telling what surprise is around the corner. For the most part, we have large grain bins that distribute feed into buckets or trucks to dispense around the ranch, but we do keep a few tons of bagged feed on hand to take to properties further away. Damaged or lost feed means higher operating costs and more inconvenience– the last thing we're looking for on this endless day.

"Nope," Shep replies, heaving a bag onto the driveway, looking a little short on patience and sociability. I cringe and wait for elaboration that comes a few seconds later from the peanut gallery.

"It's a rat, Boss!" Cooter yells over to me as he carries a bag on each shoulder, and I roll my eyes that he seems a little too excited to be the informant.

"Seriously?"

Shep nods and points to a stack of feed on the driveway with a variety of large holes on the corners. I involuntarily shudder and hold my hands about three inches apart, silently asking if we are hopefully talking about a small mouse. Shep takes my hands and spreads them a few inches to be more like six to seven inches apart and I screech in response.

"We'll clear everything out and set some traps. We need to make sure those doors are staying closed and sealed as much as possible," Shep says, heading back for more bags. He is likely saying that for the benefit of Cooter and Roy and the kids, as I very rarely make trips into the feed barn these days.

"Did you actually see the perpetrator? You saw a rat that big?" I ask, trying to inconspicuously back away from the barn without being necessarily noticed. I've grown a lot more accustomed to critters of the rodent and slithering persuasion since becoming a full-time country dweller/ ranch wife, but I'm not going to hang around and make friends if I don't have to.

"We saw a shadow of something running out, and based on holes that size, that's what we're estimating," Roy explains, tossing out two more bags. The garage door starts to open and they begin to move the stacks from the driveway into our garage. We haven't really ever used our garage for parking our cars, but using it for feed storage is new.

"Well... I've got to go start on dinner," I say, jerking a thumb toward the house and continuing to back away, praying they don't ask me to jump in and help. It's not that I won't or can't help haul feed sacks from a rat palace, it's just honestly that I really don't want to.

"Okay, we should be done in about thirty minutes. What are you making?" Shep asks, taking a second to wipe his brow and adjust his Red Rock ball cap.

"We have a few different options, but I was leaning toward ratatouille," I say while cracking a smile and throwing out my elbow jokingly, hoping he thinks my joke is funny enough to lighten the mood.

"If there's a little guy in there trying to help, let me know. Getting him in there would save us a lot of time and hassle compared to moving everything out here."

⊏⊐

"Alright, Grand Marge, you are good to go. Just give me a shout when you are ready for me to pick you up." At the stroke of 11:15 on Monday, I pull through the covered portico at the back door of the church to drop Marge off for her luncheon. While she is technically old enough to be a member of this group, JoBeth has never really chosen to socialize with them, preferring instead to attend a non-denominational study at the community center once a week, so Mom or I typically take Marge to her church bible study commitments. I reach behind the middle console and pull up a craft paper bag with a chocolate fudge Bundt cake for her to take in. She peeks inside the bag and frowns a little, like this doesn't really meet her standards and I try not to roll my eyes. I'm not a master baker by any means, but my cakes do have their own little reputation around Buffalo Creek. Plus, it's not like I'm sending her in with a bag of Cheetos and or something else equally not homemade—that fudge sauce and frosting is as from scratch as you can get. I have a feeling there is something underlying about me usurping her dish to take, and she is resistant to bring something that she didn't make herself.

Before I can ask what her issue is, I see an older pea green Lincoln Continental the size of a yacht slowly creep into the handicap parking perpendicular to the portico in my periphery. Marge seems to spot it at the same time, and instinctively slinks down in the passenger seat a little. Geraldine Farwell, Buffalo Creek's own crypt keeper, starts her crawl toward the door hunched over a Rollator piled high with a granny purse, a Tupperware bowl covered with a plastic hair cap, and an ancient Bible with worn down pages and a cover barely hanging on.

"I don't know why she carries that Bible around like she actually reads it or does anything it says," Marge quips icily, crossing her dainty bird-like arms over her chest. I will admit that Geraldine Farwell isn't my favorite person-I think she's a sour old gossip-but I wouldn't say I have a personal vendetta like it sounds like Marge does. Geraldine meets every check box to be the classic definition of a blue hair–an ancient granny car, a weekly hair appointment, her nose in everyone else's business, and a sweater/ pants set in every color of the pastel rainbow.

"What did Geraldine Farwell do to you?" I ask, stifling a laugh as I debate starting a timer on my phone to see how long it takes Geraldine to get across the portico. I'm certain I've seen solidified molasses move faster than her at this point, and I'm curious why it seems like Marge is trying to hide because

I'm also certain Geraldine Farwell couldn't see a flashing neon marquee unless it was the size of an elephant and right in front of her thanks to macular degeneration.

Marge pauses, purses her lips, and sighs, like this is very difficult for her to share, and I'm starting to wonder what top shelf drama I've been missing in the senior ladies' Bible study. "A few weeks ago, she told the ladies at a Thursday morning prayer meeting that my famous potato salad is..." She pauses again, staring up at the ceiling of my car like this is one of the worst things she's ever had to share with me. "Store bought."

She whips her head around to look at me dramatically, expecting that I will be appropriately outraged at this grievance. This is basically the Southern old lady version of saying Geraldine Farwell brutally murdered a litter of adorable puppies and wasn't the least bit sorry about it, or something equally egregious.

"Is that why you were trying to make potato salad for this?" I ask quietly, mental puzzle pieces clicking together as she seethes at Geraldine through the windshield. I have a decent tint job on my Suburban, but probably not enough to counteract the laser eyes she's giving right now. She ignores my question, choosing to stack up her own granny purse and worn-out Bible instead. "Well... I'll tell anyone who asks that your very homemade potato salad is one of my favorite family recipes." I pat her on the arm in reassurance and she rolls her eyes slightly.

Geraldine finally makes it into the building as one of the other ladies holds the heavy glass door open for her and Marge heaves a sigh. "I need to get inside."

"Do you need a hand?"

"No, I've got it, thank you. Thank you for the ride, Molly." Her attitude seems to relent a little and she squeezes my arm across the console.

"Any time, Grand Marge. Just call me when you're ready.

Or call me if you need bail money," I joke and wink at her, and she looks slightly scandalized before realizing I'm kidding and reluctantly laughs.

"I'm not planning on that, but I'll keep that in mind." She exits my car, and heads in with her unwanted Bundt cake and I realize in that moment that even the strongest of women, and the most experienced of women, can still sometimes really define themselves by what others think.

After running through my usual errands at the dry cleaners, post office, and car wash, I swing off the main street of Buffalo Creek and circle the pale pink bungalow known as Delilah's into her drive through for a little sweet treat. I idle behind a red Jeep as I wait for my turn to pull up to what was the laundry room window of the house in a former life, and pull out my phone to scroll for a few minutes. Just as the Jeep hits its brake lights like they are about to pull away, my phone rings in my hand and Shep's name and number pop up on the screen.

"Hey, can you give me a minute?" I say as I roll up to the window where Shay, Delilah's high-school aged window help, is waiting for me.

"Are you already at the sheriff's department?" Shep asks, seemingly ignoring my request.

"Hi, can I get a medium iced vanilla latte and a strawberry lemonade cookie, please?" I say to Shay with a hand cupping the microphone of my phone before turning my attention back to Shep. "What are you talking about?"

"Didn't Cooper call you? Where are you?"

"I'm at Delilah's. I gave Marge a ride to the senior ladies' luncheon and I'm waiting to pick her up. Why would Cooper call me?" I put Shep on speaker to scroll back through my call log to make sure I didn't miss anything.

"He called the landline here looking for both of us. They

want us to come in because they have a positive ID and have questions for us."

My heart quickens and I try to keep my breathing under control. No one I know is missing, and we've not done anything wrong to be in connection with this, but it's still a little nerve wracking for some reason. "Who is it?"

"Didn't say, just that they need to talk to us. I'm on my way to town now. Meet you there in ten?"

"Okay, see you there. Do you want anything from Delilah's?"

Shep pauses, and I know he's having the internal debate of wanting a coffee, but not wanting to admit that he sometimes drinks fancy (what he would call "girly") coffee. "Yeah... bring me a 'nilla latte, please?"

"ALRIGHT, Mrs. Jones, does this man look familiar to you?" A deputy slides a set of 4 x 6 photos across his desk over to me of an older man, short in stature and slight in build, with round wire-rimmed glasses over chocolate brown eyes and neatly combed hair. He looks to be in his later seventies or eighties, and is a "slacks with a sweater over a button down" kind of guy, which can be a little unusual for our part of Texas. Most of the men we know and love are pearl snaps and Wranglers men. I pick up the photos and thumb through them, hoping some of the other people in the pictures-what looks like his wife, children, etc.-will spark a memory that I might know him.

"I don't think so, sir. None of these people look familiar at all," I say, still absently thumbing until I stop abruptly at a photo of this man and Asa Shoemaker standing in front of my (well, probably at the time, their) building with a swinging white painted sign on a post reading "F&S Oil and Gas" in neat and tidy lettering. They look considerably younger, but I can still clearly tell it is Asa, and whoever this man is.

"Well, I know him, obviously." I set the photo on the table

and point to Asa. The deputy peers over at the picture, and nods.

"But not the other man?"

"No, I'm sorry. Should I? Babe, do you know him?" I ask, holding up the picture with Asa to show Shep, who is standing behind me. He shakes his head absently, taking it from my outstretched fingers and looking more closely at it.

"I assume that's Asa's old business partner, but I never met him that I can recall. That would maybe explain why he was in the building, right?"

"Ding ding ding, Shep, you are correct. At least partially," Sheriff Cooper says as he glides up behind Shep and claps him on the back so hard the picture flies out of his hand and he, I, and the deputy all scramble a little to catch it. "Do you need a refill?" He asks, gesturing to Shep's Delilah's to-go cup sitting on the desk next to us and then to the pot of institutional black coffee across the bull pen.

"Uh, no, my limit is one black coffee in the afternoon these days," Shep answers hastily, clamping a hand over the lid and nonchalantly twisting the coffee collar to make sure the initials marked on the side don't give away the contents. He may enjoy the occasional latte, but he'll never actually admit it to anyone but me. "Now what were you saying about the missing man, Sheriff?"

"That is Langley Fletcher, former business partner of Asa Shoemaker. He was reported missing about five weeks ago." Cooper pulls a chair up to the desk and takes a seat across from us, next to the deputy, looking a little more smug than I would have anticipated. He sits his own Styrofoam cup of black coffee on the top of a stack of overfilled file folders and pulls a crumpled sheet of printer paper out of his vest that he hands over to Shep and me.

The paper has a black and white current photo of Langley

Fletcher printed at the top with MISSING in blocked capital letters underneath. The accompanying paragraph explains: *Langley Roosevelt Fletcher, aged 79, 5 '8", 140 pounds, dark hair, brown eyes, and glasses, is missing from Magnolia Blossom Retirement Community as of March 5, 2025. He was last seen attending dinner at the facility at 5:15 PM on closed circuit surveillance, but family and friends have been unable to locate him since. It is unknown if he is traveling alone or accompanied. Questions and information should be directed to the Oak Hills Police Department.*

Oak Hills is not far from Buffalo Creek, but it's at the opposite end of the county from us, so not a short distance away. How does an elderly man skipping out of the nursing home make it a few towns over and into the attic of a vacant building? I check my watch to confirm that we are, in fact, well into April, and I can't believe this poor man was missing for so long that it came to this.

"Forgive me if this sounds insensitive, but how does someone just disappear, especially from a retirement community? Didn't his wife notice?" I say, reading back over the description and looking to Sheriff Cooper, assuming she is still living.

"The wife has severe dementia at this point. They have her in a different wing of the facility, with Langley in a semi-independent area. He could still ambulate and take care of his own tasks of daily living, but just couldn't care for her anymore, so they moved her into full time care and left him semi-independent. He supposedly visited her every day, sometimes multiple times a day, but she wouldn't have realized he was missing either way. Still doesn't necessarily know he's missing now, quite frankly."

A sadness washes over me as I look back at his missing photo. I can't imagine being on this earth and not knowing if Shep is around or not. As if sensing my thoughts, Shep puts his hands on my shoulders and squeezes them comfortingly as the Sheriff continues.

"Residents are charged for meals on a weekly basis by swiping in and out of the dining facility with their ID cards, or adding it to their tab when they order service brought to their rooms. The facility realized that he hadn't swiped in for a meal or ordered for delivery for a few days on March 8, and started looking into his whereabouts. The semi-independent area is pretty loosely monitored; they are supposed to sign in and out when leaving, and visitors are supposed to do the same, but the main doors are unlocked and partially monitored during the day, so someone could easily slip away. There are also back and side doors that require a key fob to enter, but anyone could walk right out without being noticed. They have two children-twins Maxwell and Madeline, age 46. Maxwell and wife Sydney and Madeline and husband Jacob all live local to the facility in Oak Hills. We haven't spoken to the kids yet, but in an earlier interview, Madeline stated she visits her parents once a week, and she visited right before he went missing, so she was unaware he was gone for several days."

"This may be a dumb question, Sheriff, but any theories on how he then ended up in my attic?"

He pauses, and it's like we all get to see him think in real time. After what feels like an eternity of his pondering, he seems ready to posit a theory. "I think he was lost and disoriented when he left, and your building was familiar to him."

Shep lets out a short, sarcastic sounding snort behind me, and I resist the urge to roll my eyes at Cooper's obvious statement. "I realize that, but how does a man who is only semi-independent end up several towns away? And locked in an attic so long he dies?"

"Or maybe he died somewhere else and was hidden in the attic since the building has been vacant for the last few years?" Shep chimes in, and I turn to give him an impressed look with a little elbow nudge. Maybe my amateur sleuthing bug has been rubbing off on him after all. Also, I never thought I'd be really proud of my husband's smart contributions to a murder investigation theory, but, hey, here we are.

"It's too early to tell, but it's possible. For now, we're going to chase down every lead we can, as quickly as we can because this is growing colder by the minute. Although, I will say this is leaning more in the accident direction than foul play right now. What we need the most from y'all is your continued discretion and to stay out of the building for a little while longer."

I smile tightly, feeling slight déjà vu at the fact that we received this same lecture only a few days ago, and I haven't forgotten. "Of course, Sheriff, whatever is most helpful to you. Did the Fletchers have any possessions remaining in the building? Do you think that is why he might have been in the attic? Maybe Asa told him it was being sold and he felt like he needed to get something out of the attic before he didn't have the chance anymore."

"We recovered a few file boxes filled with documents, and we have forensics reviewing them now to determine who they belong to and if they could be relevant. We'll continue to process the building for any other potentially relevant information, and release it back to you when we finish. Until then, keep your eyes and ears open, and we'll be in touch with any updates or questions." Before Shep or I can respond, Sheriff Cooper gets up from his chair and briskly exits the detective bull pen, pausing only to pat Shep's shoulder on his way out with his case files tucked neatly under his arm. I retrieve my bag from under my chair and hoist it high onto my shoulder as I slowly follow Shep out, since we are clearly finished after the Sheriff's hasty exit.

"So, what are you thinking?" I ask Shep quietly as we weave our way through the hallways to the parking lot. We've been silent since leaving the bullpen, and my mind feels like it's running a hundred miles an hour with all my thoughts, most of them ranging from crazy to crazier. Shep is always my chief thought wrangler—I've always been able to brain dump on him and he can organize it all and give it back to me in a neat package that makes sense and trims out everything but the logical. But sometimes when I'm really spiraling, it helps me to hear his thoughts first to create almost like bowling lane bumpers around my thoughts so all the crazy doesn't completely spill out.

"I'm not sure what to think, honestly. It's hard to believe someone would murder a man, either ahead of time, or by locking them in an attic. But then, I never thought a kid we've known since middle school would murder someone for his land, either. Just goes to show you this world is crazy, and our hope isn't here, that's for sure."

I nod in agreement, thinking that's pretty much where I'd landed. Before I can respond, my phone starts ringing in my purse and I dig around to answer before it stops.

"Grand Marge? Are you ready to be picked up?" I had honestly completely forgotten about her, and am silently relieved that she hasn't called me sooner. Thank goodness the ladies' Bible study group can go for hours, unlike the ladies' quilting club. Their little brittle arthritic fingers don't have the stamina their penchant for gossip does.

"Molly Margaret! Why didn't you tell me you found another dead body in your building?" She screeches through the line and I hold the phone away for a few seconds until she is finished to protect my ear drum.

"What? I'm sorry, who told you that?" I cringe a little and Shep gives me a sympathetic look as he pulls his own phone out of his pocket and jerks his head back in the direction of his truck like he is looking to be excused. I give him a silent nod, and head back to my own car to get over to the church to grab her.

"That cow Geraldine Farwell! She announced it to our entire table a few minutes before our time was up just to have the last bit of attention, asking me if you had shared any updates or had new details. I sat there like a blithering idiot because I didn't know anything about it, despite the fact that it happened to MY granddaughter!" She shrieks, and I cringe all over again. Of course, it had to come from her arch enemy.

"Well, I don't know how Geraldine found out, but it isn't something we're really allowed to talk about right now. She's just a nosy old gossip, and she has to do things like that so people will actually talk to her," I say, hoping that calms her down, but knowing it probably won't. "I'm on my way to pick you up; I'm just leaving the sheriff's department."

"The sheriff's department! What is going on now? Are you in trouble because of the dead body?"

"No trouble, Marge, just had to go in for questioning because they've identified the victim. If you stop yelling at me, I'll share what I can with you when I pick you up."

"Details now are the least you can do. And hurry up because I'm waiting under the portico by myself right now like a vagrant. People are going to be looking for my shopping cart and sleeping bag if I wait here much longer."

▭

After dropping Marge safely at home later and ensuring that JoBeth will keep an eye on her and keep her away from Geraldine Farwell for the next day or two, I putter through the school pick up line to grab Mia and Hayes to start our trek home. We're at the end-of-the-school-year time suck right now that feels like things are simultaneously dragging and moving at break-neck speed. Mia will finish up sixth grade in a few short weeks and head off to the junior high campus up the hill, and Hayes will move up from fourth to fifth grade and no longer be the baby of his campus. As far as Mondays go, this one has been a real doozy, so it's both unexpected and honestly completely normal to walk into our house and see Shep, Cooter, and Roy all spread around the twelve-seater dining room table working on various game cameras and accessories with hardly an open square inch in sight. Mia and Hayes peel off to head up to their rooms and I stand dumbfounded at the mess, wondering what could possibly be going now.

"Is it a hunting season that I'm not aware of?" I ask tentatively, moving closer to the table. Shep, Cooter, and Roy all look up surprised, like they were completely unaware the kids and I had even come in. "You know, 'cougar season' isn't for another few months, and I'm not that hard to find," I tease, referring to our inside joke about the two and a half months between my late-July birthday and Shep's early-October one when I am "a whole number older" than Shep, and thus deemed a "cougar".

"'Bout to be mountain lion season, Boss," Cooter snarls, jamming a battery pack into a camera and hitting the button for it to power on. Silently, Roy does the same to the camera next to him, and they begin threading the square tactical plastic boxes onto elastic bands to hang on trees. As the cameras power on, Shep takes them and pairs them to the app on his phone to have a central location for all the recording feeds. I take a seat at the end of the table and watch quietly until all the cameras are on, paired, and ready to roll. They are clearly not in the mood for jokes, so I remain silent until someone decides to let me in on the situation.

"Hank and I were talking earlier and he said they saw an adult male mountain lion up on the ridge close to that pasture where we can't find those calves. It's probably too late to get anything back but we can try not to lose anymore," Shep explains as Roy and Cooter start packing up the cameras in their travel bags to head out. Predators aren't uncommon around here, but it would be a first for us to have lost an older calf with an experienced mama to a predator. But, stranger things have happened.

"If you see one on the camera, how are you going to get to it in time?" I ask, wondering if I want to know the answer. We're no strangers to death-you get to know it really quickly in the ranching business-but there are some things I'd like to remain less familiar with, I think. Although usually I decide I'd rather not know about something after they've already shared so it's too late anyway.

"The cameras are mainly to watch his movement patterns to see the best place to put traps that won't also catch cows. They just moved into this pasture; everywhere else either has something on it now or just moved something off and needs to be rested, so we need to keep this group parked if we can. But we can't lose any more calves if we can help it." I nod in under-standing and help zip up the last of the bags as Cooter and Roy start hauling the rigs out to the UTV waiting on the driveway for this adventure.

"How was Marge when you left her?" Shep throws the remaining camera bags over his shoulder as we both move to the side door. "Sorry I left you hanging, but that was Hank calling me."

"She's fine. But if there's ever a time for Geraldine Farwell to mind her own flipping business for once in her life, now would be ideal." I roll my eyes and bite my tongue to keep from following in my grandmother's legacy and calling her a cow, too.

"Good luck with that. We'll be back in a little bit," He kisses my cheek and heads out the door to his crew. As they start to pull away, a delivery truck arrives at the driveway in a cloud of dust. I don't remember anything in particular I am waiting for at our house, so I slip out the side door to see what has arrived.

"'Evening, Mrs. Jones. Got a few for you," the delivery driver yells from the bowels of the truck and I walk around to the back to grab the packages. He hands me three medium sized boxes, and I take my stack back inside the house after yelling a thank you.

I don't recognize the labels, and the boxes aren't overly heavy, so I grab a box cutter to answer my curiosity. The top box contains several stacks of neatly folded embroidered tea towels, the middle box has tightly wrapped hand painted tea cups, and there are rows of painted floral tins of loose fancy tea in the bottom box. I stand slightly dumbfounded for a few minutes trying to figure out what I am looking at before it suddenly clicks.

Inventory. This is all inventory for the Shoppe that is currently on hold. As I gingerly pack the boxes back up to set in the garage for the time being, something catches my eye on the driveway. Covering the edge of concrete are no less than twenty-five boxes in varying sizes. I head outside and start slicing them open to find scarves, blouses, coffee table books, salt and pepper shaker sets, vintage milk glass candles, coffee cups, jewelry, and just about anything else one would find in a small-town boutique. It appears that all of my inventory has arrived, with no store opening in sight. There are large markings on each box indicating "DIVERSION" with our home address scribbled underneath because I had intended for this to all go straight to the Shoppe building, but it is here instead. Looks like we still aren't parking in the garage any time soon.

chapter
four

"SO, they just won't let you in at all? With no end in sight?" Harriet Katherine McClure, also known as Hattie Kate, resident roller-set-and-back-comb queen of Buffalo Creek, has done my grandmother's hair every Thursday morning at 9 AM since dinosaurs walked the earth. I spent the better part of my early childhood in the exact same chair I'm sitting in now-a very well-loved deep purple velvet arm chair behind Hattie Kate's operator chair every Thursday morning, and Hattie Kate knows more about the inner workings of Buffalo Creek than just about anyone else. I'm not one hundred percent sure how old she is, as she's been a staple around town since my mom was a teenager, and has looked to be in her "fifties" for at least the last three decades with no clear explanation. Normally JoBeth takes Marge to get her hair done these days, but she ended up with a sciatica attack today, and with Mom gone, I'm up, and feeling quite the ongoing waves of nostalgia and déjà vu.

"Nope, no word about anything. It's been a few days already, and absolutely not a peep from Cooper. I'm just praying this doesn't significantly delay our opening."

"What are you doing with all the stuff you've bought? Do you have a lot of inventory here yet?"

"Twenty five boxes came the other night. They were supposed to be delivered to the Shoppe, but apparently the sheriff's department called and had them diverted. Didn't even know that was a thing. They're all in our garage right now. It looks like an episode of *Hoarders* in there between those boxes and all the feed sacks they pulled out because of the rats in the feed barn. Shep is thrilled, as you can imagine."

"Oh, he'll get over it. Just whip him up some of those shortbread biscuits you're famous for, and he'll be right as rain." She waves a dismissive hand as she parks a large bin of ½" plastic rollers in varying neon colors on her operator cart next to her, along with the gel, comb, and clips she needs like little soldiers preparing for battle to start Marge's hair.

"Did you know Langley Fletcher, Hattie Kate?" I ask, picking up a copy of *Southern Living* from 2001 on the end table next to me and absently flipping through it. Modernity is not exactly a core value at the Snippin' Pretty Salon.

"I knew him, but I didn't really know him well. They went to the Methodist church when they lived here," she replies, squishing an acrylic nail into an industrial sized tub of Dippity Do and slathering the green gel onto the quarter inch section of Marge's hair in her other hand. She slicks the section over a neon yellow hair curler and rolls it up to Marge's scalp before securing it with a silver double prong clip and moving on to the next section. She repeats this time worn and perfected routine- Dippity Do, slick, roll, clip- as she works around Marge's head of stark white hair.

The McClures are probably one of the longest tenured families at Buffalo Creek Church of Christ, meaning overlap with the Fletchers would have been less than if they'd been members of the same congregation. Everyone knows in a small town you are friends with community members from other congregations, but you are best friends with your own denomination. "Did you know his wife?" I ask, continuing to flip through the twenty year old trends in front of me. "Apparently she has dementia and doesn't even realize he's gone."

"Well, that's just sadder than a hound dog in the rain. Are they gonna tell her?"

"I'm not sure. Did you ever do her hair?"

"Just a handful of times when Trina was on vacation," Hattie Kate says, dolloping on an extra measure of Dippity Do for safety before tapping Marge on the shoulder as a signal that it's time to move to the dryer chair. Marge takes off her hearing aids when she first sits to have her hair done, so she and Hattie Kate mainly communicate through gestures until she is finished up. Trina Macintosh is another main staple of the roller set crowd; I believe she's the Methodist Hattie Kate so that tracks. Hattie Kate, Trina, and Baptist Bonnie Bradford all have good enough relationships that they cover one another's clients when needed, but there is still an undercurrent of competition between them.

"Do you remember anything about her?" I grab a handful of peanut M&Ms from the cut crystal candy dish on Hattie Kate's station as she starts wiping down the chair and setting out the supplies to tease Marge's hair as big as it can go. Marge is happily nestled under the dryer and looks like she could just about take a nap and I stop to think that our grandmothers all had the right idea. How much easier is it to come once a week, let someone else wash and style your hair, and don't even worry about it the rest of the week? Why did we let that tradition die?

"She was very finicky. She would let me do her hair if Trina was gone but she wasn't ever super happy about it, and she'd pick it to death the entire time. I kinda wished she would have just not bothered coming here if it was going to be that big of an ordeal. I always wondered if she still came back to Trina when they moved to Oak Hills, or if she found someone to her standards there. She had kids by then, so probably not. Just from knowing them around town when they lived here, it seemed like he got on with everyone, and she got on with no one, so you wondered how they got on with each other, ya know?" she explains, pulling a KitKat out of the pocket of her apron and offering me one of the sticks.

"No, thank you. Did their kids go to school here? They are in our age range, but I've never heard of them. Shep wasn't familiar with them either."

"They moved when the kids were little, and Langley commuted here for work, I think. Have you talked to Asa about this?"

"No, I haven't made it over to Cinnamon Court yet, but I might try to get over there and talk to him this afternoon. I don't think he has anything to do with this, you know?"

"Oh, Asa wouldn't use a flyswatter because it might hurt the fly's feelings. Plus, he's been so torn up about his little family mess, there's no way he's part of this."

"I figured that was the case. Everything I've heard is that Langley was a well-liked upstanding member of society. How does a man who everyone loved end up dead in an attic?"

"Well, he was well liked, but he wasn't a saint. I mean, he and Asa were like brothers, but they had a little falling out when they sold the business and it was messy and brutal. No one really knew the details, but the sale was pretty abrupt and the Fletchers weren't seen anywhere around here after that. But I'm sure they made up at some point. They were too close before that not to. I can't remember if that was before or after Mrs. Ruth passed on. She was the actual real saint around here. Asa was just never the same after he lost her. Boy, you want to see true devoted love, you should have seen those two." As she finishes up her KitKat, she plops herself in her operator chair and turns to face me. "You want some coffee? I think we have a pretty fresh pot in the kitchen."

"I want some, but I already had two cups getting us over here this morning. The last thing I need right now is a self-induced round of heart palpitations from too much caffeine."

Hattie Kate stifles a giggle, and nods in understanding. "How's your mama? I'm shocked she didn't turn right around and come back down here after your last mess."

I inwardly cringe a little because despite how the entire circumstance resolved, people around town still seem to refer to the Dick MacDougal situation as "my mess", like it was my fault it was a mess, rather than the mess of the attempted murderers. In my personal, humble (ish) opinion, I basically cleaned up that mess, but the people about town will always have their own way of framing wild happenings out of the ordinary. "She wanted to come back, but I told her and Dad to stay put and get their work done. There's nothing for us to really do, anyway. They've been very explicit that our one and only job is to stay out of it and stay out of their way. They said it might have even been an accident, but either way it's nothing to do with us."

"Do you believe in accidents anymore, Molly? Because after your mess with Dick, I don't think I do," she says solemnly, raising an eyebrow to me before hoisting herself out of the chair and heading over to get Marge.

While Hattie Kate unwinds Marge's head full of curlers, combs each curl to sit on one another correctly, and teases the entire masterpiece to a wide circumference, I sit in quiet contemplation. Do I agree with Hattie Kate? What happened to Dick MacDougal sure looked like an accident and sure was not, so maybe she's right. What could have happened that someone would have just straight up murdered Langley? The off-handed nugget about Langley and Asa having a falling out is eating away at me little by little, and I'm dying to know the details. Where there is selfish ambition, there is chaos and disorder, so I'm hopeful it wasn't a conflict involving money or power- the two biggest culprits of selfish ambition.

"Alright, Ms. Margaret, what do you think?" Hattie Kate helps Marge slide in her hearing aids before spinning the chair back around to the mirror for a final inspection several minutes later. Marge picks at a few random hairs closest to her face before nodding approvingly. She shoots a well manicured hand straight out from under the bright paisley cosmetology cape wrapped around her and I silently place her checkbook in her hand. After unclipping the attached pen, she begins painstakingly writing out a check in her loopy cursive writing.

"Well, what do you think about all this new hubbub, Ms. Margaret? Especially since you missed the last time?" Hattie Kate asks a little conspiratorily, a tinge of excitement in her voice as she perches herself on the cabinet next to the mirror. May the Lord bless and keep hairdressers for their abundant pot of information they are typically all too happy to share, but dadgummit if they don't usually stir up the pot a little as they pour it out. Marge and JoBeth were on a tour group tour of Scotland and Ireland with their friends in the Red Hat Society during the Dick debacle, and were none too pleased to hear about all the drama and excitement they missed when they got home. Marge hasn't really wanted to talk about all of the MacDougal hullabaloo since they didn't get to be a part of it, so I'm curious what her answer for Hattie Kate will be. No one has FOMO quite like two single women in their late seventies to late eighties.

Marge's face sours a bit, and she lets out a small huff that sounds like the intersection of irritation and disdain. "It's not lady-like to discuss such matters," she replies, tearing her check from her checkbook. "But, don't you think it's downright ridiculous what Buffalo Creek is coming to, with two murders in two months! And there's already so much false information going around!" She hands the check to Hattie Kate and I can see almost a glimmer of exhilaration in her eyes. I knew she wouldn't be able to stand not talking about it, especially now that she's convinced herself that Geraldine Farwell talking about it is just spreading false rumors and that she knows the "truth".

"I had no idea! I guess I should have asked what the real story is before, especially since we have the source in the house. I didn't even think about people making up rumors already," Hattie Kate and Marge both turn to me expectantly and I start shaking my head.

"Nope, sorry, ladies, I can't share anything else. There really isn't anything else, honestly, but they asked us to remain discreet. That's how this gets wrapped up quickly and we can get our store open."

"Oh, no one is looking for state secrets, Molly. Surely Cooper told you who they are suspecting?" Hattie Kate prods, and she and Grand Marge both give me big puppy dog eyes in annoying unison.

"Actually, they haven't. I'm not sure they even know who the suspects are. There may not even be a reason to have suspects! I don't think it helps anyone to speculate or start potential rumors, either," I say sternly, putting the checkbook back in Marge's bag so we can get ready to go. My main priority at this point is to make this investigation as seamless and efficient as possible, and if that means forgoing a very small amount of beauty shop gossip, so be it. Also, we've talked all these details to death, and it feels like this particular horse has been beaten beyond all recognition.

"Well, you're as fun as a turd in the punch bowl," Hattie Kate ribs back as she helps Marge out of the operator chair and I try not to crack a smile. "Alright, if nobody has anything else fun to talk about then I guess I better let y'all get on. I've got about twenty minutes until Mrs. Farwell gets here." Hattie

Kate gives us a tense purse of her lips as Marge pulls on her extra sweater to get ready to leave. She insists my car is too cold–there isn't a happy medium setting for her between no air conditioner and the first setting of air, so she always wears an extra cardigan when she rides with me. It's the best compromise we've found, and I'm glad we finally got there because believe me, it wasn't the first.

A dark cloud crosses Marge's face and she furrows her eyebrows. "Listen, Hattie Kate, you don't believe a word that old cow tells you. She's a bitter old gossip and she doesn't even care if she spreads lies!" Marge is near bellowing, and I hold my arms wide behind her to prepare to catch her because she has worked herself up into a bit of a sway waving her arms as she rants.

"It's okay, Grand Marge. We don't have to throw Geraldine under the bus everywhere we go," I say gently, using my outstretched arms to start herding her to the door. I click the button to unlock my car from inside and let her get out the door before turning back to Hattie Kate. "Geraldine told the Thursday prayer group that Marge's potato salad is store bought."

"Stop! Why would she do that?" Hattie Kate exclaims, a small twinkle in her eye because she ended up with some gossip after all. I may have little power to quell rumors around here, but slipping that to Hattie Kate and letting her set the record straight should be pretty effective.

"Why is the sky blue? There's no reason to wonder why Geraldine is exactly what Marge called her, but she is, and she did. So if anyone tries to sell you that, set them straight, would you?"

"Of course, of course. I have a hard time believing anyone would actually buy that, but I've seen dumber if we're being honest. Y'all have a good afternoon, honey." She winks at me as I slide out the door and hurry to get in the car before Marge notices I'm farther behind her than she realizes.

"Alright, what else do you have on your schedule today?" I ask, buckling my seatbelt and checking my mirrors to pull back out onto the main street of Buffalo Creek. There is some light traffic for 10 in the morning on a Thursday, but I don't have to wait too long before we're back on the road out to Marge's house. "Shep is in town to get some supplies from the vet store and I think he wants me to meet him for a burger at the drug store in a little bit."

"Well, that sounds good. I can't even remember the last time I had lunch there. I need to get my vitamins anyway," she replies, settling herself into my passenger seat and buttoning her cardigan all the way up and down. And that is how my grandmother crashed my weekly lunch date with my husband.

Overton Drug Store has been on the main square of Buffalo Creek for exactly 101 years, having just celebrated its centennial last year. It's evolved over the years from a simple drug store and mercantile, to adding in the soda fountain and grill, to transitioning away from general merchandise and into more small gifts and trinkets. You won't find a better burger, hand mixed Coca-Cola, spicy fried pickle, or scoop of Blue Bell this side of the Mason-Dixon, and it has been a Thursday lunch staple for Shep and me since both of our kids started full time school-our standing Thursday lunch date.

When Marge and I push through the heavy glass front door, setting off the set of heavy brass bells hung over the door frame, I spot Shep on a stool at the end of the counter as usual. I guide Marge through the displays of hats, necklaces, and novelty cookware to the stool on his left before sitting on his right. He silently raises an eyebrow to me and I silently shrug in reply. It's not like our Thursday lunch dates are anything explicit or racy, but it is a bit of a vibe change to have your eighty-something year old grandmother present, espe-cially unexpectedly.

"How are you this morning, Shepherd?" Marge asks brightly, patting his arm as she reaches for the single sheet legal sized laminated menu tucked between two napkin holders in front of her.

"Doing pretty well, Margaret. How about you?" Shep answers, stifling a laugh. For whatever reason, for the last twenty plus years, Marge and Shep have been the most formal in referring to one another. Marge is the only person I know who calls him Shepherd, and he is the only one in the family that calls her Margaret, generally in response to her formality. I've never understood why she chooses to be so formal with him because I wouldn't consider her formal in general, but it still never ceases to make us giggle a little.

"Doing as well as expected." She pulls her readers out of her little quilted handbag and pulls the menu up over her face. She is barely five feet tall, so between her menu and her low sitting stool, she is barely visible. Shep and I exchange a look as one of the counter girls approaches with her notepad.

"Morning, Joneses. What can I get y'all to drink?"

"I'll have a sweet tea, please," Shep replies quickly, turning to me. He is the most decisive person I've ever known, and I always feel extra indecisive by comparison. I'm usually torn between the Cokes and the tea, and as I waffle between the two, Marge slaps the menu down to the counter to reveal her large bright red cat eye readers lined with giant rhinestones, making everyone jump a little.

"I'd like a Coca-Cola, extra heavy on the syrup, please," she trills before picking the menu back up to continue reading. The waitress tries not to laugh as she turns to me.

"I think I'll go with an Arnold Palmer today. And some fried pickles?"

"Sure, I'll be right back."

She heads to the kitchen to start our order, and the three of us sit in a bit of awkward silence as all we can see is Marge's menu with her long red nails clutching the bottom. Since we come here every week, we are well versed on the offerings, and honestly get the same thing every time anyway, but Marge is taking her sweet time mulling over her options.

"Where are the boys this morning?" I ask Shep, wondering if Marge will resurface before or after we order our food.

"They are moving those round bales we had delivered yesterday into the hay trap on the south side. Where did you say JoBeth is?"

"Sciatica attack."

Shep nods, and we both instinctively turn toward the door as the bells ring out and a group of men looking to be in their late twenties to early thirties enter, all wearing dri-fit polos adorned with the Crawford County State Bank logo. They all seat themselves in a line at the counter beginning with the stool next to Marge and I stifle a laugh as the man closest to her glances in her direction and then does a double take to really take in all that is sitting next to him.

"How are you this morning, ma'am?" He stammers, probably feeling like he can't look away, but knowing she clearly doesn't love being stared at. We still can't see her face for her menu, but we can hear her little high pitched trill from behind it.

"Just fine, young man, thank you for asking. Aren't you Ginny Parrish's boy?"

"Yes, ma'am, Parker Parrish," he replies, with a look that tells me he is well versed on the small town dynamic of older people knowing exactly who you are but not having a clue who they are in return. He holds out a hand for her to shake, and she bobbles her menu for a second as she shakes it daintily and then returns to holding it firmly with two hands in front of her.

"Pleased to make your acquaintance, Parker; I'm Margaret Roberts. Your mother has been in my mahjong group for the last few years. I've heard very nice things about you."

"You play mahjong, Marge?" I ask, trying to temper the shock in my voice. I've tried once or twice to play mahjong and have never been able to pick it up. I blamed it on "mom brain" because I used to love playing bunco in my college days and thought it was the easiest, most brainless game. When I tried to play after Mia and Hayes were born, I struggled to keep up and it wasn't near as fun. Now our friend group generally just meets for coffee and a catch up–trying to help our brains instead of hurt them.

"Of course I do, Molly. It's really quite a simple game," her disembodied voice answers sharply, and I stifle a laugh.

Our waitress returns a few moments later before Marge can outright shame me for not knowing how to play mahjong and takes orders from Shep and me before turning to Marge still talking to Parker Parrish behind her menu. Their conversation has become muffled until she suddenly slaps the menu to the counter. "SOB!" she cries, looking from Parker to the waitress, who is standing directly in front of them.

"Marge!" I exclaim, shocked at my grandmother's uncharacteristic potty mouth. She pulls off her readers and looks at me confusedly as she slides her menu back in its place.

"Molly, what is it?" she says exasperatedly. "I was just putting in my order; what are you getting so worked up about?" Shep starts to softly chuckle, and I roll my eyes, remembering that a double cheeseburger is called an "SOB"-a Super Overton Burger-on their menu.

"Uh, nothing, just surprised you are that hungry," I answer, trying to play it off. The waitress stifles a laugh as she finishes writing it all down, and promises to return to take Parker's group's order.

It turns out I didn't need to worry about Marge crashing

our lunch date because she barely speaks to us the entire time, and focuses all her attention on Parker. Shep and I talk through a handful of ranch business items-layout for our upcoming bull sale catalog, some new potential sires Shep is interested in, and which fence on the north side needs to be checked for fidelity before turning a group out to graze in that pasture. As we wrap up our "meeting" and finish our food, Marge seems to be doing the same with Parker. His friends/colleagues are all paying their tabs and heading back to work ahead of him, not bothering to wait for him.

"Well, it was just lovely to have lunch with you, Parker," Marge coos, and I try not to gag. I love that woman with all my heart, but she can really turn it all the way on, or shut completely off depending on who she is with.

"Somebody better pick up the ham bone she's falling off over there," Shep mutters as he picks up our ticket and heads up to the front counter to pay, jerking his head in Marge's direction. I stand and gather my bag before starting my extrication attempt. Shep's right, Marge can get to be quite the ham when she wants to be, never one to turn down attention.

"Alright, well, Parker, I'm sure we'll see you around town. You ready, Marge? I think we better get you home and check on JoBeth, don't you think?"

"Oh yes, my sister is really down in her back today. She's not as active as I am, even though I'm a little bit older. Movement keeps you young, you know," she says knowingly. He nods in confused agreement and starts to back away.

"Great to meet you, too, Ms. Roberts. Have a great rest of your day." Parker gives a nod to me and Shep that makes me feel a little like he thinks we owe him one as we guide Marge out to the parking on the street. Shep heads back to the ranch to check on Cooter and Roy's progress, and I start the circle around town to take Marge back to her duplex.

"Marge, you have a few extra minutes?" I ask, as we putter

down the main street of Buffalo Creek, adhering to the 25 miles per hour speed limit. She looks a little sleepy, and I know we are nearing the time of the afternoon that she likes to sneak in an afternoon nap that she doesn't like to tell anyone about. But I also know that she gets a little lonely in her house by herself and very rarely, if ever, turns down an opportunity to do something with someone.

"I have a few things to do at the house, but I can spare a little bit longer," she replies magnanimously, stifling a bit of a yawn.

"I just want to run by the Shoppe building and see if anything is going on and make sure none of my inventory packages ended up there by accident."

We pull up in front of the Shoppe a few minutes later, and I am surprised to see one car out front-a sleek white Lexus SUV-but no law enforcement presence or any people. Marge and I get out and I cautiously walk up the front steps, trying to remember if I know anyone who drives a vehicle like that, or if someone would have a reason to be hanging out over here.

The front door is unlocked, and the yellow caution tape is haphazardly laying across the threshold, not even remotely doing its job. I remind myself to have a word with Sheriff Cooper about that as Marge and I quietly creep in and take a look around the empty first floor to see if anything is amiss.

It's all the same cobwebs and dust as last week, which, honestly, stresses me out a little—seeing it in person and knowing there's nothing I can do about it for the time being just rubs me like a rock in my shoe. But other than that, nothing seems out of the ordinary. The car must belong to someone at the insurance agency next door or something. I spot a lone FedEx box on the porch and start to usher Marge out to grab it and leave when a loud *creak* comes from the top of the stairs. We freeze in the doorway and my stomach drops so fast I feel it in my toes. I have absolutely no desire to turn around but I have to look anyway when Marge lets out a blood-curdling scream and clutches my arm.

A tiny, bone-thin woman as pale as a ghost with long, stark white hair, and dressed in a white linen blouse and pants set is floating down the stairs silently. She barely blinks, and comes right up to Marge and me huddled in the doorway.

Marge blinks exaggeratedly once, almost like she is buffering, before fainting away in my arms, leaving us both staggering onto the porch as I really question my life choices. Add this to the long, long, long list of examples of why Shep Jones is never wrong—this place really is haunted.

The woman stands in front of us calmly, blinking slowly, and taking us in. After a few long moments, she firmly addresses us, her high and quiet voice punctuating each word. "What are you doing in my house?"

chapter
five

"MOTHER! WHAT ARE YOU DOING?" As I'm trying
to formulate an answer, I see an actual live human being
rushing down the stairs from the landing in a panic. She looks
to be about my age, maybe a little older, and is tastefully
dressed in a houndstooth sweater set and tailored jeans with
delicate ballet flats and a bejeweled headband holding back a
sleek jet black shoulder length bob. She reaches the woman in
white in a split second and checks her over before turning
to us.

"I'm so sorry. My mother has just a touch of dementia and
doesn't always understand where she is or who she is with."
She smiles apologetically and extends a hand to us. "Hi, I'm
Linny Caldwell."

I shake her hand in a stupor, staggering under Marge's
dead weight, and still trying to process the last few minutes.
While the introduction is kind and polite, it answers absolutely no questions about who they are and why they are in
our building. "Um, nice to meet you. I'm Molly Jones, and
this is my grandmother Margaret Roberts."

"Oh, you're the new owner! Asa told us about you and
your husband. We're so excited to see this old gem come back

to life." She wraps an arm around her mother and holds her firmly but kindly to keep her from wandering and brushes non-existent hair from her face like she wants to give the illusion that she is a tad flustered, but managing to keep it all together.

"Yes... I'm so sorry, do I know you?"

She smacks a manicured hand to her forehead and lets out a cross between a laugh and a sigh. "I apologize, I shouldn't have just assumed you know who we are! Langley Fletcher was my father, and this is my mother, Nora."

All the pieces suddenly fall together and I can only imagine the look on my face right now, as it usually leaves no doubt about what I am thinking. "Of course, nice to meet you. And I'm so sorry for your loss."

She transitions to a solemn nod, patting her mother on the shoulder as she keeps a firm arm around her. "Thank you so much. It was obviously a shock that Daddy was found in such a way, but in some ways a relief to know where he is. We spent many sleepless nights for weeks just wondering and praying, but not knowing what happened to him," she explains, tears starting to well in her dark brown eyes. I pause, not sure exactly how I feel about her right off the bat. She's done an emotional 180 in the last three minutes, from happy to meet me to tearfully mournful, and it smells a tad bit fishy to my expert amateur sleuthing self. I'd say she's a good actress if nothing else, but I feel like she would be more believable on either end of the emotional spectrum if that were the case. Either way, something just doesn't feel quite right with her, and I can't quite put my finger on it just yet.

"Yes, I can imagine," I say, as Marge starts to come back to life. I sit her down on the floor and stand behind her to prop her up as she wakes and looks back and forth from Linny to Nora. "Marge, this is Nora and Linny, Langley Fletcher's wife and daughter." I bend down behind her and say this quietly to her to keep her from making more of a scene. She silently nods in some semblance of understanding and I help her up off the ground to her feet.

We stand in awkward silence for a few long minutes until I can't stand it any longer. "I'm so sorry, were you looking for something? Or is there something I can do for you?" The intersection between *'sorry I found the unexpected corpse of your dad'* and *'why are you trespassing in the building I just bought'* is a weird and delicate one and I could not feel more uncomfortable right now. A look of understanding washes over Linny and she suddenly looks sheepish.

"My apologies again, you were probably quite shocked to find us in here, huh?" She laughs lightly and I nod casually while keeping a lid on my real thoughts-*yes, quite the shock to find you and your ghost of a mother haunting around here with no context or prior meeting.* "Once they identified my father, Sheriff Cooper said we were welcome to come in and look around to see if there was anything that seemed out of the ordinary to us, or anything we recognized that might help them. Mother's short term memory is basically non-existent, but her long term memory can be fairly detailed at times, so they thought there could be a chance she would spot some-thing that might be helpful." She has a knowing tone in her voice and her words should have sounded believable enough given her extra measure of confidence, but something still just doesn't sit right. We were explicitly told to stay out, so why in the world would they be invited to come right in and essen-tially tamper with a potential crime scene?

"Sure... just curious... Did you see anything? We haven't been allowed to be in here since the sheriff closed it down and it was basically vacant before that." I try not to make it sound like I find her suspicious, but I do want her to know that I'm not going to believe just any random yarn she spins. Marge is giving her the full on skeptical old lady glare and I'm praying to the Lord Almighty she keeps her thoughts to herself. She has a knack for digging up answers, but her method leans more toward dynamite than hand trowel—and, unsurprisingly, it can get a bit... inflammatory.

"Oh, no, we've not really seen anything. Just memories and reminiscing," she says wistfully, hoisting a Louis Vuitton Neverfull higher on her shoulder. "My brother and I were up here all the time when we were small children. It's been awhile, obviously, but my goodness, some things just stay the same... Well, we should probably get out of your hair! Mother needs to get back to her room anyway. She does alright with small outings, but she can start to get really cranky and disoriented if she's out of her normal routine for too long." Cranky and disoriented seems like an understatement as she accused us of being in her house. As far as I'm aware, no one has lived in this building since Asa's wife's grandparents in the early 1920s, so disoriented definitely applies as well.

Linny starts to shuffle Mrs. Fletcher out the door before I can ask any other questions and I panic for a second about losing my chance to learn anything else from her. "Um, wait! Linny?" I quickly call after her and run out to my car as she settles Mrs. Fletcher into her passenger seat. I dig through the console and come up with a stray Chick Fil A receipt and a sharpie, which is quickly turning into my signature business card. "This is my phone number. If you think of anything you might be looking for in the building or that I can keep an eye out for, please let me know. I'd love to do whatever I can to help figure this out." Linny gives me a million watt stunner of a smile, giving full beauty pageant/ homecoming queen vibes. I'd like to say it's heartwarming or comforting, but it is really just reading *'I've got something to hide, but I'm hoping I can distract you from that'*.

"How thoughtful, thank you so much. I can tell that Daddy would have loved you. And he would have loved that you are taking over their legacy and bringing life back to this gem of a building. Best of luck with your next steps, Molly." She pulls me into an unexpected hug, and the strong cloud of Baccarat Rouge combined with her strong grip almost knocks the wind out of me.

"Thank you so much," I barely gasp, and pat her back hoping it will act as a release button and she'll let me go. She backs off and takes me square by the shoulders in both of her hands.

"Also, please know that my brother Maxwell and my father did not have a good relationship. If he or his family pops up around here, please alert the authorities. He would undoubtedly be up to no good and doesn't need to be privy to any sensitive information related to this." I have nothing to say to this, so I merely nod like a goober and then take in another of her pageant smiles. She gets in her car and starts backing out to presumably head back to Oak Hills while I stand on my front steps wondering what in the heck just happened.

I hear Marge clear her throat and I jump a little in surprise, as I swear she wasn't even outside two seconds ago, and she's now standing close enough to me that I can hear her wheeze a little as she breathes. "Up to no good, she says? I think it takes one to know one."

<hr>

A few hours later, I've dropped Marge back at her duplex, picked kids up from school, and started the evening shuffle of getting kids to and from dance class and baseball practice. As I'm sitting in my Suburban in the parking lot of the dance studio trying not to doze off, my phone starts to ring. I don't recognize the number, which usually means I let it roll to voicemail, but it is the correct area and prefix to be a local number, so I roll the dice and go ahead and answer it.

"Hi, is this Mrs. Jones?" A perky, high pitched voice comes through the speaker of my car at a nearly unbearable volume, and I cringe down to my toes. The only time I am typically ever addressed as 'Mrs. Jones', I'm about to get roped into something I'd probably otherwise say no to.

"Um, yes, this is Molly."

"Hi, Molly! This is Kaci Whitfield from the middle school!" She is pert near shouting with enthusiasm, and I quickly roll back the volume knob on my car to bring her down a notch as I rack my brain to remember who Kaci Whitfield from the middle school is. Her name doesn't ring one single bell, but I've found that doesn't necessarily mean anything around here. I probably also couldn't tell you what I had for breakfast, or name my entire family's birthdays in one sitting, either. But do please ask me to sing the Phil Collins banger *"Easy Lover"* word for word because that I can remember flawlessly for some unknown and useless reason.

"Mrs. Whitfield? What can I do for you?" I am kicking myself because Buffalo Creek truly isn't that big, and I should probably know exactly who she is, even if she hasn't taught the kids yet. I go ahead and call her "Mrs." because chances are around here, she is.

"I'm so sorry, I guess I should introduce myself! I haven't officially started at the middle school just yet. They've hired me to teach seventh grade English and coach the cheerleaders next year!" Ding, ding, ding, we have a winner-I should have guessed this would have something to do with cheerleading given that it feels like each and every sentence she says is punctuated by a flurry of exclamation points.

"Oh, yes, I thought I heard that they'd found someone to take Becki's place," I say, rummaging through my purse to find my day planner. I know I'm going to get asked to do something-I can feel it in my mother's intuition soaked bones-so I might as well be prepared to take down the details.

"Oh my goodness, what a wild story, right? I haven't heard all the nitty gritty, but I can't believe she was encouraging the girls to cheat off one another! Is that right?"

"Uh, yep. That's not even the half of it, sister, but that is true." Honestly, attempted murder and a workplace extortion driven affair are probably more than just the other half, but I don't want to trip up the pep in her step. I drum my felt tip pen on the steering wheel and wonder when Cheer Barbie is going to get on with it. I've never been known to say no to much of anything when it comes to school or sports volunteering, but I'd like to know what I'm getting into before Mia gets out of ballet class and we have to hit the road again.

"Anywhoodle! I met with the girls today to discuss logistics for summer camp, and summer workdays, and we talked about our fundraising efforts. After the bake sale y'all had a few weeks ago, it would seem that no one can locate that money." She pauses, and I nod knowingly to just myself alone in my car. Of course Becki took that money along with everything flipping else she was up to–I wouldn't have expected anything differently. I open my mouth to tell her the parents can likely just cover the remaining amount before she cuts me off and continues. "We talked through different options for fundraisers, and they were most excited about one that I shared that we used to do for our college cheer team that was always a big hit. It takes some planning and some execution, and we'll definitely need parent participation, but it can be a big money maker."

If she says the words "car wash", I'm going to roll myself out of this car and right into oncoming traffic. That feels like something that would make a ton of money when manned by college age girls in small swimsuits, but not so much with middle-aged moms in swim dresses trying to keep perverts away from their preteen daughters in tankinis. "Well, the moms are usually pretty supportive and willing to help. What are we looking at here? Another bake sale? Selling something? A GoFundMe page?" Maybe there's still a chance I can curb her into just letting the parents cover the camp. It can't be that wild of an amount. I used to think it was entitled for parents to just pay for things instead of having kids earn the fundraising money or necessary funds. Then we actually had kids, and I realized how often activities and extra-curriculars expect your kids to beg other people for money, and you see very quickly that it's sometimes just the polite (or, you know, easier) thing to do to pay it yourself and move on. Plus, it's just so much less work.

"A community wide karaoke night! And Mia said you'd love to be the chairperson!"

A loud record scratch reverberates in my head as I sit up in my seat to make sure I heard her correctly. "Wait, what? A karaoke night? And I'm in charge?"

"Yes!" Her excitement fills my entire empty Suburban and I take a second to glance around outside for cameras because surely I am being *Punk'd*. If Ashton Kutcher circa 2003 doesn't pop out from behind a bush post haste, I might lose it.

"I'm in charge of a karaoke night for the entire community to come to?" I ask again, like my brain is the human equivalent of the frozen spinning rainbow wheel and I can't refresh to the next page. Kaci laughs, and I wonder if I've said something legitimately funny, or if she now thinks I'm dumb because I can't seem to process what's going on. Like I said, it's not my first rodeo as a parent volunteer, but this would be my first rodeo being an entire event coordinator. Not to mention that I have an entire boutique I'm supposed to be putting together to open in a matter of weeks and the other small matter of figuring out why there was a corpse in my attic with no explanation.

"Yes, it's going to be so much fun! We used to look

forward to it all year at Southern Baptist; it was one of our favorite things to get to do. Mia said you are great at event execution and have plenty of experience, so this should be a piece of cake for you. For right now, we're shooting to have it in about four weeks, so we'll need to start getting the rough details going, and pushing advertising out. I'd like to meet with you sometime early next week to see what you have lined up at that point, okay? Let's plan for Tuesday at 10 AM. I don't have a classroom at the school just yet, so we can meet at your house if that's convenient for you." Suddenly little Mary Sunshine has turned into GI Jane, and I manage to stammer an affirmative reply, wondering why on God's green earth my precious baby daughter would throw me under the bus like this. This is a gross misuse of the phrase '*if you want something done, find the busiest person in the room*'. We end our conversation just as Mia's class comes pouring out of the double glass doors of the hundred year old building that houses the ballet studio. She jumps in the passenger side and gives me a grin.

"Guess who got a solo in the recital piece right before intermission?" she beams, holding up a photocopy of a long list of names and dance numbers.

"Gee, is it the same girl who volunteered her mother to organize a community wide fundraiser without telling her?" I answer, trying to sound more joking than accusing. This feels like one of those things where you are thankful your kids know that you are there for them no matter what, but you kinda wish they'd ask permission first. Mia looks a little sheepish, and nods slowly.

"I know it's a lot, but you are definitely the most fun mom that's also still organized enough to get it done. And I have a plan for something else, too."

"Are you saying there are other team moms more fun than me?"

"Of course. But generally speaking, the more fun they are, the less organized. You hit the middle pretty well."

"Thanks?"

"No problem!"

"Okay, but seriously, how are we going to organize a whole fundraiser that actually makes money, not just costs it, at the same time we are opening a boutique?"

"That's just it, Mom-let's have it *at* the Shoppe!"

I am certain my face reads mainly dumbfounded curiosity at this point, but she seems so sincere. "Babe, how are we going to do that?"

"I have it all pictured in my mind-we set up a cool temporary stage in the backyard area with lots of eclectic mismatched tables and chairs all over the lawn, and twinkle lights and paper lanterns. We don't have to do dinner or anything, probably just drinks and maybe some snacks? Ooo, like a popcorn bar! Savory and sweet, let people throw in whatever mix-ins like M&Ms or cheese or maybe both if they're weird! That can be part of the fundraiser-people pay for different sizes like the movies, or a big refillable bucket. I think the school has a popcorn machine for parties and stuff. People will have to walk through the Shoppe to get back there, so people will probably buy things on their way out there. You could maybe even say a portion of proceeds are donated back to us? It's great exposure for the Shoppe *and* the cheerleaders!"

It's honestly not a bad idea, and in a perfect world, it would work without a hitch. There is a large backyard area that is privacy fenced, and with a little work to the existing pavers and flower beds, we could get everything looking pretty good. But unfortunately, there is one very obvious fly in this ointment. "I think that's not a bad idea, but there is one problem. We don't have access to the building right now. By the time we do, it will be super crunch time to get everything for the Shoppe in place by then, plus setting up a large scale fundraiser out there, too. How would we get all that done?"

Mia looks contemplative for a moment, and then looks to me like the answer is so simple and obvious. "Mom, we'll all help!"

Mom, we'll all help. That's her ringer of a plan. Lord, be near, either for her naivete or my lack of faith.

I shake my head as I start pulling out of my parking place to head to the ballpark to meet Shep and Hayes. As we wind through town, I think about the fact that I may not be able to remember breakfast or birthdays, but this might actually be a real use for my *"Easy Lover"* routine. *Finally.* Boy, if that isn't a perfect example of the Lord preparing me for such a time as this, I don't know what is.

"Wait, you said you have a plan for something else. What is 'something else' that needs a plan?"

"Oh, you'll see. Let's just say that Coach W is single and in her early twenties', and I know two handsome and funny cowboys who are also. One of them has got to be her Mr. Right."

She has a bit of a mischievous glint in her eyes, and I wonder where this intense matchmaker energy for Cooter and Roy is coming from. As far as I'm aware, neither one of them has been actively looking to settle down or even date seriously. I'm not sure either one of them would even be interested in being set up, and I'm not sure how I feel about setting them up in essentially a competition between the two of them for the heart of one girl. She gives no more explanation before launching into a detailed recap of her day and I am left with my imagination creating what this redneck west Texas version of *The Bachelorette* that Mia apparently has in mind is going to look like.

chapter
six

"THANKS FOR GETTING BACK to me, Sheriff Cooper. I was just curious if you have any updates on the case?" The next morning, as I dump creamer into my second cup of coffee, I put the sheriff on speakerphone and I am praying he is in an amiable mood today. There are times that I would say we're decent friends, and times I wonder if he'd spit on me if I were on fire. My fingers are crossed that it's a friendship kind of day.

"Yes, yes, Molly, I've been meaning to touch base with you. The CSI unit is wanting to do one final sweep in the next few days and then we think you'll be able to get back in there. Thank you for your patience. Since it's such an aged crime scene, it's been really important to preserve what fidelity we can." He lets out a little harrumph and I try not to roll my eyes, thankful this is a phone conversation and he can't see my face.

"Yeah, about that," I start, trying to temper the attitude in my voice as I walk my coffee cup into our office and sit down in front of my computer. I dropped the kids at school about an hour ago, and am about to start tackling my long to-do list that seems like it's now twice as long since the addition of this fundraiser business. "I was under the impression that no one was allowed in the building. Why did we stop by yesterday to check for straggler inventory boxes only to have the bejeezus scared out of us by Fletcher's wife and daughter?" There is a brief pause on the line before Cooper's voice comes out in a higher pitch than usual.

"Beg your pardon?"

"We stopped by the Shoppe yesterday to see if any of my inventory was accidentally delivered there, and Nora Fletcher and Linny Caldwell were milling around inside. I don't know if you've met her, but Nora Fletcher can give someone quite a fright, as they say. Linny said you'd given them the go ahead to look around the building and report back anything that seemed out of the ordinary to them. That seemed a little suspicious to me since we were told it was locked down, right?"

He pauses for several long moments, and I feel like his politically correct filter is formulating his response in real time. "Well... uh... did you say they were in the building?"

I work hard not to roll my eyes. "Yes. In the building, upstairs specifically. Does that sound correct to you?"

He sighs heavily, and I confirm my suspicions before he says another word. "No, we did not give anyone permission to be in the building. Can you give me a statement about what you saw?"

"Just like I said, Coop. My grandmother Margaret and I stopped by to check for inventory boxes and the door was unlocked. We looked around the first floor and didn't see anything, so just as we were about to leave, we saw Nora Fletcher on the landing. She came downstairs to tell us to 'get out of her house' right before her daughter, who introduced herself as Linny Caldwell, came down and told us the story of why they were allowed to be in the building. We talked for maybe ten or fifteen minutes and then they left at the same time as us, about 1:15 PM."

I wait for what feels like an eternity for a response before I finally get another heavy sigh. "I promise you that we will finish our final sweeps and give you access back by the end of the week."

"Thanks, Sheriff. And that is free and complete access, like I can start setting up my store?"

"Yes, that should be unhindered access. But do one thing for me—if anyone from the Fletcher family comes back around, will you let us know ASAP?"

"Sure. Anything else?"

Another long pause fills the line, and I hear nothing but the clicking of typing and phones ringing in the background. I wonder for a split second if he thought he hung up but really just left the phone face up in the bull pen and walked away. He finally comes back sounding a little quieter and more shaken than I'd like. "Honestly? When you get in there, I would recommend changing your locks. We left that building locked. Sounds like the Fletcher family might still have a key."

I hang up the phone and sit in quiet contemplation. What I gleaned from that is that essentially the Fletchers let themselves in to snoop around. Why? Were they looking for something in particular? Did they find what they might have been looking for? And if they let themselves in this time, have they done it before?

I'm pulled from this train of thought rolling full steam ahead by yells, whoops, and hollers outside the front office window. I get up from my upholstered computer chair and watch through the shutters as Cooter runs full speed down the driveway with Roy on his heels. It looks like Shep is still standing down at the horse barn, but the boys are headed in the direction of the feed storage barn as fast as they can. Intrigued by the hullabaloo, I walk out the side door of the house and down to Shep.

"What's going on?" I ask, and he turns around laughing and shaking his head.

"We got an alert that one of our rat traps deployed. The boys are excited to see what they got. It's like two little redneck kids trying to trap Santa or something."

I shudder involuntarily, just as Cooter comes running back with a rat trap the size of a textbook and what looks like a kill to match. I hold up a hand to signal that I don't want to see whatever they've caught just as he and Roy make it back to us. "I think we got 'im! Take a look at that ol' boy, Boss!" He thrusts the trap in my general direction and I try not to vomit on the dirt. Again, my ranch stomach has toughened up a lot over the last several years, but not that much.

"I'll be back inside if you need me!" I manage to side step and avoid a full view of the dead rodent as I head back up to the house, leaving the boys to dispose of their friend no longer with us. "And please don't need me for that," I say under my breath as I let myself back through the side door.

I sit back down at my computer and start punching out some fundraiser details since it seems the most pressing. I put out a call on the Buffalo Creek Moms Facebook page for tables, chairs, and tablecloths to borrow for the night. A quick call to the middle school administration office confirms that they do in fact have a popcorn machine they are willing to let us use for the occasion. I make a list of beverages and popcorn toppings and additives to purchase closer to the event, and jot down a note to ask Coach Whitfield if she wants to borrow a karaoke set up or rent one from a party company. I'm honestly wondering if she might even have one of her own given the fervor she has for the entire karaoke night concept, and that would be the most convenient. As I'm dropping some tentative details into a flyer template on Canva, my phone starts buzzing across the desk with my best friend Mandy's picture on the screen. I swivel in my chair away from the computer and toward the window as I answer it. Out the window, I see Cooter and Roy moving feed sacks over their shoulders one by one down the driveway, presumably back to the feed barn. I assume the rat from the trap was in fact their intended target, and they now feel comfortable moving all the feed back into the barn. Talk about changing on the turn of a dime–in one fell swoop the garage went from normal operation to feed barn/ inventory storage, and in one day, it is headed back in the opposite direction, praise the Lord.

"Any chance you have any large scale auction items you'd like to donate to the middle school cheerleading squad?" Mandy says with a healthy dose of frustration before I can even greet her.

"Wait, what? What do we need large scale auction items for? When are we having an auction? Live or silent? For the love, what is going on around here?"

She sighs and launches into her explanation. "I saw on Facebook you got roped into the karaoke night thing, right? Well, apparently to raise additional funds, Coach Whitfield wants to have a silent auction table for people to bid on and announce winners at the end of the night. Guess whose kid threw them under the bus for that one?"

"Geez, we gotta get some protective gear for these buses we're getting thrown under. Any luck so far?"

"I just got the call so I haven't really started yet. Four weeks is quite the turn and burn for a full silent auction."

"It's quick, for sure. So... is now a bad time to ask if Scott-cha Covered can make the centerpieces for this shindig, too?" I ask, referring to the in-house floral counter she is planning to open inside the Shoppe. Mandy has been a flower wizard for as long as I've known her, and one of her spiritual gifts is being able to take any bunch of grocery store flowers and turn them into a *Southern Living* magazine spread. She has been wanting to take it to the next level, but isn't ready to open a full flower shop, so having a counter at the Shoppe felt like the perfect compromise for her to get started. After much brainstorming over coffee and cookies in our friend group, the perfect name (just in case she does ever branch out on her own) emerged-Scott-cha Covered, a play on her last name.

"Well, that depends. Is Scott-cha Covered going to be operational at the time or will it still be homeless pending a sheriff's department investigation?"

"Fair question, and luckily, I have good news. Cooper told me this morning that we should have access by the end of the week. Is that enough time?"

"It should be. Are you going to be able to be open at all before we have this whole thing in the backyard?"

"Probably for a whole five minutes. At this rate, I could probably combine everything and call it a fundraiser/ grand opening/ Molly loses her mind extravaganza."

"Hey, that's honestly not a terrible idea. Soft opening? I say let's shoot for that. Hey, speaking of shoot, do they have any leads on Attic Man?"

Our friend group took to calling Mr. Fletcher "Attic Man" before we knew his true identity, and it has clearly stuck long after his identification. They've had a field day positing all manner of theories about what happened to him, ranging from completely mundane (he climbed up there in a dementia fueled confusion and got trapped), to the completely deranged (he was an escaped member of a circus mafia and was "taken out", then hid up there post mortem). I'm wondering at this point if they've all taken out legitimate bets on what the real story is because I've gotten a steady stream of texts and calls over the last week asking questions that I don't have the answer to–quite frankly, I don't think anyone does, and probably won't at this rate. It is still nagging me that Linny and her mom were in there clearly looking for something, but there shouldn't have been anything to see.

"No, but I got to meet his daughter and wife yesterday. If you would like to see a ghost in real life, you should meet Nora Fletcher. She fits the role perfectly. She scared Marge so good she fainted."

"Oh sheesh, that's scary. Wait-did you go up to Oak Hills?"

"Nope, they were down here. In the Shoppe. I would say they broke in, but Cooper thinks they may still have an old key and let themselves in without permission, although they tried to sell me that they did. Supposedly they were looking to see if anything looked out of the ordinary to them to help solve the case. Now, I'm trying to figure out what they were looking to take since they weren't supposed to be in there and were clearly trying to grab something they didn't want anyone else to see."

Mandy pauses, and I can tell she's thinking through her own theory. She has always been the quietest one in our group, but she's gained some confidence to really speak her mind in the last several months, and it proved invaluable with the Dick MacDougal situation. "What if they weren't taking something? Did you see them leave with anything?"

"Well, no. But she did have a huge Louis Vuitton tote, and whatever it is could have been small enough to put in there and leave with it unsuspiciously. I know they were upstairs, but I didn't go up and check anything after they left. Why? What are you thinking?"

"I'm just wondering... what if they weren't taking something, but putting something up there to find. Some sort of false evidence, or something. I'm just really curious if they will find something now that they've been in there," she says, trailing off. "I'm sorry, that probably sounds crazy! What are the chances that she'd be involved in her own dad's death? This isn't an episode of *Dateline* or something."

"Not as crazy as we probably think. She was very quick to

tell me that her brother was not to be trusted, which tells me she is likely to not be trustworthy, either."

"Have you talked to Asa at all about this? I'm sure he knew them well and could help you put some of the pieces together."

"No, but I've been meaning to. That may jump to the top of my to-do list this afternoon. Hey, I have a random question for you." I jump subjects a little bit before we wrap up our conversation, mostly looking for confirmation about Mia's theory from yesterday. "Did Emily give you a reason for why she volunteered you to head up the silent auction?"

"She said I was the most organized of the moms. I think she was just trying to butter me up. You're really organized too; I don't think I'm the most organized of everyone."

"Well, I learned yesterday from Mia that there is apparently an inverse relationship between organization and fun. Did you know that?"

She pauses before letting out a dry laugh. "Didn't know that, but it tracks with the fact that my family calls me Captain Buzzkill and the Taskmaster."

"Well, well, well. To what do I owe the pleasure of the one and only Mrs. Molly Jones calling on me this afternoon?" Asa Shoemaker's quiet gravelly voice calls from his small living area as I slip through his apartment door at the Cinnamon Court Retirement Village. I wrapped up my fundraiser work, including commiserating with Mandy, a few hours ago, so after feeding the ranch men a hearty lunch, I packed up for town to pay a visit to the one man who might be able to make a little sense of everything that's going on around here.

We've known Asa for several years now-he was previously the owner of a large scale Hereford cattle operation down the county road from us, on the other side of Dick MacDougal. While most other people in town seemed to love to cheer for us to struggle as we started ranching, Asa was always a quiet, but steady voice of encouragement for us, and we've never forgotten that. As it seems to go around here, he was widowed fairly early, and they never had children, so he's been flying solo for a few decades now, but still seems content in this life, despite the handful of heartaches he's been dealt.

"My goodness, where do I start, Asa?" A small laugh pops out involuntarily, and I think he must know at least partially why I'm here. News, or rather gossip, travels like wildfire around here, and typically does more damage, too. I sit down in a brown corduroy La-Z-Boy recliner opposite of him as I drop my bag on the linoleum floor next to me. He holds out a cut crystal candy dish from the end table next to him, and I happily take a Werther's Original before reaching down into my bag and coming up with a white paper bag and offering it to him.

"Now, Molly. You know they're telling me I have the pre-diabetes. I'm not sure I'm supposed to have those," He says a little despondently, looking down into the bag full of Delilah's strawberry lemonade thumbprint cookies.

"But you can have the Werther's?" I ask jokingly, pushing my wrapper in my jeans pocket after popping the caramel into my mouth.

"Touche, my girl. I'm sure just one won't hurt," he nods, pulling one out, but putting the bag down on the table next to him instead of giving it back to me. "I've been waiting for you to come and see me, you know. I need an update on all your goings-on."

"It's been a little wild around here lately. But I'm sure you know most of that. How are you holding up? It can't have been easy to hear you've lost another friend," I say quietly, hoping that appropriate rides the line of specificity in what I want to talk about, but open to letting him share whatever is on his heart.

He sighs heavily and nods. "Yes, it was quite a shock to hear Langley had passed in such a manner. But honestly, I'd lost him as a friend many years before that. It's never easy to lose a friend, but typically speaking, you just lose them once."

"I see. I had heard something to the effect of y'all having had a falling out at some point. Is that what you mean?" I ask gently, knowing I am toeing the line of empathy and nosiness very closely.

"I figured you would get up here to ask me these questions sooner than later. I think I'm going to need a cup of coffee to go with these cookies if you want all my secrets, Mrs. Jones," he laughs, gesturing to a single cup coffee maker on the counter in his kitchenette.

A few minutes later, I walk back to our chairs with two Buffalo Creek Booster Club coffee cups full of generic decaf medium roast. I pass one to him, and try to sit as gently as I can so I don't spill mine. He takes a few long sips of his, and I wait quietly because I think he's going to get this going on his own and I don't want to seem insensitive by prying.

"Alright, so you want to know about my relationship with Langley, and what I know about the Fletchers, don't you?" he asks, and I nod silently. "I won't guarantee it will be helpful, but here we go. Langley and I met many, many years ago in graduate school. I had been ranching and running the family's mercantile business for several years, but was wanting to have opportunities to get something bigger and better. So, Ruth convinced me to go back for my MBA over at Southern Baptist. Langley was in a similar situation-his family had an oil business that he was trying to run. He knew all the oil ins and outs, he had double degrees in engineering and geology, but the actual running of the business was killing him so he enrolled for an MBA, too. I knew nothing about oil, but I knew I could run a successful business if I had the chance, and had the right partner that could handle the proprietary side while I did the business management side." He pauses to pull another thumbprint cookie out of the bag, and then holds the bag open to me. I take one because, one, I can't resist those cookies either, and two, I think commiseration over cookies together tends to work better than interrogation.

"Well, for whatever reason–I like to think it was the Lord's hand, because I think His hand is in everything–Ruth and I became fast friends with the Fletchers. By graduation, he and I had a fully formed business plan to transition his family's oil holdings into our mercantile building and really start rolling into the most successful oil and gas business of the valley. And we did well for a lot of years. Langley and Nora had the same struggles we did to have children, and that kept us close for a long time, until they just couldn't stand it any longer. They went to Dallas and had what they call IVF now. It was so new and so experimental back then, and I just knew it wasn't going to work and was just setting them up for more heartbreak."

I nod, thinking I honestly have no idea when IVF became mainstream. I've had friends that have used it with success without much worry, but I can't imagine what it would have been like on the cutting edge.

"Miracle on miracle, it worked after a few tries, and they had Madeline and Maxwell in one fell swoop. One fell swoop of terror."

"Did Ruth ever want to try since it worked for the Fletchers?" I ask, hoping that wasn't insensitive. I brush a few stray cookie crumbs off my jeans while he ponders for a second before continuing.

"No, she felt that the expense for the unpredictability was too much. My Ruth believed in the Lord's providence more than anyone I've ever known, and she felt to her core that He would give her children as she was meant to have them. We were respite foster parents for many years, and she took delight and purpose in caring for children when they needed someone the most, but we just never had the chance to be someone's full time parent, and she had peace about that. Now, where was I?"

"The Fletchers had their twins?"

"Oh, yes. So, Langley and Nora now have Madeline and Maxwell, and they are both hell on wheels. Imagine having miracle twins in your forties-you are tired, you are old, you don't know how to parent, and you are so unimaginably thankful and grateful to have these babies, or just babies in general. They wanted to give those kids every good thing and blessing on this earth, plus they didn't even sniff the word discipline ever in their lives and were all the worse for it. We used to gird our loins for the days Nora would bring them up to the office, especially as toddlers."

"Really? I met Linny a few days ago, actually at the Shoppe, and she said the building was full of fond memories for her as they came up there all the time as children."

He harrumphs loudly, and his coffee teeters over the edge of his cup. "I'm sure she does have fond memories of strewing geology maps from hither to yon and leaving leaking sippy cups of apple juice on multi-million dollar contracts."

I laugh, trying to picture a younger, probably more rigid Asa in the middle of an "Eloise"-esque office raid in the late eighties/ early nineties. I'm wondering if this is exactly where their falling out happens-I would wager that parenting is the thing that people are the most sensitive and least receptive to opinions about. "That couldn't have been easy. Did you ever discuss their parenting style with them?"

"Ruth and I broadly broached it a time or two. We had a handful of valuable things broken in our home, but felt it wasn't worth it overall to ruin our friendship over it. The louder sentiment about it was the fact that the entirety of

Buffalo Creek and Oak Hills refused to babysit for them. I learned to shut and lock my office door whenever I would hear them storm the downstairs. Our office girls would stow away anything important on the first floor when they saw Nora pull into the parking lot. But, more than anything, they made Langley happy, and we wanted that for him, and didn't want to spoil it."

I nod in agreement, thinking that that's all any of us want for our friends. But that doesn't sound like the end of the story. "So... did they get any better as they got older?"

"Well, when they got to elementary school, they were tamed a little after a year or two. They had a few no-nonsense teachers right off the bat thanks to their reputation and that helped to curb their wild behavior. I had heard that they were quite the rebellious teenagers, but that was no surprise given their toddlerhood and early childhood. Even though the teachers helped take the wild off at school, they were still raised with no respect for Langley or Nora, and it never changed."

"That's pretty sad, given the circumstances. Did their relationship improve when the kids became adults? I guess maybe not because Linny warned me that her brother and father had a poor relationship."

"No, they reaped in adulthood what they sowed in childhood. It was difficult for Ruth or I to comment throughout the years because we were deemed as an invalid opinion since we weren't parents, at least in the traditional sense. But that wasn't what drove Langley and I to the break in our relationship."

He pauses and sighs, and I try not to look too eager. I appreciate the story time, truly I do, but I only have so long before it's school pick up time, and I'd love to get as many answers as I can before I have to hit the road. "When the kids were in late elementary school, I noticed a change in Langley."

"A change? Like he was sick?"

"No, like he was worn down by the strains of his family and wasn't making decisions he would have made in better conscience. Linny and Wells were out of control, and Nora would not hear of them ever being disciplined or having boundaries of any sort. Langley knew they were headed down a bad road, but he just never had the will to cross Nora. And instead of working it out within his family, he sought comfort elsewhere." Asa hangs his head and looks near tears. I feel my own tears well up, mostly out of empathy for the fact that this man has seen so much human messiness, and remained strong throughout. How can one man stay so resolute in the midst of absolute chaos like he has?

"He had an affair?" I ask quietly, not wanting to nudge him too quickly, but wanting to confirm my suspicions.

"He began an inappropriate relationship outside his marriage, yes." Asa confirms, like he's too dignified to even use the colloquial term.

"What happened?"

"It seemed to begin innocently enough, but as with all things worldly, it spiraled beyond his ability to control. Ruth and I had minded our own business for ten plus years about the raising of their children, but I couldn't watch my very best friend and business partner become mired in that destructive trap and not try to help him. I confronted him, and it went very poorly."

"But if y'all thought they wouldn't take it well to comment on the raising of their kids, why would you go there? That feels like something someone would be even more sensitive about."

"Did you know that we are called to judge one another as believers?" he asks evenly, looking up to meet me in the eye. I nod, as I know what he is referring to, and it is generally a deep cut compared to what most people like to reference when it comes to judging. "The book of Matthew tells us to 'judge not lest we be judged', but the apostle Paul tells us in his first letter to the Corinthians that we are not meant to judge those outside the church, but we are called to judge sin among us to hold one another accountable in the Spirit. I don't take that charge lightly, and neither should any of us. And there are plenty of examples in which we are called to come before one another with a humble heart, both when giving and receiving counsel. I felt like I did that, but Langley disagreed, and he very much resented my assessment of his situation. We remained strained, but professional for several months as the situation was in a deadlock, but when he came to me later to tell me that he was going to be a father again, I could not abide being in business with him any longer."

"He got his mistress pregnant?" I blurt out, clapping a hand over my mouth in disbelief. Asa frowns, like he is disapproving of this terminology, but that I'm not incorrect.

"We were doing well in our business venture–better than either of us had imagined we would. There had been an offer of a buyout from a larger company during that time, and we'd both considered it, but had not made a firm decision. Once he shared his predicament, I told him we were no longer of similar mind, and it would be best for us to part company, both in business and in friendship. So, we dissolved F&S Oil and Gas and went our separate ways."

I'll admit, in all the possibilities I ran through prior to visiting him about why they had their "falling out", that was not one of them. And I cannot believe the general grapevine never got the lid off this one. "That is crazy. But you did reconcile at one point, didn't you? Surely that didn't completely end your friendship forever? Linny said you had spoken to them recently about us buying the building."

He solemnly shakes his head and looks down. "I believed wholeheartedly I was doing the best thing I could to hold him to the truth in firm, but no-nonsense, love. But this was also during the same time that my sweet Ruth received her terminal cancer diagnosis. Ruth was my whole world, and I couldn't fathom how someone who had their one true love right in front of them with no expiration date would squander that while mine was being unfairly ripped from me. It made me bitter and unkind to Langley, and I regret that I couldn't have helped him find a better solution to his situation, or that we couldn't have remained friends despite our disagreement."

I sit quietly for a few moments, thinking through everything he's revealed in the last few minutes. "So, what happened? I assume Nora forgave him and they stayed together since they were still married when he went missing? Does he have any contact with this third child?"

"As far as I'm aware, Nora never knew that this happened, or if she did, it was swept completely under the rug and never spoken of. And Langley had a third child, but he was not part of raising it that I know of. The child's mother was also married and I believe the plan was for her to raise the child as her husband's without him the wiser and she and Langley dissolved their relationship once it reached that point. It was my understanding that their relationship was not one of romantic interest, but more of mutual friendship and commiseration. And probably excitement, to an extent. I never had an interest in that sort of thing, but you could say that Langley didn't get a lot of positive attention at home, and you could see where a man would take a shine to it if he found it elsewhere. But, nevertheless, once the business sold, we went our separate ways, and that was that. I never spoke to him again, and I've not seen or heard from the children, either."

"Do you think that this will all come to light now that he's passed? Would he have acknowledged that child in his will?"

"I'm not sure. I'd like to believe that he softened in age and realized the error of his ways and would have wanted to make amends. But when you live a lie for that long and you've deceived even yourself, it's that much harder to discern the truth from your alternate version of events."

"Wow," I say, still a little in disbelief. "I can't believe that there is a third, possibly unknown to them, Fletcher child walking around somewhere. What happened to her?"

Asa frowns again, but yawns before correcting me because we are likely closing in on his afternoon nap time. He sinks a little further down in his armchair, and works hard to keep his heavy eyelids open. I thought our conversation would come to a halt when I would have to jump ship to go pick up kids from school, but it looks like it's going to be here when Asa peters out on me and falls asleep. He stifles another yawn, and reaches for the small multicolored afghan in the floor basket near him. "His mother was one of our secretaries, although I was never sure exactly which one."

chapter
seven

"MOM, how many dollars have I earned?" A few days later, we are armed with dust rags, mops, brooms, and various cleaning sprays intent to make the first floor of the Shoppe shiny and clean so we can start setting up the displays and bringing in the inventory. Shep, Cooter, and Roy are cleaning and repairing all the stone work on the wrap-around porch, and Hayes and Mia are inside helping me with the promise of earning extra money. I have a little kid flashback of when I would bribe the kids to help me clean our house with the promise of "dollars". Hayes was always very aware of the number of dollars he had earned back then, and apparently some things stay the same.

"Uh, how long have you been working?" I ask distractedly, getting a bucket of mop water ready to mop behind the counter. Since we got the go ahead yesterday to get back in the building, it has felt like a whirlwind of tasks and to-do lists. I know we've gotten a fair amount done, but I'd be lying if I said I clocked the exact time we got to work or even what the current time is.

Hayes takes the opportunity to stop his halfhearted

wiping of the baseboards and sits back on his heels to think. "Probably like six, seven hours, right?"

"Try more like two, bro," Mia snorts sarcastically, rolling her eyes as she sprays a thick "M" of foam glass cleaner on one of the large picture windows to the east, then wipes it down. Hayes's body sinks in defeat, and I try not to laugh, as I would have completely bought that we'd been at this for six or seven hours. They've been pretty good sports about giving up a Saturday morning to do this, but I know it's not ideal.

"You're doing good, bud. Hang in there a little while longer and then maybe you and Mia can take a break and go down the street to grab us lunch. I'd say you've earned twenty dollars so far." I wink at him as I dunk my mop in the water and wring it out. The benefit to snagging this particular building is that it is already set up to function as a store, so we really aren't having to install any infrastructure. The downside, of course, was just the spare corpse in the attic, but you take the losses with the wins around here.

As I mop behind the counter, I let my mind replay my conversation with Asa earlier this week for the millionth time. Just as we were getting to the juicy part, he zonked out and left me hanging. I didn't have the heart to wake him up, so I ended up leaving Cinnamon Court that day with more questions than I came with, and precious few answers. But at least we're back in business as far as getting the Shoppe on the road. I realize that the obvious answer is to visit Asa again and really get down to the nitty gritty, but that just doesn't feel right at the moment. While I would love whatever answers he could give, the line between casual conversation and harassment can get thinner and thinner the more attempts at a subject. I've decided to let it ride for a little while on the subject of Langley's death and turn my full focus to a successful Shoppe opening instead. The authorities can sort it out, I'm sure. And if they don't—well, it's like Jesus told Peter about John: what's it to you? Or in this case...what's it to me?

The kids make it another thirty minutes or so with their cleaning tasks, and I get to the point that I need them out to mop the rest of the floor, so Shep sends them with cash down the street to the drug store to get lunch for everyone. They will either team up together to get in some sort of ridiculous trouble that requires the both of them, or they will kill one another in the process, so I look forward to seeing how that shakes out. Shep and the boys take to the back yard to start working on some karaoke night preparations, and I set myself to finishing the downstairs cleaning before the kids get back with lunch.

I slip my headphones on to wrap up mopping, and am just finishing up around the front window nooks when I see a shadow of someone coming up the steps to the front door. "Shep, I just mopped there, don't come in, please!" I shout over the Brandon Lake song blasting through my headphones. The windows are cracked, so I figure he can hear me, even outside. It's a hundred-plus year old building, but it's not that fortified. I scrub the corner and turn partially to the door as I run along the baseboard, still seeing the same shadow of a person lingering in the doorway.

"I'm mopping in here, babe, please don't come in and step on the floor!" I shout again, a little frustrated that it seems like he's ignoring me. Shep is sometimes in his own head getting jobs done and it takes a second to grab his attention, but he never intentionally or purposefully ignores me.

I finish up on the west side of the building and start rolling the mop bucket toward the east side just as the door swings open. "Shep, I've asked three times! Stay out of here while I'm mopping, please!" I rip my headphones off and drop my mop in the bucket, getting ready to have a real throwdown about this when I see that the man coming through the door is not Shep. He looks to be mid-to-late forties with slicked back jet black hair, dressed in golf shorts a tad on the short side and a polo, with a smaller, somewhat lanky build. One slick bottom loafer hits the wet hardwood floor as he steps inside and he immediately goes down, knocking his back on the threshold and wincing as he goes. Every single mom fiber of my being wants to smother him in *"I told you not to"* and *"If you would have just listened to me"*, but I take a deep breath instead and hold out a hand to help him up.

"Well, you really ought to put up a sign or something that it's not safe for folks to enter, don't you think," he muses, a hint of sarcasm in his voice as he dusts off his backside. "You sure wouldn't want people to get hurt and leave yourself open to liabilities or anything." He gives me a smarmy smile and I can feel my inner self absolutely screaming with rage in response. Who is this complete scumbag and why is he not only in my building for no apparent reason, but low-key threatening me with litigation due to his own stupidity and lack of listening skills. I shouldn't have expected any differently considering he is sockless in those loafers. Obviously a lack of good decision making. And, just ew.

"I didn't think we'd need a sign since I yelled at you not to come in thrice... That means three times." I give him a tight, but unimpressed smile, suppressing what I'd really like to say and holding up three fingers. The downside of opening a store is that we are about to become public figures essentially, and how we behave in public matters. It's always mattered, no doubt, but now it's the difference between *"we love doing business with them because they are really great people"* and *"we'll never go back there because of that one time they kinda came off as rude"*.

"Oh, well, I guess I missed that." He shrugs and takes a tentative step forward as he looks around. I swear on all that is holy, if he is dumb enough to fall again, I will let him writhe like an upside down turtle until he gets himself up.

"Is there something I can help you with?" I sigh, watching as he tracks footprints through the areas I've mopped already, milling around near the back counter. This man has less wherewithal than someone trying to teach a blind man to read a map, and I've beyond had it. I consider myself a pretty patient woman, but I'm no patience millionaire and that account is about to be overdrawn.

"This is where Debbie used to work," he says wistfully, running his hand down the length of the countertop. "She would keep hard candy just for us in a dish right here." He thumps the corner of the countertop, shaking his head like he is trying to control his emotions. "Connie had her desk right over there by the door. She would always give us pennies from her purse. And Ginny's desk was right there in the middle. They were all like second mothers to us; they loved us so much." He chokes up a little bit as he walks through to the front windows, giving me quite the imaginary tour. My whole body cringes down to my toes every time he makes a footprint on my wet floor and the longer he puts on this little show, I start putting together all the pieces of who this blowhard is and why he is in my building. He clearly went to the same acting school as his sister. And he seems like the kind of guy that doesn't get questioned about who he is or why he would be somewhere.

"I'm so sorry, do I know you?" I ask, hoping to throw off his pompous charade by not playing into it. I know exactly who he is now, but I don't want to give him that satisfaction.

He stops and stares quizzically at me, and the pause he takes makes it seem like this isn't part of the script for his show– I've thrown him an improv curveball and he's trying to decide how to proceed. "My apologies, I suppose I should have introduced myself. You must be new around here. Wells

Fletcher," he says, as he extends a hand. Shep would have more than one thing to say about how soft and uncalloused (a.k.a., how girly) his hands are, but I'm certain that meets my expectations given what I've seen so far. Also, how did these people decide on nicknames? Linny and Wells? Have they ever heard of the much more obvious Maddie and Max for Madeline and Maxwell? Talk about taking the road less travelled.

I watch as he waxes on about his childhood in this room as he continues to make trails of footprints, tempering that with Asa's admission that they were very ill-behaved children that no one liked to have in the office. "I just can't believe after everything, this is where Pops met his end. But, of all the places in the world, he loved it the most in this office. I think it's where he would have wanted to go," he concludes, making it to the bottom of the stairs. I frown a little to myself, thinking that it sounded like they only owned the oil and gas business for 15 years tops before selling out for what I assume would have been quite the payday. Combine that with the fact that the driving force behind the sale was a moral rift between two very close friends, I highly doubt this building was Langley Fletcher's favorite place in the world, so much so that he would have wanted to meet his Maker in the attic. I'm not sure exactly what I expected "Wells" to be like in person, but he's turning out to be quite the tool. Probably on par with what his childhood self sounded like.

"Right, well, we are actually in preparation for opening the building in a new capacity. Can I help you with something specific? Otherwise, we probably need to have you move it along so we can get back to work," I say, gesturing to all the cleaning supplies and the Marauder's Map of very not-invisible footprints he has left me. I clearly have not managed his mischief well.

He chokes out a very fake sounding sob and I try not to visibly roll my eyes. "I just... all of this has been so hard..." He puts a hand over his face, his shoulders crumbling a little as he tries to sell that he is truly griefstricken and distraught. "I just wanted to see where Pops met his end before you potentially erase his legacy here. You know, for closure. I'll just pop upstairs quickly and be right back down." He starts jogging up the stairs when I hear a loud wolf whistle that makes him jump. Honestly, it made me jump a little, too, even though I saw Shep coming in the back door out of my peripheral vision and knew it was coming. Thankfully he got here just in time to put a stop to this nonsense.

"No, I don't think you will. This is legally our building now and going anywhere in it without permission is trespassing," Shep says evenly, standing behind me to both literally and figuratively back me up. We stand there silently as Wells stares at us from half-way up the stairs like he is gauging how serious we are about this.

"Well, I beg your pardon. My father was unexpectedly found dead upstairs, and all I wanted was to have a moment of remembrance, but sure, by all means, get back to your cleaning. I wouldn't want to ruin anything for you. There very well could be treasured family belongings up there that belong to us, but as you say, it's yours now," he smirks, taking heavy, loud steps on each stair to come back down. He saunters with little intention in the direction of the door, like he is trying to formulate another excuse, either through guilt or pulled heartstrings, to get his way up there.

"Sir, you're a day late and a dollar short on that. Or rather, two weeks late. The sheriff's department has thoroughly combed every inch of this building and there are no belongings left here. Plus, your sister and mother have already been up there too, without permission, might I add. I can assure you, there is nothing left up there. I hope that helps ease the pain," I say, adding a little fake sweet to my voice to match his as I gesture to the door, indicating he can go ahead and see himself through it. As soon as I say "sister", he stops abruptly in his tracks and whips back around to face me and Shep with genuine concern, maybe even leaning toward panic.

"Did you say that my sister has been in here? Recently?"

"Yes, earlier this week. Your mother was in here too. I'm not a gerontologist, but I would recommend not taking her from her facility with her level of dementia, if you want my honest opinion. She was rather confused about it all." I push a few stray hairs back up into my messy bun and wave the hem of my oversized t-shirt to generate a little breeze. We've got all the existing ceiling fans on the first floor going, but it's still not enough to keep up with the heat of the day rolling in. I'm hot and tired with a to-do list longer than my arm and this dude has really worn out his welcome.

"Yes, I see. Well, let me be honest with you. My sister and my father did not have a good relationship. If she was here snooping around, it was pretty likely she was up to no good. I think the sheriff should be alerted," he says with authority, almost like he is doing me a favor to warn me of her unsavoriness. He is standing in the doorway, with one hand on the large doorknob, and no indication he is planning to make his exit all the way through it any time soon. I wave both hands to essentially shoo him through, taking hold of the inside doorknob to shut the door behind him. "And funny you should warn me about her. Because she said all the exact same things… about you."

***

"Alright, boss, where does this one go?" Roy squeaks out, holding one end of a round wooden table that he and Cooter have carried in from the trailer outside a few hours later. Once we knew that the Shoppe was greenlit, I began scouring garage and estate sales for old dining tables and bookcases that I could strip and stain to the same dark gray/ oaky finish so they would match but still have visual interest. We've stored all the chairs up in our old bunkhouse for a time that we might need extra chairs (ironically, probably in a few weeks when we open the doors to greater Buffalo Creek to join us for karaoke), and are now about to start staging these tables with merchandise. In between directing the boys on where to place the furniture, I am measuring and taping a line on the wall heading up the stairs to lay my blue chinoiserie inspired wallpaper. Once the wallpaper is up, Shep is planning to trim it off for me, and I'll finish off the wall with some vintage photos of Buffalo Creek that I found in our library and had enlarged and framed. I'm probably naively optimistic, but I think opening by our original date in a few weeks is not too crazy to think possible. The refrigeration people will be here Monday to install the coolers for the meat, plus one display cooler for pre-made floral arrangements, as well as back coolers for extra stock. Shep has already rigged up the wooden dowels to hold large rolls of wrapping paper on the wall behind the counter, as well as a small set to sit on the back counter to hold different colors and textures of curling and fabric ribbons and bows. The internet service will be installed on Tuesday, so point of sale units will come in on Wednesday. We can be pulling out inventory to style and display all the while. We are by no means close to the finish line, but a clear plan is starting to fall into place, and I'm starting to relax a little. The only little nagging I can't clear from the back of my mind is why both Fletcher siblings are telling me the other is the problem. That, combined with wondering if either of them know there is a third in their midst, just won't give my mind a rest.

"Let's put it right here, guys. That should be the last of them, right?" I direct them into the nook of the window bay on the west side, and then stand back to make sure everything looks even and easy to navigate through.

"Yeah, that's the last table. You want us to start bringing in the boxes?" Cooter asks, wiping the sweat from his brow and popping his top pearl snap to expose a little more chest for more air flow.

"Easy, killer, this is a family establishment," Shep teases as he walks by with the first of the aforementioned boxes. "Save it for your karaoke night routine."

"Karaoke night? We ain't getting up in front of everyone for karaoke night," Roy protests, shaking his head. He is typically the more shy and reserved of the pair, so his response doesn't surprise me, but Cooter is adamantly nodding his head in agreement.

"Yeah, Boss. We ain't singers. That's for sissies. And Johnny Cash. But only Johnny Cash."

I roll my eyes and join Shep at the counter where he is stacking the boxes. "I can't believe y'all. This is for charity. You wouldn't sing one little song for charity?" I ask as I begin to unpack the top box. It is general office supplies, like sticky notes, scissors, paper clips, and rubber bands, all meant to go in the built-in drawers behind the counter.

"Boss, that would pert near ruin our reputation, I'm afraid," Roy counters, and I can tell he is truly serious.

"Well, you don't have to sing for everyone, but how about you get to those other boxes out there waiting," Shep suggests, heading out to grab another load. "Maybe y'all just need to post up as security for the night. Protect everyone from all the ghosts we can't seem to get rid of around here." Roy and Cooter look at one another with concern, like they want to believe Shep is kidding, but are also aware of the series of events that have been unfolding around here. I mean, I couldn't rule out ghost infestation at this point, either.

"I don't want to be a ghostbuster," Roy mumbles as they shuffle for the door.

"I ain't afraid of no ghost." Cooter puffs out his chest and answers confidently as they head outside for the trailers. I head back to the counter and get back to unpacking my supply boxes before they bring in any more inventory boxes, humming the *Ghostbusters* song to myself because it's now obviously stuck in my head. After a few minutes, the back door creaks open and I jump, snatching up the scissors on the counter near me and turning back with my weapon. All of my people are in the front, so I'm definitely on guard for whoever is making an appearance through the back uninvited.

"It's just me, just me!" Mandy laughs as she struggles through the back door with a clear plastic tote box full of various vases and buckets. I take a deep breath and relax, setting the scissors back on the counter.

"Sorry, we've just had a weird day with visitors. Why the back door though?"

"I could park closer to the back door," she says, winking and nodding toward all of our vehicles and trailers parked in the front. "I figured I'd try it, and if it was locked I'd head to the front. What other visitors have you had today?" She slides the box onto the side counter under the stairs where her flower counter will be and dusts off her athletic dress.

"The infamous nefarious brother came by today."

Mandy's eyes widen and a small smile spreads across her face. "Was he trying to get upstairs?" she asks, a little giddiness in her voice.

"He was, but Shep stopped him. This guy is something else. One of those adults that reeks of '*I have no idea what a spanking spoon is*' but should have had a great familiarity. He tried to tell me that his sister was the problem."

"It's both of y'all. Hi, y'all are the problem, it's both of y'all," Mandy warbles badly, trying to make a joke of the popular Taylor Swift anthem. I laugh and nod, agreeing that generally speaking, if someone is adamant that someone else is the problem, they are likely just as much the culprit as well.

"Seriously. He was not happy that she was here, and here first. I don't know what they are all looking for, but it must be something important for everyone to have made a pass through here to look, you know?"

"Have you been up to look?" Mandy asks, jerking her head toward the second floor. I shake my head, and she bounces toward the stairs. "C'mon, we gotta see if we can see what they were looking for!"

I silently follow her up the stairs and through the stained glass door at the landing into the second floor hallway. Honestly, I should probably admit that I haven't been upstairs since we found Langley Fletcher. I mean, technically speaking, today is the first day we've been in the building with permission anyway, but I've had no interest or desire in coming up here. Post traumatic stress disorder feels dramatic to describe our situation and how I feel about being back upstairs, but I would say the thought of being up here gives me a small to medium sized knot of dread in my stomach. I know there's no getting around it in certain situations, but I don't think we were meant to see drastically decomposed remains of other humans.

Mandy pokes her head in and out of the bedrooms, not seeing anything eye-catching right off the bat. "Do you think the daughter and the wife looked in the attic?" she asks, jumping up to catch the pull down string for the attic door. My whole body tenses and I squeeze my eyes shut as she yanks it down. I wait expectantly for the thud of something unsavory, like muscle memory, but it doesn't come. I peek one eye open and see Mandy scurrying up the stairs to look around.

"It smells terrible up here!" Her voice wafts down from up in the attic, and I try to stay nonchalant, hoping that she won't notice that I'm not right behind her.

"I mean, there was something dead up there!" I call, unsure what to do. As I stand there like a bump on a log, shifting weight between my feet, I hear the thunder of Mandy's footsteps across the attic floor over my head. "Be careful! I don't know if that floor's sturdy enough for you to be running on it!"

"You gotta get up here! I think I found something!" She pops her head through the door opening and excitedly beckons me to join her. I take a hesitant step, and then stop.

"Something like what? Do I really need to come up there or can you just bring it down here?" I can't really explain it, but I could just about seal off the entire second floor and beyond of this building and not miss it one bit. Just being up to the point where I am is making me much more anxious than I typically am, and I can feel my heartrate running through the roof as it is.

"I really don't think I should move it. What if it is a really important piece of evidence? I don't want to be in trouble for tampering with the crime scene." She sits down on the top step and I cringe down to my toes because she looks so precariously perched there, like she could fall through to the floor, just like Langley Fletcher, at any second.

Before I can decide if I'm going to suck it up and go up there or stay down here like the big chicken that I am, Shep thankfully pops up on the top of the landing.

"What are you looking for up there?" He looks up to Mandy skeptically, and I can tell the logical part of him thinks she is not making super smart decisions by being up in the attic and sitting up on the steps.

"I found something that might be important up here, but I don't want to move it in case it turns out to be like evidence or something," Mandy calls back down, gesturing up into the attic. She pulls herself up through the hole and Shep moves to the pull down ladder to follow her.

"Thanks, babe," I whisper, and he nods, with the air unspoken between us that I just don't want to go up there.

I hear some bumps and thumps around upstairs, but no talking. I feel thumps of my heartbeat up in my ears as I wait for them to come down, telling myself there's no way they could have found something important. The sheriff's department combed every inch of this place over the last week or two, and there's no way they missed something. Although, they did miss a whole murder a few months ago, so maybe I shouldn't give them so much credit.

A few minutes later, Shep comes down the step ladder and turns to face me. "I think Mandy did actually find something. I sent pictures to Cooper and he said to go ahead and pull it out and he's on his way." Shep holds up a large sealed manila envelope with a faded typed label stuck to the front. I take the envelope gingerly and try to make out the label. "Cassius Renfro, Esq." with a local Buffalo Creek address is printed on the sticker from what I can make out.

"I have no idea who Cassius Renfro is, do you?" I stare at Shep quizzically, and he shrugs.

"Beats me. Cooper said they would open when they get here."

"I can't believe we found a real clue, y'all!" Mandy beams, bouncing up to us after coming down the stairs. "What do y'all think is in there?"

"Not sure, but I think we can at least meet them downstairs. There isn't enough air up here to wait around to find out," Shep answers, starting for the stairs. Mandy and I follow him, but we leave the attic ladder pulled down for when Cooper gets here in case he wants to look up in there again.

"Alright, Joneses, what did we find this time?" Cooper asks when he arrives a few minutes later. He is in civilian clothes, and I wonder if we've pulled him from some sort of Saturday night activity with his wife, as he is not wearing his typical cowboy hat, and his salt and pepper hair is neatly combed. I could see Mrs. Tammy not allowing hats on their evenings out.

Shep hands over the envelope, and he examines the label and the seal thoroughly, taking pictures with his phone as he flips it over and back. "Did we interrupt a date night for you, Sheriff?" I ask coyly, unable to contain myself as he does his inspection.

"Ms. Tammy and I may have been enjoying an early dinner at the country club."

"Oh, my goodness, I'm so sorry to interrupt your evening! We're definitely going to be on her bad side now."

"Eh, she doesn't really have a bad side. She's the world's most forgiving person. That's how she's managed to stay married to me for forty six years. Well, are y'all ready to see what's inside?"

Mandy nods with glee, and I have to admit, I'm pretty curious myself. Shep hands him the pocket knife from his back pocket, and Cooper uses it to slice down the top of the envelope to open it cleanly. He peeks inside and frowns, turning it over in his hands before looking back up at us.

"What is it?" Mandy asks with bated breath, hardly able to contain her excitement.

"Nothing," he says gruffly, flipping the envelope over and shaking it to the ground. "It's empty."

eight

"I JUST DON'T UNDERSTAND it. I can't find anything about who Cassius Renfro is. Esq is short for Esquire, right? And, Esquire still means attorney, right?" By the beginning of the next week, we are no closer to answers about the mysterious empty envelope than we were Saturday night. Cooper put the envelope in a large ziploc evidence bag, and Mandy and Shep showed him the small cranny the envelope was wedged into between floor supports in the attic. Further inspection showed that someone had likely never sealed it in the first place, so taking the contents out was easy, and then the heat of the attic sealed it afterward. Coop took it all to be impounded as evidence, but we haven't heard any updates, and it's driving me a little crazy. Nothing is coming up on Google, which means I'm at a dead end. I am still talking through the little that I do know with Shep over our morning coffee and I can tell he is beyond tired of this discussion. There is truly no explanation as to what this was meant to be, if it means anything at all, but I need to pause this to turn my immediate attention to my planning meeting for the karaoke night with Kaci Whitfield this morning.

"I believe it does. He probably existed before the internet, and never made it on there. I think I would have loved to have existed pre-internet," he replies, dropping his breakfast plate and coffee cup in the sink. "Well, I'm headed up to check cows and cameras in that north pasture. Call me if you need anything." He kisses me on the cheek and heads out the side door as I pick up the rest of our breakfast dishes and tidy up before my guest gets here.

"Molly! It's so great to finally meet you in person! I'm Kaci Whitfield!" Coach Whitfield is exactly as I pictured-barely five foot tall, bouncy blonde curls, cartoon sized blue eyes, and a figure that would make a Sports Illustrated model jealous. She has arrived on our driveway right on time in a Barbie sized Mini Cooper convertible, and is wearing a hot pink crop top and short set that looks vacuum sealed to her body. I walk out to the end of our driveway in my Ugg slippers and matching pale pink quarter zip pullover and drawstring pants sweat set (what Shep calls my "Arthur Spooner suit") to meet her. I raise my coffee cup to her in salute and prepare myself for the high energy meeting to come.

"Thanks for coming out to our neck of the woods. Hopefully it wasn't too bad of a drive," I say as I gesture to the door for us to head inside. I see Cooter and Roy approaching on the UTV and start to panic a little about getting her in before they see her. I have no idea if Mia has shared her "genius" plan with them or not, but I don't want to encourage it in any way.

"Hey, Boss!" Cooter yells from a few hundred feet away as they draw closer. "Shep said he forgot his calving book and wanted us to grab it for him!" They swing onto the driveway and bail out both sides as the Gator rolls to a stop. They are dressed in matching red plaid pearl snaps with the Red Rock Ranch logo embroidered on the chest with relatively unstained jeans and their less worn out looking cowboy hats. Either some part of their schedule for the day is happening in town, or someone gave them a heads up about our visitor.

"The little black hardcover one? I think it's on his desk in the office." I gesture for them to go in ahead of us, hoping if I don't address the elephant in the room (aka Kaci), maybe they won't even notice.

"Well, look at us forgetting our manners! I don't believe we've had the pleasure of being acquainted yet, ma'am. I'm Coudreaux P. Cogburn. But you can call me Cooter." Cooter completely side steps me and makes his way right up to Kaci. He extends a hand in front of her, and winks while tipping his hat with the other, and she lets out a long, ridiculous giggle in response. Lord, have mercy.

"Oh, it's wonderful to meet you! I'm Kaci Whitfield. I'm the middle school cheerleading coach. And you are?" Kaci looks up at Roy, who is shyly standing a few feet behind Cooter, and bats her eyelashes a little. I feel like I'm watching some weird redneck version of National Geographic and I'd love nothing more than to change the channel.

"That's my business associate Roy G. Blackburn. You can call him Roy," Cooter explains, stepping slightly to the side so that Kaci can shake Roy's hand, too. Roy daintily shakes Kaci's fingertips with a little bow, and I strongly consider just walking the other direction and leaving them out here to whatever this is. But I think the front door is locked and this is my only way back into the house.

"Now, to what do we owe the honor of your fine presence this morning, Ms. Kaci?" Cooter croons. He is pouring it on thicker than caramel on an apple, and could probably give you the same level of toothache. Roy is nervously swaying ever so slightly from side to side, and I can tell he probably likes Kaci, too, but is going to be much too shy to try to outshine Cooter.

"Well, we've got to get all the details for our karaoke fundraiser lined out this morning! I'm going to see you there, right? Both of you?" she chirps, batting those dang eyelashes again. Here's where the rubber meets the road-Shep and I got one answer for that question, but I'm betting my bottom dollar that she'll get a different one.

"Why, we wouldn't miss it for the world! Roy and I love karaoke. It's one of our most favorite pastimes, 'a-course." Cooter smiles widely and Roy looks like he might just sway right over. "You got a favorite song we can sing?"

"Oh, goodness, I love all kinds of music! Texas Country is probably my favorite, though. You know, like Wade Bowen, Randy Rogers, William Clark Green," she giggles, smoothing some non-existent wrinkles on her Spandex outfit and hoisting her large LL Bean tote bag higher on her shoulder.

"Shoot yeah, we know all those guys! We'll make sure to find a real good one, and dedicate it just to you," Cooter maintains an uncomfortably long amount of eye contact with her in silence until I clear my throat and head for the door.

"Alright, alright, y'all get back to work. Roy, come get this calving book. Cooter, leave this poor girl alone, for the love. Kaci, we'll be right in here," I shoo them all inside and try to disperse everyone to their intended destinations. After I set Kaci up in the dining room, I make sure the boys do, in fact, leave the house and then we get to work.

"So, I think we can presale some VIP tickets ahead of time to get at least a base amount of funds, and then continue with ticket sales at the door for tables further back, or standing room if we get to that point. At SBU, did you typically have entrants sign up ahead of time to perform to make sure you had people that would participate, or did you roll the dice?"

"We did have a sign up sheet in the Student Center just so we could make sure we had tracks for the songs people wanted to sing, but with a community event like this, I don't think we necessarily need to. We can just plan for our set up to have a large availability of commercially popular songs. Do you think tables and chairs are better than just rows of seats? Which do you think would fit more people?"

"I think you could likely fit more with rows, but I think people will be more likely to hop up and go on stage if they are at a table versus having to climb over a bunch of other people on their row. We have plenty of chairs, and there are already six or seven families that have volunteered probably 15 tables so far. If we need to, we can also open the back upstairs balcony for just seating," I say, thinking about the little landing over the backyard out the back upstairs hallway. I sure as heck wouldn't sit up there, but I'm sure there's some crime junkie who's itching to get up there and see everything. As I jot down a few notes on my legal pad, I hear the garage door opening in the back. I assume Shep is back and wait for him to make a drive-by through the house.

"Okay, we'll go with ground floor tables and overflow balcony seating. Do you have any thoughts on ticket prices?" Kaci asks, ticking through her list on her iPad.

"Maybe $15 a person? What do you think works better-a set ticket price or an open donation for seating? We've had good luck in the past letting people be as generous as they like instead of setting it to a specific number." As we discuss the pros and cons of each fundraising method, I see movement out the window of the dining room. The shutters are pulled completely open to let in as much natural light as possible, so we have a full view of Cooter and Roy carrying feed sacks back down the driveway to the feed barn. I knew they had a handful of bags left to move back to the barn, and it looks like Cooter and Roy are trying to use this opportunity to their advantage. Roy is easily carrying his feed sack down the driveway, looking strong and nonchalant as Cooter prances by with a feed sack on each shoulder, occasionally shifting the weight, but trying to pass Roy like he is faster. Roy sees that he is being passed by twice the weight and picks up his speed, nearly running toward the barn with his extra fifty pounds across his shoulders. Cooter realizes he can't keep up with Roy's near full speed run, so he drops into a lunge, and starts moving down the driveway in alternating lunges, presumably to show strength rather than speed.

I watch this ridiculous show of the World's Goofiest Ranchhands for another minute or two before excusing myself for a coffee refill and heading off to find Shep. He is flipping through a stack of mail at the kitchen counter and sipping another cup of coffee. I pour myself another, too, and sidle right up to him at the counter.

"Whatcha doing?" I ask sweetly, wondering if he has any clue what's going on outside.

"Just going through the mail. We got a sale flyer for Bullock in July. Do you remember him? He bought that yearling bull out of Fearless at the spring sale and has tried to convince social media he is the next coming of Patriarch. He is collecting and selling straws for $150 each." Shep shakes his head disdainfully and I laugh a little to myself that this is one of those incredibly niche conversations that would mean absolutely nothing to 99% of the population, but I weirdly know exactly what he's talking about. Patriarch is, fittingly enough, one of the heaviest-hitting names in seedstock Angus. And while we're proud of the genetics we're raising, a yearling bull from a lesser-known line just doesn't make the same splash as one of the old granddaddies who's sired generations of greats. I know Bill Bullock to be an older, boisterous, blowhard of a man that thinks anything he touches turns to gold, particularly in Angus breeding, but since he lives in Oklahoma, we really don't cross paths that often. For some reason, he attended our spring bull sale back in February and bought from us–a first for him, but we didn't think much about it as that's the goal- you want people to come buy your bulls, and you don't really have expectations or stipulations on who or what. We've never been to one of the Bullock sales, and I'm curious if Shep has interest in going since his breeding philosophies and ours don't necessarily align.

"Yes, I remember. So, sorry to interrupt, but do you know what's going on outside?"

"The boys are moving those extra bags of feed back to the barn. We have a few tons on pallets that we'll move with the skid steer once the loose ones are out, but Roy and Coot are gonna move the loose ones quickly. Why?"

"Just curious if you knew that it's Redneck Ninja Warrior out there trying to impress Mia's cheerleading coach. Have you ever watched Cooter do lunges and carry two sacks at a time? Because now's your chance," I say, giving a Vanna White wave toward the front windows for him to see for himself.

Shep walks past me into the dining room and up to the window just in time to witness Roy grapevine by with two sacks over his shoulders toward the barn as Cooter sprints empty handed back toward the garage, presumably back to get another load.

"Oh my goodness! Your ranch hands are so strong," Kaci giggles, looking up like she's just noticing all the hoopla going on outside. She sets her stylus pen on the table and turns her complete attention outside and I clear my throat a little to pull Shep from his staring in disbelief.

"I'll be right back," he says and hastily leaves as I slide back into my chair with my coffee refill.

"Oh, I'm sorry, Coach, did you want some coffee?" I ask, starting to get up before she waves me back down.

"Oh, no, I'm good! I don't drink coffee. It just tastes kinda yuck to me. Besides, I brought my own matcha!" She pulls a clear glass bottle full of pea green liquid out of her tote bag and I nod and smile. Yes, my coffee tastes "yuck", but her drink that looks like the color of a baby's diaper tastes good. Make it make sense.

"Right, of course. Okay, where were we?" I say, flipping back through my legal pad and trying to regain my train of thought as I see Shep herding the boys back to the garage as they exchange words in my periphery.

We continue our meeting with no more interruptions, completely planning out the night and our logistics leading up to it. I'm honestly proud that we're able to put together something that seems like it will be pretty successful, plus kinda fun, after it fell in our laps such a short time ago.

"Okay, well, thanks so much for meeting with me, Molly! This has been... fun," Kaci says, cracking a large smile and darting her eyes around the driveway as she gets into her car. Shep took Roy and Cooter down to the horse barn to clean stalls and tack while we finished our meeting, so I'm not sure she'll get the satisfaction of seeing the boys again before she leaves.

"Yes, thanks for coming. I'll email you those ad flyers, but let me know if you need anything before then." I close her door behind her and pat the top of her tiny little car to indicate she should just go ahead and move it along. I can already tell this little rivalry is going to cause us issues on top of the issues we already have.

Just as I head back inside to tackle my ever growing list of laundry, dishes, fundraiser prep, and curiosities related to murder investigations that are none of my business, my phone starts ringing.

"Molly? It's Sheriff Cooper." As the sheriff's gruff voice comes through the line, and I go through that same old waffling- is today a day he likes me or no?

"Hi, Sheriff. What's going on?" I ask, stopping at the kitchen counter and leaning against the butcher block. As I wait for his answer, I flip through the stack of mail that Shep was sifting through earlier and stop when Bill Bullock's smarmy face is staring up at me. He's done absolutely nothing to any of us, but I would put him into that category of people I have no reason not to like, but just don't for whatever reason. It's like a gut instinct that tells you to stay away from certain people, and he's on my red flag list. I flip the large postcard over so he isn't staring at me anymore, and skim the details. The sale is in mid July (one of my least favorite times of the year) at his ranch in western Oklahoma on a Monday morning. If you decide to come the night before, you are treated to a prime rib dinner and special acoustic concert by Pat Green. Pat Green? How did someone like Bill Bullock convince someone as big as Pat Green to come do a concert just for his bull sale?

"... so can you meet me?" Sheriff Cooper's bark rips me from my mental argument about Bill Bullock and Pat Green and I silently chide myself for not paying attention to whatever it was he was saying because it apparently was important.

"Um, sure, I probably can. I think you cut out there for a second; can you repeat what you just said a minute ago?"

"I said we found Renfro. He's at a nursing home in Franklin. I'm told he's a little off his rocker so I think talking to him would be easier with the calming presence of a woman. All my lady officers are busy, so can you go with me?"

"You only have one 'lady officer', Coop," I snort sarcastically, thinking of Patty Hastings, long time deputy of the department, typically in charge of monitoring the schools and directing traffic at funerals. She's a bit on the gruff side herself, and I might be more scared of her than I am Sheriff Cooper. You try to turn the wrong way out of a parking lot she's in charge of one time and she'll be on your case for life.

"Exactly, and there's a funeral today at the Baptist church. So can you go or not? I'm leaving in forty five minutes."

I glance up at the clock to see that it's only ten in the morning, despite the fact that it feels like I've lived a week since getting up this morning.

"Can we be back by 3:00 for me to pick up the kids from school?"

"I'll do my best, but no promises."

"Alright, I'll see you at the station in thirty minutes."

———

"Crawford County Sheriff Michael Cooper and Special Agent Molly Jones to see Mr. Cassius Renfro, please." A few hours later, after swapping out my Spooner suit for jeans and a nice blouse, Sheriff Cooper and I are walking into the Shady Acres Nursing Home in downtown Franklin, a very, very small community about twenty miles from Buffalo Creek. While the Cinnamon Shores facility that houses sweet Asa Shoemaker seems like a resort for older people, I would say Shady Acres leans more toward a traditional nursing home. For starters, the smell is a dead giveaway, no pun intended. The facility itself is much more locked down, and there is only one entrance/ exit that requires us to check in with a front desk attendant. She flips through a rolodex by her computer and comes up with a card. After scanning the card, she dials an extension on her phone and waits for an answer.

"Hey, Nancy, I have visitors for Mr. Renfro. Is he up to it?" She pauses to wait for an answer, and then nods to us and points down the hallway to the right. "Head down there, room 114."

Cooper and I take off down the hallway before she says anything else, and I tick down the numbers on small placards next to rooms as we go starting at room 100. Most doors are fully open or ajar, and we see resident after resident lying in their beds fairly lifeless. I'm getting less and less optimistic about what condition Cassius Renfro is going to be in when we get there to talk to him the further we make it down the hallway. When we finally approach room 114, the door is partially open. Cooper knocks as we enter and see an older Black man sitting up in an old medical grade reclining chair with his eyes closed. He has on a mustard colored sweater tucked into brown plaid tweed pants and his black wiry hair is gray at the temples. He stirs a little as we walk in quietly, trying not to startle him. Or at least, I'm trying not to startle him. Cooper has a little less couth, and I can see decades of law enforcement coming out. He clears his throat as we get closer and I shoot him a look of disapproval as Mr. Renfro starts to wake. I thought he was exaggerating or just looking for an excuse to bring me when he said he needed a woman's touch, but I'm starting to see he was completely right.

I kneel down next to his chair and place a calm hand over his, hoping to keep him from freaking out when he wakes up completely.

"Mr. Cassius! Wake on up now! You've got you some visitors, sir!" And just like that, his nurse (Nancy, I presume), barrels through the door with a cart full of gadgets and supplies. She wheels up to him noisily and starts pouring water into a small paper cup from a plastic pitcher on her cart. After dumping a handful of pills from a tray into another small paper cup, she bends down at his other side and jostles him a little to finish waking him up.

"Alright, sir, just take your afternoon meds here, and then these people are here to talk to you, okay?" It is obvious poor Cassius Renfro is quite disoriented in waking, but he takes both small paper cups from Nancy and takes the pills before looking first at me, then Cooper, then back at me. Once Nancy careens out as quickly as she flew in, he tries to speak.

"Ddd...do... I... kn...know you?" His voice is deep, quiet, slow and unsure, and I try to seem upbeat and reassuring so we don't scare him. Cooper decides to go in an opposite direction with intimidation tactics.

"Mr. Renfro, I'm Sheriff Michael Cooper with the Crawford County Sheriff's Department. Were you previously a practicing attorney in the Buffalo Creek area?" he asks, pulling large color photos of the envelope out of his vest. "Does this look like an envelope that would have come from your office?"

Mr. Renfro slowly takes the photos from Cooper and studies them intently. "Yes... I w...w...was an ... att... attorney," he gets out in pieces, like speaking is a real struggle for him. In watching him, I'm realizing he is likely less "off his rocker" and more post-stroke, or something that would give him some degree of expressive aphasia. "That... was my envel... envelope."

I pat him on the hand and slide myself close to Cooper so I can have a sidebar with him. "Coop, he sounds like he has some type of aphasia, like he has difficulty with the mechanics of speaking. I think this would go more smoothly, and you'll get better responses, if you stick to simple yes or no questions. He has no issue understanding you, but it is hard for him to speak to you. Just remember, more flies with honey than dumping vinegar, you know?" I whisper, giving him an encouraging smile, and hoping this will ease our conversation. "You want me to try?"

Cooper shrugs and gestures for me to give it a go, so I lean back on his bed and think for a minute. "Mr. Renfro, I'm Molly. I'm just a friend helping Mr. Cooper here today, and we just need to see if you have some information that can help us. Is it okay if I ask you some yes or no questions? You can just nod or shake your head if you prefer, ok?" He nods in recognition and I take a deep breath to start.

"Did you practice law in Buffalo Creek?" Another nod.

"Did you know a man named Langley Fletcher?" Nod.

"Were you his attorney?" Nod.

"Did he ever have you draw up documents for him?" Nod.

"Would you have mailed him documents in an envelope like that?" Nod.

"Did you do his business documents?" Nod, accompanied by a waving hand. I take that to mean that he did probably some of the business, not all.

"Did you handle his personal business documents?" Nod with no qualifier, so I push in on this. "Did you draw up his estate planning?" Confident nod.

I look back to Cooper to see if he wants to jump in at any point. He gives me another gesture to continue, so I stop and think for another minute.

"Mr. Renfro, as far as you know, did you handle Mr. Fletcher's most up to date last will and testament?" He nods, and I wonder if my next question is going to open a complete can of worms. I'm assuming that if I've been to Asa to talk about all this, then surely Sheriff Cooper has, and none of what I'm about to say is going to be a surprise.

"Did his will split assets between two children?" Renfro frowns, and then shakes his head no. This is the theory I'm leaning toward at this point– that will is missing because it might name a child no one knew about or acknowledged.

"Did his will split assets between three children?" He nods, ducking his head a little. I look back at Cooper, and his eyebrows have shot up clear to his forehead and he leans forward a little. I'm thinking this is perhaps not old news to him.

"Do you happen to have a copy of that will?" Cooper asks, trying to jump in on the action. He has at least picked up my rhythm and method, so the question lines up with the series. Renfro frowns again and gives us a halfhearted shrug. He gestures around to his nursing home room, and I take that to mean that he isn't really sure what possessions he has left.

"Do you have anything left in storage? Or a house still somewhere?" I ask, knowing that is a muddy question, but worth a shot. Most people let go of houses in order to have the means to move to a nursing home, but there's a chance he still has something left.

He nods and tries to add detail, but he struggles with each word. "My... files... with... son..."

"Great, what is his name?" Cooper jumps in, pulling out his notepad from his chest pocket to take down a name and anything else that Mr. Renfro might share. I smack his arm lightly and gesture for him to put it away. I'm unsure how old Mr. Renfro is, or the true severity of his condition, but it feels like we are taxing him to his limit and the last thing I want is for him to crash out because we pushed too hard.

"Does your nurse have contact information for your son?" I say gently, and he lets out a deep breath and nods. "Okay, we'll ask her to share that with us if that's okay with you?" Another nod.

"Thank you so much for speaking with us, Mr. Renfro. We really appreciate it." I pat him on the forearm, and nod toward the door to indicate to Cooper that I think we should move out while we're ahead. He agrees and just as we are about to make it through the doorway, Renfro chokes out a strangled noise that stops us both. We turn and see him struggling to get himself out of his chair. He gives up for a second and stares us both down with wide, nervous eyes before wrestling out a few more words:

"That... w...w...will... is trou...trouble."

"WHERE DO you want the salt and pepper shakers, Molls?" A few days later, I have the best unpacking team that zero dollars but decades-long friendships can buy helping me unpack inventory at the Shoppe while the kids are in school. We're T-minus two weeks until our opening weekend, and things are progressing fairly smoothly. Mandy has all of her supplies set up for the floral counter and has opened up her online order taking portal to begin at the soft launch, and thanks to Lucy and her creativity, we are nearly finished with our table displays. I'm feeling cautiously optimistic about this aspect of my life, which feels at odds with the pit in my stomach about the Langley Fletcher unknown will situation.

"We can spread them to different tables where there is room," I say, directing Lucy and a set of tractor shaped salt and pepper shakers to an empty spot near a barn shaped cookie jar, and a stack of red gingham melamine plates on a table near the back counter. She nods in agreement and begins distributing the different shaped sets-flowers, monkeys, succulents, tiny cowboy boots, just to name a few - throughout the store. I am making sure the pricing stickers are scanning into the online point-of-sale system, and Mandy is stacking clear vases on the open shelving above her floral counter to double as decor and sample options for customers. She is playing it pretty cool, but I can tell she is itching to talk about everything going on and what we found out talking to Cassius Renfro.

"Alright, how does that look?" she asks, stepping back for us to both get a good look at the display. It looks very artsy and intentional with different heights, widths, and thicknesses of glass giving varied visual interest.

"I think it looks good," I offer, taking a minute to look at the wall before staring straight at her to see how long it will take her to crack. "I know you want to ask, so just ask."

"Of course I want to ask! What did you find out with Cassius Renfro?" she exclaims, like a tea kettle finally whistling out its steam as it comes to a boil.

"Not much, unfortunately. According to his son, he had a series of several strokes about four months ago, and he has pretty severe Broca's aphasia. He remembered doing the will, and what should have been in it, but he didn't know where it would have been. We were pretty limited to yes or no questions, so that made it harder to get additional details. His son has some old file boxes of his, and I told Coop I'd go with him to get them this afternoon, but it doesn't sound like the son has any information on any goings-on or anything."

"So, what should have been in it?" Lucy calls, still adjusting displays on the front tables.

"That his assets should have been split between his *three* children," I answer, cringing a little. This is a detail I haven't shared with them yet, as I'm not sure it's completely common knowledge, but probably will be shortly as more investigation details are released.

"What?" They both shout in near perfect unison, and I try not to laugh at their matching scandalized looks.

"So... when I had my chat with Asa, he shared that this was the dissolution of their partnership, but professionally and personally. Langley had an affair with one of the secretaries here and she ended up pregnant. They supposedly ended their relationship, and it was never made public that he fathered another child, but Cassius Renfro indicated that he did include that child in his will."

They are both staring at me dumbfounded, and I wait to see if either will reply, or if I need to pull the conversation along again. "Who is the third kid?" Lucy asks breathlessly a few seconds later.

"Not sure. From descriptions I've heard, there were three secretaries working here at the time. Asa didn't know exactly which one. Supposedly, the woman never told her husband, and he raised it as his own."

"Okay, well, it can't be that hard to figure out-everyone knows everyone around here. All we have to do is figure out which secretary had a kid in the correct time frame. The kid would be around their early thirties, right? Do you know the secretaries' names?" Mandy says, setting her empty box that once held the vases down and grabbing a legal pad from behind the counter. She poises a pen over the paper, ready to take notes and make a chart of what we do know.

"Wells, the Fletchers' son, said there was a Debbie that worked back here," I say, gesturing to the counter we're standing at. Lucy and Mandy think for a few minutes before Lucy rings in with an answer.

"Debbie Frazier? Don't they have a son that age?"

"Yeah, their son Kyle is around thirty, I think?" Mandy adds, jotting their names on her paper.

"Alright, we can check to see if she worked here. He said Connie had a desk here in the middle of the room. Who knows a Connie?"

"Oh, oh! Connie Wallace!" Mandy shouts, like she has buzzed in first on *Family Feud*. "Her son Matt is in his early thirties." She slaps the counter in triumph, and adds their names to the list.

"Okay, let's check on her. And the last secretary was a Ginny, right there up front in the window."

Mandy and Lucy pause to think quietly but both shrug after a few minutes. "I don't think I know a Ginny," Mandy finally says, looking from Lucy to me. Lucy nods in agreement, and I suddenly have a lightbulb moment.

"Actually, I do. Ginny Parrish has Parker, who has to be in his early thirties."

▭

"You know, Sheriff, if I didn't know any better, I'd think you are actually taking a shine to me as your associate detective," I say, as Sheriff Cooper and I exit his department truck and head up the front sidewalk of a two story modern farmhouse on a quiet street in the heart of Franklin. Sheriff Cooper has confirmed with Augustus Renfro that he will be home this afternoon, and is willing to share his father's back files from his time practicing law, so we are back in Franklin to pay him a visit. Mandy and Lucy decided to do some research on their own this afternoon to see if our hunches were correct on the Debbie, Connie, and Ginny we identified, and if so, which of the three possible sons is really a Fletcher.

"You are not my associate," he harrumphs, yanking down his flak jacket that seems to be in perpetual odds with his generous mid-section. "More like my assistant."

"Assistant, associate, po-tay-to, po-tah-to," I reply in a sing-song voice, making it up to the Ring doorbell first and giving it a push. "The point is, I think you know now what an asset I am, not a hindrance, right?"

He stays silent for a second before responding. "You ever heard the phrase "keep your friends close, and your enemies closer"? It's kinda like that, but keep your assets close, and your distractions closer so they don't cause more of a mess," he says with a straight face, staring ahead at the closed door and waiting for it to open.

"Rude," I mutter in response, frowning at him before turning back to the door, too. I'm not usually this clingy, but so help me, he will admit that I am a necessity before this investigation is over.

We both go silent as the door slowly cracks open, and a young girl with a mess of dark curls and a gingham short set peeks around the edge. She stares at us with dark chocolate brown eyes with curiosity, and I glance back and forth between her and Sheriff Cooper to see if she is scared of us or just intrigued.

"Hi, sweetie. I'm Ms. Molly, and this is my friend Mr. Michael. What is your name?" I ask, bending down to her level and hoping I'm coming off as kind and comforting, not a creeper stranger.

"Fwowa," she replies, gliding her "l" and "r" sounds in what I assume is meant to be "Flora".

"Flora! What a pretty name! How old are you, Flora?"

She holds up three pudgy fingers to us. "Fwee."

"Oh, my goodness, three years old! You are so grown up! Is your mommy or daddy home right now?" She nods and disappears, leaving the door open a few inches.

"You're pretty good at talking to that kid," Sheriff Cooper offers, gesturing to the empty doorway and giving me what I assume is a compliment.

"Um, thanks? You raised kids, you don't think you know how to talk to kids?"

"Nah, I think that's a woman thing. You were good with that old man, too. Maybe you are more of an asset than I realize."

I beam, thinking this may be as close as I get to him admitting that I am a necessity, and I was really expecting him to hold out longer than this, quite frankly. Before I can put together a snappy reply, a middle aged man who looks like a younger Cassius Renfro arrives at the door.

"Hi, August Renfro," he says, extending a hand to Sheriff Cooper, and then to me. He invites us into his home, and I decide that if this is police work, I'm totally down. There is nothing more that I love than seeing inside random homes and getting a behind the scenes look at their lives and inner workings.

As we walk from the entry way into the heart of the home, Flora skips off to a corner of the living room to a miniature table buried in coloring pages and buckets of crayons, markers, and pencils. As we stand in the first few moments of awkward silence, a tall Black woman in a set of rumpled hospital-blue scrubs and curls just like Flora held back by a large colorful headband runs between us from the kitchen to the stairs without so much as a glance, and my curiosity peaks.

"I'm so sorry, that's my wife. She is a nocturnist at the hospital here in Franklin. Her shift is supposed to start at 6, but the day shift hospitalist had a family emergency so she's rushing to go help cover." August looks a little embarrassed that she completely ignored us, but I wave a dismissive hand to try to make him feel better.

"I was married to a physician for a long time. When duty calls, they just gotta go. It gets better on the other side," I laugh and he nods knowingly.

"Have you remarried, then?" he asks cautiously, and I startle at the strange question before realizing how my original statement sounded. I can't tell if it's a question of curiosity, or almost permission, and I quickly shut down the latter.

"Oh, gosh, sorry, no! My husband was a physician, but he transitioned from medicine into full time ranching. I meant the other side of life away from medicine, not away from my husband. My bad," I cringe, thinking that as per usual, I have dug a verbal hole that is getting increasingly harder to jump out of and my attempt at assuaging his embarrassment seems to have just prolonged it.

"Right, well, how about those files of your father's?" Cooper says, stepping in to get us back on track.

"Of course, right through here," August replies, scurrying ahead of us into the kitchen where there are old, worn file boxes sitting up on a white marble island counter. "This is all Dad had in his office whenever he had to quit working. He was still practicing up until his strokes a while back. I have no idea what any of it is, but you're welcome to look through it and take anything that could be helpful. We just boxed up his office space and moved out as quickly as we could so he could sell the building."

Cooper claps August on the back appreciatively and whips the lid off the first box. A thin layer of dust flies up, and I reflexively let out a small cough and step back to see if I can talk with August a little longer. He likely knows nothing about any of this, but it doesn't hurt to build relationships with people just in case.

"How long have y'all been in Franklin, August?" I try to sound breezy and casual, not like a one lightbulb interrogation, but he still looks a little surprised I'm talking to him. There are some bumps and thumps coming from upstairs, and he glances toward the stairs nervously a few times before responding.

"Um, about three months. We moved back from Dallas when Pops got sick and it seemed like he wasn't going to bounce back like we'd hoped."

"Oh, I see. Is your wife from this area, too?"

"No, Celia is actually from Chicago. She did fellowship at Southwestern. I work for a hedge fund firm based in DFW, now remotely."

The pieces of the current scene are fitting together a little better after just a few sentences–this isn't where Celia Renfro wants to live, and if she is fellowship trained, it is likely that being a general nocturnist isn't her first choice of career. His set up has likely changed minimally, but hers probably drastically.

"My husband was a gastroenterologist. Fellowship can be kind of a bear to get through, especially in somewhere big like Dallas. Does she enjoy the smaller hospital?"

"Not at all. She's trained in neuroradiology so essentially everything she does now is outside her scope of expertise, or rather, enjoyment. She only enjoys things she's an expert at. This is supposed to be temporary until we can get Pops a spot at a stroke speciality rehab in Dallas. There's a really great one that deals with his type of stroke and aphasia, but the waiting list is long. Celia tried to pull some strings, but there's still a bit of a wait. I convinced her to come here for a little bit until we can get him in. Her job was eating her up anyway, so I thought a little break and a slower pace would be good for us."

I consider asking how that's going, but quite frankly, it seems pretty evident, and asking feels like additional salt in the wound.

"Here we are! Fletcher!" Cooper exclaims, and I am snapped back to our true reason for being here- trying to find the full will of Langley Fletcher. I smile weakly at August before jumping back to Cooper's side so it looks a little more like I'm actually helping. Cooper pulls out an overstuffed file folder and hands me half of the papers inside.

August gestures for us to spread out on the table in the kitchen, and we start silently sifting through to see if anything is useful. I flip page after page filled with legalese about land leases and mineral rights, wondering if Cassius really didn't handle much of Langley's personal business at all when I get to the last set of stapled papers in my stack. At the top of the page, it reads "The Last Will and Testament of Langley Roosevelt Fletcher" and it seems to be the paydirt we were looking for.

"I think I found it!" I shriek quietly, not wanting to bring too much attention. I have no idea how much Celia and Flora are aware of, but having the sheriff and a random lady searching through boxes at your house is out of the ordinary enough without undue hysterics.

Before I can blink again, Cooper has swept the papers from in front of me and is scanning through them. "Yes, I think this is exactly what would have been missing from the envelope we found. It says there is a trust assigned to the care of Nora, and that remaining assets are to be divided into three equal parts, mineral rights are to be split into thirds, land is to be sold and split three ways, blah blah blah," he reads aloud, skimming the pages as he flips through them as quickly as he can.

"Okay, so who are the three beneficiaries?" I say anxiously, thinking we already knew the part about splitting everything into the thirds. What we don't know is who the third is, and if that third person is potentially a murderer.

"Says here that beneficiary parties are named in Appendix A," Cooper replies, quickly leafing to get to the back of the packet where the appendices typically are. He stops when he gets to the last page, and after looking it over extensively, he sighs in frustration. I give him a pointed look, silently asking for an explanation.

"The appendices aren't here."

▭

A few hours later, I am slowly pulling up our driveway, full of the frustration of yet another dead end, only to see Cooter and Roy once again carrying feed sacks up the driveway-this time in the opposite direction as the feed barn. I cringe, wondering what has happened now that it looks like we've begun another evacuation.

Shep is on the driveway when I pull to a stop, and the look on his face tells me that he is likely not in the mood for a conversation. I grab my purse from the passenger seat and slowly exit my car, waiting to see if I'm offered an explanation of the growing feed storage in the garage. I grabbed the kids on my way home, and they both immediately bail to the house without a word as I linger in Shep's general vicinity.

"So... how's it going?" I ask tentatively as he remains silent.

"Turns out there's more than one rat."

"Ah, I see. Are you having to put traps out again?"

"I guess. This sucker got ten bags since we put them back the other day. We'll dump those in the grain bins, but I don't need to lose many more bags."

"For sure," I say, not really knowing what else to add. I'm more than aware that this sucks, but I'm not sure how to help the situation, and nothing I can say will really change anything. We both head for the side door into the house and he lets out the heavy sigh of a long, stressful day.

"Were you at the Shoppe?" he asks as I open the refrigerator and start pulling out my ingredients to start dinner.

"Um, yes, for a little bit this morning. It's starting to really come along. We got most of the merchandise tabled this morning, and I think we'll be finished setting up sometime tomorrow."

"What was going on this afternoon?" The look on his face tells me that he knows I've probably been up to no good, but that he's maybe a little afraid to find out exactly what I've been up to. He's been incredibly cautious to the point of discouragement about my unneeded involvement in all the goings-on the last few months, and I'm not really interested in a lecture about my place in it all. But on the other hand, I have at least been invited on the last few outings, and it's harder to argue with that.

"Cooper asked me to go with him to look through the boxes from Cassius Renfro's son. We're trying to locate the missing will that should have been in that envelope," I reply slowly, knowing that I can't truly be in "trouble", but again, would like to be spared a lecture if possible. He opens his mouth to deliver his rebuttal, but is distracted by what looks like two trees scurrying down the driveway out the front windows. Intrigued, I drop the sealed package of ground beef I am holding into the sink, and follow Shep out the side door to see what is going on now. Tacos can wait when our trees have apparently grown legs.

"What in the world are y'all doing?" Shep asks as two figures covered head to toe in grass, moss, and bits of nature-a.k.a., full Mossy Oak ghillie suits–are swishing by, headed to the UTV parked in the garage.

"Shep! We'll finish the feed in a bit. We just saw him on the cameras! We're headed up to the northside to see if we can get 'im!" Cooter hoots, raising the face mask portion to reveal the overwhelming glee on his face. Roy unloads two rifle cases into the back of the Gator, and gives us a silent thumbs up and they both slide onto the bench seat and Roy fires up the engine.

"Y'all saw who? Who is on the cameras and why do we need rifles?" I ask, wondering why I feel so far behind. I'll admit, I haven't been paying much attention to the antics around here, which clearly, there are plenty of, but I didn't think I was this far out of the loop to be so shocked by the appearance of high-powered firearms and ghillie suits.

"The mountain lion, boss! We're missing another two calves, so this sum-buck's got to go!"

"Y'all be careful, and radio me if you need help," Shep

responds, nodding his approval as Cooter covers his face back over and they back out of the driveway at a less than safe speed.

"Another two calves?" I say quietly as they careen away, and Shep nods silently. "Same ET group?"

"Yes, and two of the better ones, of course. We're going to move that whole group to this closer pasture in the morning and just combine them with the March calvers for now until we can get this thing," he sighs, and I instantly feel guilty that I've been so wrapped up in my own self-importance that I didn't even know what was going on. I squeeze his shoulder as we walk in, knowing that losing any calf, but particularly an embryo transfer calf, and three of them at that, is less of a blow than losing one of our own children, but not by much.

"So, you were saying y'all went to find Renfro's son and Fletcher's missing will today? How did that go? Did y'all find it?" Shep pulls himself up to the island on a stool to watch as I start dinner. I start browning ground beef in a skillet and pulling out spices to mix together for taco seasoning as I get Shep up to speed.

"We did but we didn't. We have the initial pages of the will that specify how everything should be split up-i.e., three ways to include both legitimate and illegitimate children but the actual parties are listed in an appendix for some reason, and the appendix pages are missing."

"So what is the verbiage in the actual will?"

"It lists all the specific things, like land, mineral rights, cash money, investments, etc. that are to be split equally by Party A, Party B, and Party C. I don't understand why he wouldn't just list them there."

"Maybe some parties are the kids themselves and some are kid plus spouse. Do you know anything about the Fletcher twins' spouses? And we don't even know who Party C is, right?"

"I knew I married you for a good reason, Shep Jones. I bet that's it! Rich people are always weird about making sure their stuff goes very specifically to who they want, and not anyone else. I bet there is an in-law that was persona non grata and they needed to make it clear, and that was the easiest way to do it. And yes, we are still narrowing down Party C. Hey, can you chop and mix these?" I slide an onion, two jalapenos, and two Roma tomatoes to him on a cutting board with a food chopper to start our pico de gallo. There's no reason he can't be a help in more than one way as long as he's sitting there.

He begins quartering the vegetables to fit in the chopper as he looks to be pondering. "What do you know about Party C? Any leads at all? Why can't Asa just tell you who it is?"

"We have a narrowed list of who we think might have been the secretaries at the time. Asa said all Langley ever told him was that he had a relationship with one of their secretaries, but never specified which one, and they dissolved the company pretty quickly after he found out that one was pregnant by Langley. Wells Fletcher told me first names, and we have three possibilities based on who has kids in the right age range. What do you know about Debbie Frazier, Connie Wallace, and Ginny Parrish?"

He ponders again as he lines up vegetables on the chopping grate and smacks the lid down to push them through. "Not much. Debbie Frazier's husband is Dutch, who runs the feed store. I see her balancing books in there sometimes. I couldn't point out Connie Wallace if you paid me a million dollars. Didn't we eat lunch the other day with the Parrish kid?"

Not a lot of intel, but quite frankly, more than I was expecting from the guy that couldn't reliably tell anyone our address for the first decade of our marriage. It wasn't necessary information he used on a regular basis, so it understandably got buried under other, more useful, information. "Connie

Wallace runs the front desk at the utilities district, but I'm not sure that would make her easier for you to place. Yes, Parker's mom Ginny is the one Marge plays mahjong with, apparently."

He nods, like some of the pieces are clicking together for him as he dumps all the tiny cubes of onion, jalapeno, and tomato in a large mixing bowl and douses them with garlic salt before stirring to combine. "Well, sounds like maybe you need to see if you can get in this month's mahjong game."

chapter
ten

"HI! IS THIS SEAT TAKEN?"

By what I can only describe as interference by the Holy Spirit, when I called Marge later that night, she told me their next mahjong game was the following night, and they actually did need a sub to fill in for Dottie Price. Her precious Shih Poo, Sprinkles, was just spayed and she couldn't possibly leave her home alone so soon after her surgery. And to that I said, one woman's over the top ridiculousness is another woman's golden opportunity. So, the next night I find myself with a pink plastic Solo cup full of church-lady punch in one hand and a cheat sheet card for those funky patterned dominoes in the other, trying not to look too desperate to get the empty folding chair next to Ginny Parrish.

"No, darlin', you go right ahead! I don't think we've met– I'm Ginny Parrish." Ginny smiles warmly, and I get a pit in my stomach that reminds me why I'll never be a full time (a.k.a., real) detective–no way this woman had an affair on her husband and lied to him for decades about the paternity of their son. I mean, does a woman who has the sweetest white bob you've ever seen, wearing a pastel yellow sweater set with embroidered ducks across the collar, seem capable of having an affair?

Yes, Molly, she does. Just like a boy you'd known since he had coke-bottle glasses in middle school tried to kill your mutual neighbor. Focus.

"Wonderful to meet you! I'm Molly Jones." I extend a freshly manicured hand–had to get them redone this afternoon after all our Shoppe cleaning so they wouldn't look haggard as we played tonight–and slide down onto the burnt orange upholstery of the folding chair. Marge told me whose house we are currently in on our way over here, but I honestly couldn't tell you her name or point her out at this point. All I know is she seems to be a big figurine collector of all kinds, and she has nestled four square card tables to accommodate sixteen players amongst her normal living room furniture–two black tweed upholstered recliners, a red leather sofa, and two large credenzas (full of the aforementioned figurines) lining the back walls. My chair backs up to her glass coffee table, and I lay down a pink cocktail napkin on the glass to act as a coaster before setting down my punch cup so I can really focus.

"Lovely to have you here, Molly. I see you came with Margaret?" She daintily sips her own punch cup, and racks up the tile sets in front of her to prepare. I hate that I have to balance the nerves of trying to investigate with the nerves of not looking like a complete idiot with this game that I really don't understand. But this is probably as close as I'm going to get without being suspicious, so I'll take what I can get.

"Yes, Margaret is my grandmother. I was telling her the other day that I'd really love to learn to play, so when y'all needed a sub, it felt like the perfect opportunity!" I giggle, trying to stay natural and casual. "But, y'all go ahead and forgive me now because I really don't know what I'm doing!"

Ginny gives me a strange smile- one that looks kind at first glance, but maybe seems a little sinister upon further inspection. And a few minutes later, when I'm informed that they exchange actual cash money per hand, I realize why Marge came in with a gallon size Ziploc full of quarters and why it was really dumb to admit I have absolutely no idea what I'm doing. I just put a huge bullseye on my back and I have a feeling that Ginny and my two other tablemates are about to exploit it.

"Molly, sugar, just pick one. You're discardin' it, not marryin' it." Less than fifteen minutes later, Bea Dupree, seated to my right, looks about ready to shove me out of my chair and take my turn for me. I blink back tears and take a deep breath as I stare at my pile of tiles that all look different, but not in a discernable way. I have never in my life been in such a complicated and stressful game, and cannot fathom for one second why anyone thinks this is fun. I've never spent more than ten minutes in the same vicinity as Bea Dupree. I've only seen her once before—at a Buffalo Creek girls basketball game, as she has been a rabid superfan since her daughter and the rest of the '79 team won the state championship. I'd say now that I've gotten enough disdain from her in the last fifteen minutes to last me a lifetime, and I'd love to never be in the same room as her again ever.

In a moment of rising panic, I just grab a white tile that looks to have a red Chinese character swept across it because it looks the most different from anything else I have, and toss it out into the center of the table, relieved that I should have a few moments of peace now. Upon seeing my discard, Bea's eyes expand to the size of saucers and Wanda MacMillian—directly across the table from me—looks like she might faint. Ginny shakes her head slightly, like she is a little disappointed in me, but didn't expect anything less, before Bea screams "PUNG!" loud enough to make everyone jump, slamming a wrinkled hand over the top of the tile formerly belonging to me. Her long, blood red nails drag it back to her pile and her smile is so large, I contemplate telling her *"you're welcome"* since she was so sassy about me just taking my turn. It seems my lengthy contemplation was actually to her advantage.

While Bea is still clearly on cloud 9, Wanda slides a random tile from the center pile to her stacks, and then Ginny silently lays down a large line of tiles and quietly declares, "Mahjong."

Bea's massive grin falls flatter than a cake in altitude, and I surmise that while Bea was loudly enjoying her small victory, Ginny just won the whole game. We each hand over one of the small tokens we received at the door and push all the tiles back to the center to be shuffled and redistributed to start the next game.

After another two rounds—one Bea victory, and another Ginny victory—our hostess calls a snack break. I take the opportunity to indulge in a plate full of Hawaiian roll sliders, deviled eggs, homemade cheese straws, and a variety of desserts. You won't find a better plate of finger foods than at a social gathering of old Southern ladies, and the plate full of deliciousness is a decent consolation to humiliating myself. I sit back down in my chair a few minutes before Ginny rejoins me, her plate of just one slider, one cheese straw, one deviled egg, and one petit four, looking like self-control next to my gluttony.

"Do we all stay in our same spots or rotate for the next round?" I ask wearily, wondering if I'm in for three full rounds of Bea's competitiveness. The thought feels like a cheese grater on my nerves, but a necessary sacrifice to get a little more time to talk to Ginny.

Ginny shakes her head silently as she chews the world's smallest bite of deviled egg. "No, the highest score and the lowest score at each table stay, and the two in the middle move," she replies once she swallows. She daintily wipes the corners of her mouth before looking at me a little pointedly.

"Oh! I have the lowest score right now?" I ask, wondering why I sound as surprised as I do. Of course I have the lowest score. I don't have the slightest idea what I'm doing, and every piece of advice they've all given, whether out of generosity or frustration, seems to have gone in one ear and right out the other.

"It's okay, it felt like it took me a long time to figure out, but it's not too hard once you are in the swing of it and playing regularly. I had some co-workers teach me when my son was young, and I've just stayed in the habit of playing. It can be really fun, with the right group, you know." She winks and gives the slightest of head nods to Bea at the next table, looking like she's about to wreck shop on a group that includes Marge. I can't wait to dissect that dynamic on the drive back to Marge's duplex. But, for now, I need to focus on what information I can get out of Ginny.

"Sounds like your co-workers are more fun than mine! But mine are my husband and two ranch hands in their twenties. Working with boys doesn't usually mean a lot of game nights," I joke, cringing at the very unnatural laugh that honks out of me. We can file this as an additional reason I would not survive as a full time detective.

She thankfully smiles and nods. "It was a really special place to work, and I miss it. You're probably too young to remember Petal Pushers, the flower shop? It was on the square near the drug store. Ida Mae Newman owned it for years, and they closed it down when she passed away, probably ten years ago. I was just the counter help, but Ida Mae and her partner, Mavis, were true artists. And when we had down time, they taught me all the good games-mahjong, bridge, 42."

"How fun! How long did you work there?"

"Just a few years. I was working as a secretary for an oil

company, and they closed a little unexpectedly, so Ida Mae took me when I couldn't find anything else."

"Oh, was that Asa Shoemaker's company? My husband and I recently bought his building and he was telling me a little of the history. Sounds like they sold out and closed down pretty quickly."

Ginny maintains an even face, and I wonder if she is now piecing together who I actually am. If she's holding the metaphorical cards (or tiles) I need, she's definitely not showing it. "Yes, I worked for Asa and Langley for about seven of the fifteen years they were open. It felt like the worst timing when they decided to sell out because we had actually just found out that we were going to have a baby, and we really needed me to keep working, at least for a little bit."

Bingo. If Ginny had just found out she was pregnant when they sold the company, then Parker has to be Langley's. "Oh, my goodness, that must have been so much to have all that uncertainty. Were the other women able to find new jobs quickly, or was it tough for everyone?" I try to sound nonchalant, and I feel like my casual detective working has drastically improved since several weeks ago when I was legs up in the air having turned over my chair in Buffalo Creek's one and only five star restaurant just desperate to get a little more information while eavesdropping. At least both of my feet are on the floor right now, and who would have considered that progress.

"Well, the three of us were quite a trio out trying to find jobs, that's for sure. I mean, I know they're not allowed to discriminate, but imagine three women all about to have babies trying to find jobs in a town not bigger than a minute," she laughs, stacking her napkin and plastic fork on her empty paper party plate. I nod in agreement, and then abruptly stop when what she said completely sinks in.

"Did you say all *three* of you were having babies?" I ask, trying to temper what hopefully does not sound like judgement in my voice. "What are the odds of that? Must have had something in the water in that office!" A somewhat fake sounding laugh slips out of me, and I cringe inwardly that I might be ruining everything. Ginny looks a little taken aback at my sudden line of questioning, and I try to reel back down to casual.

"Um, yes, Debbie, Connie and I all had our boys within two months of each other, if you can believe it. We were such a little family there—I felt like I'd finally found the sisters I never had. We grieved splitting up, but the Lord provided. Ida Mae and Mavis at Petal Pushers took me in and treated me like one of their own. They even helped with Parker when he was tiny." She pats my hand with gentle conviction. "Molly, just remember—the Lord is always preparing a new way, and He doesn't do anything less than the best. If it feels like what's next might be worse, that just means He isn't finished yet."

Before I can answer, two other ladies take their seats at our table with excited smiles. Ginny greets them, and starts shuffling up the tiles before giving me some additional last minute advice. "Now, just remember-try to just get three or four tiles that all look the same. Don't worry so much about what the picture is, just match up three or four and go from there, okay?"

"Um, yes, thank you. That should make it a little easier," I reply, giving her a weak smile. In a matter of seconds, I've gone from thinking I'd laser-located exactly who we were looking for, to blowing it back open to an even wider field than I'd first thought–Langley's third kid could literally be any of the three possibilities.

"Well, how did you mahjong?" Shep asks when I come in the side door a little while later. The kids are already in bed, and he is sitting at the kitchen counter with a cup of (probably, or at least should be) decaf coffee and a stack of spreadsheets and bull EPD sheets. If I had to guess, he's probably selecting bulls for a round of breeding, one of his favorite things to do.

"Not well. Luckily Marge brought an extra 120 quarters for me because I lost every single one of them." I sit on the stool next to him and plop my bag on the counter. "How was y'all's night?"

"Not bad. We had hot dogs and I wrecked Hayes at FIFA. Mia read a book or something... Did you just say you paid $30 to lose at mahjong?"

"I think so? I'm not really sure, I just know that I got tokens when I walked in, and I had no tokens at the end of the night. Marge walked in with a bag of quarters and left with an empty bag. Those ladies don't mess around so there's really no telling how much I actually lost."

He pats me on the back and I can tell he's trying not to laugh at me. "Well, did you at least get the information you went for? Did you get to talk to Ginny Parrish?"

"Oh, I talked to her alright. And she was pregnant with Parker when Asa and Langley sold the business," I reply, taking a chocolate chip cookie out of the jar on the counter. I had more than enough calories earlier, but these are more emotional calories than nutritional calories.

"There you go. Now you can tell Cooper that Parker Parrish should be the missing Party C, right?"

"I wish. All three of them were pregnant. The Wallace, Frazier, and Parrish boys were all born within two months of one another."

"Geez, what was in that water?"

"My exact sentiments."

I sigh, feeling like this is a bit of a dead end that I hadn't expected, and I'm unsure how to move my way out of it. Shep pats me on the shoulder supportively and I give him a grateful smile and rest my head on his shoulder.

"Well, the good news is that at the end of the day, you don't really have to worry about it."

My head pops back up almost immediately after I lay it down, and I stare at him. "What do you mean?"

He looks a little sheepish, like he knows I'm not going to like what he's about to say, but he is going to say it anyway. "I'm just saying... you aren't actually in charge of investigating this. You've got the building released, and we aren't related to any of this, so you really don't have to worry about it, right?"

I let his words sink in and really think about them before deciding how to respond. He's not wrong. In fact, he's annoyingly right, as he has been for the entirety of our relationship. Whether I've wanted it to be so, or sometimes not, if there's one certainty I've been able to count on for the last twenty plus years, it's that Shep Jones is right. Why does this matter to me? I debated this the last time–why am I inserting myself so fully into this mess like my life depends on it?

"Am I too nosy?" I ask instead, wondering if he can help me tease this apart. "Like, why do I feel so strongly that other people's business is my business. I mean, I almost got us shot a few weeks ago. Why can't I just mind my own business?"

"Because you care about people, and because it's so in your nature to help people. Which isn't a bad thing. Just maybe not the best thing to be doing sometimes. Plus, I think this is clearly a thrill for you."

"It's certainly not boring, that's for sure. I don't know where to go from here, babe. I think we're at a bit of a dead end."

"If we're honest, do we really think someone killed Langley Fletcher? I mean, what is the motive there?"

"Honestly? I have no idea. But I would have been more

inclined to believe that it was just an accident had his family not come out of the wood work acting weird as all get out right afterward. I don't think I'd call it motive, but don't you think it's strange that both kids were desperate to get in that attic? If your dad was found dead somewhere, wouldn't you want to be as far away from that place as possible?"

He ponders for a moment, and then involuntarily shudders. "Fair enough. So do you think one of the kids really offed him? Like on purpose?" I shrug in response because I truly have no idea. One of them is the most likely scenario, even though it seems terrible to think that a child would do that to their father. "So... which one would it be?"

Before I can answer his follow up question, my phone starts to buzz on the counter with Sheriff Cooper's name scrolling across the top.

"Molly?" His gruff voice booms through the phone as I answer and put the call on speaker. "We went to the family to see about Fletcher's official will."

Shep looks at me with surprise in his eyes and leans in so he can hear as well. "Did you find anything?" I ask, wondering how I managed to be on the list to get the update on this.

"More than enough. Each kid says they have his official will."

"Let me guess. They aren't the same?"

"Nope."

"Let me guess again-they don't mention an extra sibling?"

"Nope. Hers has her as the sole heir, and he has the two of them splitting equally. Neither mentions a third sibling."

"So... which one is right?" I say tentatively, thinking I was maybe kidding just a little bit about being his actual sidekick, but now that the opportunity is here, I'm sure not going to turn it down. I knew I was growing on him, but this is real, actual inclusion, and I am so here for it.

"I think it's neither. It's the third one we haven't found. Yet."

chapter
eleven

"OKAY, so... they are pretty similar here as far as I can tell?" The next morning, after dropping kids off at school and leaving Shep and the boys to work on freeze branding a set of yearling bulls, I head into the sheriff's station to lay eyes on the two versions of Langley Fletcher's will. In the department conference room, Cooper has copies of each of the versions that he was given by the Fletcher twins, plus our incomplete version from Cassius and August Renfro, all lined up on the table side by side to compare page by page.

So far, there haven't been any differences at all-both lay out a trust meant to care for Nora Fletcher until death, with her assets being distributed upon his death, aside from what was meant to care for her. It seems like all the versions are fairly up to date to reflect the state of Nora's health, which has my wheels really turning about how we have so many versions that look legit.

"Is there any way to authenticate these for legitimacy?" I ask, thinking that I had no idea people took updating these officially so seriously. There's a decent chance that our will still just lists who would take an infant Mia in the event of our deaths, and there's maybe a possibility that one of us penciled in "You get Hayes, too" at some point after he was born, but we definitely have not been in an attorney's office in over a decade.

"Not really, a lot of it is just word against word. Both of these jokers have attorneys swearing theirs is the real deal. Clearly someone is lying. And my bet is on both of them." Cooper leans back in a rolling desk chair pulled up to the table and rests both hands behind his head with his elbows back. I sit in the middle of the table, and continue to read each version paragraph by paragraph to compare until my eyes start to blur.

"Here's a question–why would her version cut him out? What is the reasoning that she should be the sole heir? I know they've each said the other is the problem, but why would his still name both of them and hers leave him out?" I lean back in my chair also, pushing my readers up into my hair for a few moments of pondering with Sheriff Cooper.

He runs his hand over his beard a few times in succession, staring up into the corner of the room as he thinks. "You think his version should have left her out?"

I shrug–I'm just spitballing here, like basketball sized spit-balls–but it's not a crazy train of thought. "I just think it's suspicious that he would have been left out. What did he do that was so egregious he would have been removed from the will? It's fairly well established in their lore that neither of them was a saint, at least as a child, so I have a hard time believing that he would have done something to have Langley cut him out and let her inherit everything outright," I say as I look back to the current page I have up–the listing of what is inherited by each party. Nothing changes about what is being inherited–just the division between the parties. Or a lack of division in the case of Linny's version.

"So who sounds more guilty in that scenario–her for being the sole heir, or him for thinking he might be cut out?"

Cooper muses back, and I stop to think about his reasoning. I had assumed that meant Wells looked more guilty in that case because he was trying to get back in, but I see Cooper's point that she has just as much to gain by him losing his half and her getting it.

"I don't know; all this legalese is giving me a headache," I answer, laying my head down on the table and wondering if we'll ever figure this out. Every discovery feels like one step forward and two steps back to the point that I think we could just about give it up and it wouldn't make a difference.

"Does knowing what happened to Langley change anything, Coop? Like, if by some miracle, we figure out what happened to him, does it really matter?"

"Well, it matters that justice prevails," he starts, giving me a bit of a harrumph that I would dare ask such a question. "And depending on what happened to him, it could change what happens to all this. " He gestures to the papers spread across the table, and I assume he means the estate that one or the both of them stand to inherit. Not to mention the third unnamed child that fits into this somehow.

"Fair enough. If you're indicted for murder, you don't get to inherit millions."

"Um, convicted, yes, you are forfeiting the inheritance. Indictment is a whole other story. Indictments tie up estates for years." Cooper lifts his legs with what feels like more effort than it should be and drops both boots on the table with decisive thunks before crossing them at the ankles.

"Interesting... At this point, I'm not sure the goal would be to tie everything up, but that is an interesting point to note. Who are you thinking is this third kid, Coop?" I take his lead and put both of my feet on the table facing his feet so we are just two hardened, crime busting partners, shooting the breeze over a case. Or at least I'm going to pretend that's what we are until further notice.

"Who did you say our options are?" he asks, resting his hands across his torso and leaning back in his chair a little further.

"Well, Ginny Parrish said that she, Debbie Frazier, and Connie Wallace were all expecting babies at the time they closed F&S, and Asa Shoemaker said this affair and subsequent baby was basically the main driving force behind the sale of the company. He was unsure which secretary was the mistress, and I thought it would be a slam dunk of whoever was pregnant at the time, but of course it couldn't be that easy. How big of a ruckus would it be to just order DNA on each of the boys? I know it will turn town upside down, but it's kind of our only option, right?"

He shakes his head in frustration and pulls his feet off the table. "Nope. At this point, we have no evidence of wrongdoing, either by a confirmed child or a non-confirmed child, meaning the existence or non-existence of a third heir is a civil matter. A probate judge would have to order that, not us. I mean, uh, me," he puffs, like he's suddenly remembered that I'm still a civilian. Incredibly helpful, but a civilian nonetheless.

"So... what's our next step?" I ask tentatively, hoping I get to be involved in whatever it is. I mean, I'm going to be either way, but I'll admit, it's been much less stressful to be involved with his blessing instead of against his wishes.

He scratches his beard and ponders for another long moment with a heavy sigh. "The best next step is finding the complete version of this third will, then figuring out which of them is the most up to date. My bet is that the missing one is the one we want, otherwise it wouldn't be missing. And that kills two birds with one stone because it should tell us who the third kid is, right?"

"I think so. Someone is a Party C-either an unknown child or someone else that Langley took time to put in for an equal share. Am I allowed to talk to Connie Wallace or Debbie Frazier?"

"Molly Jones, I am not your mama. I can't tell you who you are and aren't allowed to talk to–unless you are being belligerent and harassing," he replies, sounding worked up, but with a slight twinkle in his eye that tells me we are on the same train of thought. "Just don't make anybody mad or things might get a little harder down the road, you know?"

I nod in agreement and gather up my things to head for the door. I'm not sure exactly which one I'll talk to first, or how to even start a conversation in the right ballpark, but I know it will start out there and not in here. Before I get up from my chair to get going, I pause and look Cooper straight in the face with a seriousness I don't typically have. "You think this was a homicide, don't you? I know it's just an open, unsolved investigation, but we're not barking up trees that don't exist, right? You think he was murdered?"

"If I thought this was an accident, I would have closed it two weeks ago, Molly."

I give him another nod of agreement and pat him on the shoulder as I head out the door. Once I get back into my car and am debating between heading to the water district or the feed store, Shep's name buzzes across my phone in my hand.

"Hey, what's up?"

"Are you busy right now?" he asks, sounding out of breath and a little perturbed. Shep has always been incredibly even-keeled emotionally, so "a little perturbed" is typically Shep code for he's incredibly irritated but isn't showing it.

"Not overly so. Do y'all need something?"

"Apparently this cooler is cracked, and all the dry ice we got last night leaked out. We've got everyone penned up and ready to go, but we need thirty more pounds of dry ice. Can you run by Bluebonnet and grab us some?"

That is not exactly the turn I planned for my next move,

but there is no way I'm going to tell him no. "I can do that. You need a new cooler, too?"

"Yeah, you're probably better off stopping by Taylor's to get that, just a 110 gallon with a flat bottom. Thanks, Molls."

"No problem, I'll see y'all in a bit."

After securing the cheapest 110 gallon flat bottomed cooler I could find at Taylor's Sporting Goods on the main square of Buffalo Creek, I take a turn into Bluebonnet Market to grab dry ice so I can head home. Knowing that Shep and the boys are essentially stuck waiting on me has me a bit flustered, and I race through the front sliding doors to the nearest checkout.

"Hi, I just need thirty pounds of dry ice, please," I tell the cashier, waving a hand to the large cooler by the exit door and pulling out my wallet. The cashier blinks at me silently, and I quickly type in my phone number on the pin pad for my rewards account, thinking this must be what she is waiting for to complete the transaction. As she reaches under the counter and rummages around, a line starts to form behind me, and I feel even more flustered, as I don't like to make people wait or draw attention.

After a few long seconds, she pops back up from under the counter and hands me a small stack of brown paper grocery bags. This time, I am the one to silently blink, as I have no idea what she is wanting me to do.

"Ok, sugar, you just got to go over to that cooler and pull out however much you think you need, and then bring it on over here for me to weigh it. You can put it in them bags," she explains, popping her gum as I stand there with my bags, more than a little dumbfounded. Admittedly, I have never been the one to buy dry ice for branding before, but I assumed it is similar to buying regular ice-you pick up the bags of standard weight and you go home. I am not feeling very confident about this process right now.

"So, how much does a bag weigh?"

"Just depends. You just gotta get however much you think and I can weigh it for you here at the register."

I glance back at the growing line behind me and my fluster starts to grow rapidly into a panic. "Okay, can you just check out the next person while I'm getting the bags?" I nod to the person behind me who looks less than thrilled with the antics of my inexperience.

"No, sugar, you already typed in your rewards number. I can't cancel your transaction without a manager and he's on lunch. Just go grab whatcha need, and get back over here. They'll wait." She flashes a smile to the growing crowd and pops another bubble with her gum as I snatch the paper sacks off the counter and rush to the cooler, grabbing a shopping cart on my way.

I whip the lid open and see plastic sealed sacks of 12" x 12" blocks of dry ice about 1" thick stacked up on top of one other. As I reach inside the cooler, I let go of the lid and it immediately drops down and smacks me on the back of the head with a decisive *thwack*. It makes me instantly angry, with a side of not thinking straight, and I grab a block with my bare hand to shove in a paper sack.

While I am completely aware that touching dry ice can burn your skin, I apparently (stupidly) thought the plastic was enough of a barrier to combat this– spoiler alert: it's not. I yelp in pain, and drop the block back in the cooler as the lid comes back down on my head. At this point, I'm contemplating crawling in the freezer for good and just calling it a day.

After a few more seconds of struggle and one block wrestled into a paper bag, I feel the weight of the lid lift off my head. I look up and see a kind stranger–the man from the couple in line behind me–has taken the liberty of holding the freezer open for me. I choke out a battle worn "thank you" before gingerly filling five more paper bags with ice and dumping it into the cart. I wheel it back to the checkout counter to complete this bizarre round of *Supermarket Showdown* feeling defeated, both mentally and physically. Bubblegum lifts out the first three paper sacks before declaring to me that they cumulatively weigh 32 pounds before pausing and raising an eyebrow to the remaining three bags in my cart, silently asking how I would like to proceed.

"Well, I guess that's all I need then," I say, pulling out my card and jamming it in the card reader. The transaction runs for $95.68 and as she hands me the receipt, she gestures to my cart of rejects. "I'll hang on to the ones you bought and you can go ahead and put those back so we don't get 'em mixed up."

I'm certain my entire body physically falls at this point as I wheel the cart back to dump the extras in the freezer, and then return for my purchases. "Thank you for your patience," I say to the couple behind me as I gather everything to finally get out of the way.

"You're fine, honey. That looks like more work than anyone else is doing in here. Have a good day," the woman says, shooting a sideways glance at the cashier as she starts swiping their groceries down the belt. I pause for one final second, trying not to stare, but putting the pieces together in that moment that the couple behind me the whole time was Debbie Frazier, and her son, Kyle.

After I get the dry ice loaded in the cooler, I turn back to see Debbie and Kyle walking through the parking lot to a large white truck with the *Frazier Feed and Seed* logo on the side. I hesitate, and then think that if I don't take my chance now, it may not come again.

"Hi! I just wanted to say thank you for helping me with that cooler. And again for your patience. You did a good job raising a gentleman, mama," I say tentatively as I walk up. Debbie snaps her head up and then waves a dismissive hand with a small smile.

"My Kyle is a good boy," she agrees quietly as he gets in the driver's seat. She stands silently for another moment or so and I panic about what to say next before she gets in to leave with him.

"It's so funny to run into y'all because we were just talking about you!" I blurt out, and Debbie's face instantly turns sour. I don't really know them at all, and now it sounds like I've been sitting somewhere in town just gossiping about her. I mean, that's not out of the ordinary in a small town like Buffalo Creek, but it is out of the ordinary to admit it to the person in reference.

"Not in a bad way! I met Ginny Parrish a few nights ago and we were talking about when y'all worked for F&S because my husband and I just bought that building from Asa Shoemaker. She was telling me how they closed the business when all three of y'all were pregnant and how crazy it was for everyone to go get new jobs." I laugh nervously and hope that I haven't overcooked my grits. It was a bold move to just lay it out like that, but my mouth was moving faster than my brain. Sometimes that works out better, and sometimes it really bites you in the butt. We're about to see which way it's going to land this time.

Debbie's sour look turns toward confusion. "I wasn't pregnant when F&S closed." She leans against the side of the truck and hoists her purse up higher on her shoulder. Now my brain has come to a screeching halt, and my mouth is trying to drag it along.

"Oh, I'm so sorry! Ginny just said that all three of you were expecting and had your boys within two months or so of each other. I must have misheard the timing or something. I apologize," I stammer as I try to discreetly peer in the driver's side to confirm that Kyle does in fact look to be in his early thirties. Maybe he was born before all this? Or after?

Debbie lets out a short laugh and playfully smacks my arm. "Oh, that Ginny, always having to be so proper. She probably said it that way so it didn't make me feel left out or something, but it's fine. Yeah, the boys were all born about two months apart from each other, and we were "expecting" him, but I was never pregnant. Dutch and I just couldn't ever make that work."

She trails off and I stand there, still confused and trying to put all these unexpected pieces together.

"So Kyle is..." I begin, hoping she can fill in the blank for me.

"Kyle is adopted. A teenager in Winchester placed him with Baptist Family Services when she was four months pregnant, and he was born right in between Parker and Matt. We adopted him at birth."

"Hey, did they have enough?" Twenty minutes later, I pull onto our driveway where Shep is waiting to unload the dry ice. I am absolutely reeling from the last thirty minutes of my life, between the dry ice incident and the revelation that the Fraziers are ruled out of this paternity question. I try to snap out of it, and focus all my attention on Shep and getting the dry ice out to start branding.

"Yeah, there should be. I could have used a little warning about that whole experience," I gripe, helping him pull the cooler out of the back cargo area and into the waiting Gator.

"Warning about what?" he asks absently, opening the cooler to start breaking apart the blocks. He has leather work gloves on, which makes him impervious to potential burns, and I absently rub my palms together where they are still smarting.

"What an ordeal buying dry ice is! Having to grab however much it is and have them weigh it and all that. It was so stressful," I reply, probably leaning into victimhood a little too hard. He looks up at me from breaking up the ice with a confused expression.

"What do you mean? You had to weigh out the blocks?"

"The cashier said they all weigh something different, and I grabbed way too much, and it burned me through the plastic, and then I had to put half of it back. There was a huge line behind me, and it was so overwhelming," I pout, hoping to garner a little sympathy for my trouble, all while knowing I'm barking up the wrong tree-Shep Jones typically does not dole out sympathy. He is best known for handing out large, steaming bowls of what he calls "Suck it Up Stew".

And I'm right. Instead of concern or reassurance, he starts laughing. The laugh grows from a soft chuckle to a loud belly laugh and I want to be irritated, but it honestly just makes me laugh as well.

"I guess I should have told you that I usually call ahead to order and pick it up. I've never had to weigh it out myself."

▭

Later that night, I'm putting the finishing touches on all the details of the Shoppe for our soft opening the next day. We put out on social media and through some local ladies' groups that we would be open for a few hours to test systems and have "early shopping", but I want everything to be just as smooth as a real opening. Shep and the kids are holding down the fort at home and everything is essentially ready, but I'm fussing about little elements just to calm my nerves.

I'll admit, it's a little bit creepy being in this building by myself at night, but I keep telling myself that ghosts aren't real, and I highly doubt we have a murderer on the loose who would be looking for me. If Langley really was murdered, I feel like it was probably him-specific and not just someone looking to murder anyone they might have the chance to. But that doesn't mean I haven't stopped dead in my tracks every time I hear the slightest little noise out of the ordinary.

All the merchandise tables are perfectly arranged, and I walk through to add even spacing between the wooden hangers on the hanging racks of clothing next to the tables. Mandy has already dropped large floral arrangements on the counters, and my gift wrapping station is poised and ready with large spools of craft paper and a rainbow of curling ribbons. The coolers are packed to the gills with fresh beef, humming quietly along the underside of the stairs, and all in all, I'm pretty pleased with how everything has turned out.

Deciding to call it a night and head home, I turn off all the lights and head out the back door, trying not to psych myself about being there alone in the dark. My Suburban is less than twenty feet from the back door–just right outside the back gate–so I sprint off the back porch and through the gate, hitting the unlock button on my key fob as I go. Less than thirty seconds later, I am safely in my driver's seat, and lock the door behind me before sitting for a minute or two to scroll my phone.

After a quick turn through all the social media options, mostly checking to make sure my posts about tomorrow's opening are still scheduled, plus a quick peek at my general feeds, I put myself in reverse to back out and head home.

Just as I straighten out onto the side street, the slightest bit of movement catches my eye up on the roof of the Shoppe. I quickly throw myself in park and fumble for my phone to record what is happening, and to call Sheriff Cooper.

"Coop! You've got to get guys down here!"

"Molly, where are you?" Panic is in his voice, I assume matching the panic in mine.

"I'm at the Shoppe, and there's someone on the roof! They are trying to get in the second floor window!"

"Where exactly are you? In the building?" I can hear him grabbing keys and slamming doors, which I assume means he is heading out to meet me.

"No, I'm in my car on Sycamore. I was leaving and I saw the movement as I went to pull away!"

"Molly, you're alone in your car?" he asks flatly, the sound of all his movement stopping momentarily.

"Yes!"

"Then why in tarnation are you whispering?"

I stop for a second and realize I have been whisper shrieking this entire time, and I am, in fact, completely alone. "Oh... sorry, Coop. Anyway, the person was on the roof and they are trying to break in the second floor back window near the attic stairs."

"Alright, video what you can, and we'll be there ASAP. I'll get my closest unit to get over there and I'll be as close behind him as I can get. Just sit tight." He hangs up, and I keep my phone camera zoomed in on the shadowy figure on the second floor balcony. He or she is in all black, and appears to have a thin frame, although I can't really tell much about their physique due to the lack of light- our street lamp on the corner is out, conveniently. It seems like they aren't having much luck getting the door or window to budge, and I'm praying some sort of law enforcement shows up before they decide it's worth it to break one of the antique stained glass windows.

Like a knight in shining armor, a few seconds later, I first hear a siren, and then see the lights careening around the corner. A deputy truck parks along the side of the Shoppe and a uniformed man jumps out, so I jump out and run over to meet him.

"They're right up there!" I say breathlessly, pointing up to the second floor balcony. The officer nods in recognition, and silently moves through the gate. I watch as he nears the back porch like he plans to climb up, and the intended intruder realizes what's happening. He or she jumps back to the roof, runs around to the front, and slides down one of the front columns before heading off running into the night.

I get most of it on video, turning it off as I come back around the corner and find the deputy halfway up the back column to get to the back balcony.

"You can just forget it. Whoever it is is gone," I say sullenly, waving a dismissive hand as he slowly shimmies back down to the ground.

"Man, I almost had him, but my pants leg got caught on a nail in that column," he explains, and I nod silently, not wanting to be the one to burst his bubble that he wasn't even remotely close.

"It's okay, I got most of it on video. I'm not sure you can tell anything since it's so dark, but it's worth a shot," I say, patting him on the back to reassure him as Sheriff Cooper's truck screeches to a halt in front of us on the side street.

"Where's the perp?" he hollers as he flies out of his truck and looks frantically around us. The deputy and I stay silent and I slowly shake my head and give a subtle point to the north where the "perp" has fled. Cooper drops his shoulders in defeat and starts unclipping his radio from his belt. I hand him my phone to watch the video as he calls in the situation.

"Calling all units—suspect on foot, attempted B&E at the southwest corner of 25th and Sycamore, heading north. Unknown gender, black clothing, medium height, thin build. Apprehend and detain." He turns off his radio and looks back at us. "Dammit, Randy, what happened?"

"My pants leg got caught on a nail, sir," he reasons,

holding up his leg to show where the fabric of his pants is ripped. Cooper rolls his eyes and hands me back my phone.

"I should've known not to send you after you barely passed your physical last week. This ought to be more your speed–go see if you can apprehend some donuts for the station instead." Randy hangs his head and gets back in his truck, and I'm unsure if the request for donuts is sarcastic or not until I see his truck turn right at the corner, headed in the direction of Happy's Donuts down the street. Bless his heart, this one is going to be hard to live down.

"He did his best, Coop," I say gently as we slip into the backyard to head upstairs and check for any damage. He nods, and I know he's not really mad at Randy, but more so frustrated at the situation. The likelihood of any other units tracking down a generic black figure in a large portion of residential Buffalo Creek is slim to none, but hopefully there's something on the balcony that could help us at least.

Cooper and I turn on every light in the building as we head upstairs onto the small balcony overlooking the backyard. There are some light scratches where it looks like they were trying to pry open the window, but no footprints. Cooper waves a black light flashlight over the area but nothing hits.

"This won't show prints themselves, but if they left any residue of any kind it should show up. Looks like whoever this was covered their tracks pretty well." He mills around a little more with his black light as I shine my cell phone flashlight around. Just as I'm about to give up and head back inside, something glints off my light and catches my eye. I bend down and use a stray twig to loop under a thin silver band lying innocently on the balcony.

"What about this, Coop?" He turns around and gingerly takes the twig from me, a small gleam of excitement in his eyes.

"A wedding band?" He pulls a small Ziploc bag from his pocket and drops it inside. "That ought to get us somewhere."

"THANK you so much for shopping at the Red Rock Shoppe! Come see us again soon!" Laramie, our adorable college aged counter help, is finishing ringing up a purchase for Luann Melton, long time resident of Buffalo Creek and all around small town critic extraordinaire, mostly maintaining eye contact with Mrs. Melton, but darting her eyes to me standing twelve inches behind her a handful of times. I nod discreetly in approval before we both flash Luann giant smiles as Laramie slides her bag across the counter. Luann gives her own nod and smile of approval as she pulls her brown craft paper bag full of trinkets and a few pounds of ground beef down and goes to head out the door.

"Thanks kindly, girls. Everything looks just darlin', Molly. I think you're going to do alright, despite all that dead body nonsense."

I maintain my smile but I once again feel dead on the inside. All anyone has commented on is the fact that the store looks, feels, smells, and *is* great, despite the circumstances of a few weeks ago. Any hope I had of people moving on and forgetting evaporated after the fifth customer out of five couldn't help but bring it up. At this point, I could probably slap it on flyers and use it as a marketing gimmick- come shop where dead bodies fall from the attic. What a pull.

"I appreciate that, Mrs. Luann. Tell Mr. George we said hello, and I hope he enjoys that ground beef." I give her a wink and pull back the corners of my mouth a little so my smile isn't fading as I pray she takes that cue to leave. She heads to the door, saying hellos to a few other Buffalo Creek old timers, before finally exiting. Laramie and I breathe a collective sigh of relief, and I straighten up the handful of office supplies on the counter that we've displaced during the last few rushes.

"I think everything's going really well, Molly!" Laramie gives me an encouraging smile, and I nod in agreement. All in all, for a soft opening, it actually has been going well, aside from trying to get out from under the negative press we've started out with. Laramie is a smart girl and doesn't need me to stand behind her as she rings up purchases, but I've been hanging out more so to answer everyone's invasive questions so she doesn't have to. The only thing nosier than women in a small town is a raccoon in a trash can.

Unsurprisingly, the sheriff's department wasn't able to find any suspects last night, and our only lead is the silver wedding band. I know from conversation that both Fletcher twins are married, but I can't remember if I spotted wedding bands on them when I've seen them in person or not, and I don't really have a reason to go track them down now. Sheriff Cooper has been in the shop intermittently, just to keep an eye on things as we've opened to the public. Nothing has been really out of the ordinary, though, aside from everyone's fixation on our little discovery before opening.

"Do you want me to straighten tables before we get another rush?" Laramie asks, breaking me out of my daydream about busting the unnamed intruder from the night before. I obviously have no idea who it might be, but I think a short list would include either Fletcher twin, and whoever their unknown half sibling is. I haven't had a chance to "bump into" Connie or Ginny yet, and there's a part of me that is hoping more than I probably should that one of them will just wander into the Shoppe at some point and present me with the opportunity I haven't had the chance to manufacture.

"Sure, thanks, Laramie." I give her a grateful smile and she heads out onto the floor to reorganize all the display tables. Laramie belongs to our long time dear friends Hank and Tiffani, and when it came time to consider hiring part time help at the Shoppe, she was the obvious no-brainer choice. The last of ladies in the store come to check out a few minutes later. For the briefest of moments, the store is empty, and all is quiet.

"Molly Margaret! When were you going to tell me you were involved in a police chase last night?" The back door suddenly flies open a few minutes later and smacks into the wall behind it, immediately reminding me that I forgot to have Shep fix the door stop for that door. If there's not a doorknob sized hole in that wall now, I'll be truly shocked.

"I wasn't in a police chase, Marge," I answer warily, taking my grandmother's purse from her and setting it on the back counter before guiding her to an overstuffed royal blue corduroy armchair in the corner in front of the checkout counter.

"Margaret! You could have at least closed your damn door!" Before I can get the back door closed, JoBeth appears in the doorway, huffing and puffing like she's been chasing Marge down the alley or something. She looks viscerally irritated, and I try not to laugh as she pushes her teal rimmed glasses higher on her nose and gives me a hug.

"Hey, JoBeth. Who's been talking to Marge?" I whisper in her ear, and point to a stool behind the counter. JoBeth has always been the coolest great-aunt. For my entire lifetime, she's had short hair that she keeps chopped in a pixie cut, and the smallest of figures that she dresses in the most eccentric of outfits. Today, she is in a white oversized t-shirt with a pair of loud, multi-colored quilted pants and orange sneakers. She and Marge have a very classic oldest daughter/ baby daughter dynamic, and I am usually both exhausted and amused after any interaction with them.

"Language, JoBeth. No need for vulgarity," Marge quips back before JoBeth can give me an answer, settling into the chair like it is her throne in the Shoppe. JoBeth sticks her tongue out and gives her a mean face, despite the fact that she is behind Marge and can't actually be seen.

"Oh, I beg your pardon, madam. The next time you get your ass out of my car, please shut your own damn door!" she squeals, her face starting to redden, and I am immediately grateful that we don't have any lingering customers in the Shoppe.

Marge just harrumphs in reply, and straightens her silk scarf as Laramie brings her a cup of coffee. I mouth a silent thank you as she scurries off to do some invisible work in the front that removes her from the line of fire between Jo and Amy March here.

"She's been yapping with Geraldine again. And Geraldine lives with her police scanner shoved up her butt, so she heard all about the break-in call last night. But I do believe some details were exaggerated," JoBeth advises quietly, sliding up on the aforementioned stool. "But, how is business going, though? What happened last night?"

"It's been pretty steady, which is good considering we didn't do a lot of advertising just yet. I just wanted a little traffic to test the systems before we do the full grand opening. We're planning to do the big opening along with that karaoke fundraiser for Mia's cheer team. Nothing crazy happened, just someone trying to break into the second floor that we caught before they got in. They ran off before anyone could get them."

"Good deal, sugar; I'm glad it's all going well. And you just be careful about all these crazies around here. I've always said there isn't anyone crazier than small town people."

"Noted. What are y'all up to today?"

"We are just running around town doing some errands. We wanted to check on you before we go over to Connie's for book club." She pats me on the shoulder and I let her words sink in before whipping around to face her.

"Did you say Connie?"

"Yeah, Connie Wallace? Do you know her?"

"No, but I need to. How do you know her?"

"She started a book club a couple years ago and Marge and I have been going the last few months. I'm on the library board with a few other ladies that go. Marge goes so she can sound smart to everyone and I go because someone usually makes the good homemade cheese straws. We read *To Kill a Mockingbird* this month like we didn't all see the movie sixty years ago when it came out." She rolls her eyes and I try not to laugh. "Why do you need to know Connie?"

"Boy, it's a long story at this point. Do you think she would have had an affair with her boss thirty years ago and covered it up?"

JoBeth's eyes swell to the size of Oreos and a slow smile spreads across her face. "I have no idea, but that sounds more like what I signed up for when I agreed to do a book club."

"What are you two clucking about over there?" Marge tries to turn around in the armchair to look at us, but the stuffing of the chair makes it difficult for her to get herself turned around.

"Marge! Do you think Connie would have boinked her boss back in the nineties?" JoBeth asks loudly and bluntly, and

I cringe down to my toes, again, so thankful we are the only ones in here.

"Josephine!" Marge cries in horror, literally clutching her scarf in shock.

"Lord, JoBeth, that's one way to put it. So, supposedly there is a version of Langley Fletcher's will that we cannot find that names a third child as an equal heir. Asa said Langley had an affair with one of their secretaries, but he didn't know which one, and they all had boys within like two months of each other. We've been trying to find this copy of the will, or at least figure out who might be the third child. We've ruled out Debbie Frazier's son Kyle, so Connie Wallace's son Matt, or Ginny Parrish's son Parker are the two other options."

"Well, I don't know Connie that well, but I do know that Ginny would absolutely never," Marge declares confidently and we get another eye roll from JoBeth.

"You'd be shocked how often "never" actually happens, Margaret."

"I mean, I didn't get those vibes from her at mahjong night, either, Marge, but it's got to be one of the two," I explain, inserting myself into their verbal ping pong.

"Well, how much longer are you supposed to be here?" JoBeth asks, gesturing around to the empty store. I flick my wrist to check my watch—1:45.

"We said we'd be open from ten to two," I answer, craning toward the front windows to check for anyone on the sidewalk. "We just posted in the community Facebook group and relied on word of mouth, so who knows how many people actually know we're open."

"Perfect, book club starts at 2:30. You come with us and we'll figure this out."

"Okay, let me just see if Shep or the guys can grab the kids from school," I say, thinking that this is an interesting turn of events for the day. Just when you aren't sure how you're going to get something done by yourself, it's just like the Lord to give you the answer in the most unexpected of ways.

Marge sets her coffee cup up on the counter behind her and rocks back and forth until she finally gains enough momentum to rise from the armchair. She straightens the scarf over her short-sleeved pastel sweater and, in what I can only describe as a brief possession by Shania Twain, looks at me and JoBeth and commands, "Let's go, girls." Then she strides straight out the back door, leaving it wide open behind her.

⬜

"You've read *To Kill a Mockingbird*, right? You were kind of a nerd in school, weren't you?" JoBeth asks as the three of us make our way up the front sidewalk in front of Connie Wallace's home in a fairly new subdivision on the outskirts of Buffalo Creek. I know better than to be offended by JoBeth's question- I've known her my whole life and know she's not trying to be mean or hurt my feelings. But she definitely leans more on the "truth" aspect of "speaking the truth in love" than the "love" part.

"Yes, I have. Don't worry about me embarrassing y'all," I say, hiking my bag higher on my shoulder. I am in a pair of black workout tights and one of our oversized "Red Rock Shoppe" Comfort Colors tees, and feel like this wouldn't have been my first choice of wardrobe to go to a book club full of judgy older women, or to investigate a possible suspect in my now side gig as a detective. But, you gotta take the opportunities as they come, I guess.

"Oh, you can't embarrass me. I just didn't want you to embarrass yourself if you didn't have anything to contribute to the conversation," she clarifies, gesturing for me to head in ahead of her as Marge leads the way inside Connie's unlocked house.

I open my mouth to give her a rebuttal, but walk straight into a gaggle of squealing older ladies in Connie's foyer with Marge holding court in the middle of them. "Margaret! It's so good to see you!" A woman with medium auburn hair sprinkled with grays and curled up like she is trying to look younger than she is emerges through the crowd and envelopes Marge in a hug.

"Connie, thanks for having us! I hope you don't mind, but JoBeth and I brought a guest today." She flashes her charming smile that few have ever attempted to argue with, and gestures to me standing behind her. I tug my t-shirt down, hoping I don't look completely dumpy, but knowing I can't do anything about it. Looking back, I should have at least grabbed a cute top from one of the Shoppe racks and dressed myself up a little bit, but too little too late now. "This is my granddaughter, Molly."

Connie's face falters as she looks from Marge to me, and I wonder why she would have such an immediate visceral reaction. "Hi, thanks for having me. I love *To Kill a Mockingbird*. I wrote my senior thesis on it when I was in college," I say, trying to fill the silence while working to decode Connie's increasingly sour face.

"Of course, wonderful for you to join us. If you'll excuse me, I need to make sure the coffee is going in the kitchen. The food is set up in the dining room, and all the chairs are up in the living room for the discussion." Connie quickly elbows her way back through the crowd toward what I assume is the kitchen as Marge looks back to me and JoBeth behind her.

"Well, who peed in her Post Toasties?" JoBeth mutters to us as we bring up the rear of the crowd headed to go get a snack and sit down.

"Must you be so vulgar?" Marge scolds again, and I stifle a

laugh. I agree that it seems like Connie's mood shifted on a dime, and I'm curious if there is something that she knows that she'd rather I didn't. Either way, she's clearly not thrilled that I am here. And something tells me the reason why is likely very important.

"It's really an overarching commentary on how the court of public opinion is just as powerful—if not more powerful—than the actual judicial system," Susan Phillips says, perched on the edge of her chair. She's a darling little lady not bigger than a minute, but she's commanding the room like she's back teaching high school English. "Atticus didn't just lose the trial —he lost the town long before the verdict. And that made all the difference, don't you think?"

"So what should Atticus have done to combat the court of opinion?" Sandy Bennett asks, and I weirdly find myself completely invested in this exchange.

"Honestly? Nothing. People decide what they want to believe, and then they go looking for proof. Not the other way around." Susan shrugs, leaning back in her chair and sipping her tea.

"So, Tom Robinson was doomed from the get-go, don't you think?" Sandy bats back, sipping her own tea. I've seen Sandy and Susan around town and I know they are both widows that spend most of their social time together. Their back and forth is one of besties completing each other's thoughts, not of an argumentative nature, and I am fascinated watching their entire discussion and glad that no one is trying to butt in to add to it or derail it.

Their collective thought that we as people convince ourselves of something and look for the evidence to support afterward has me spiraling a bit. What does it say about society that things have remained essentially unchanged since 1960, or really the 1930s when the book is set? And how much are we doing this now-convincing ourselves that something has happened to Langley when maybe it hasn't? Either way, whether his demise was purposeful or accidental, it's clear that the division of his assets is contested, and there is something to solve there.

As Susan and Sandy continue, I see Connie quietly rise from her folding chair on the back row closest to the kitchen and slip away. She remained as far away from me as she could get while we all filled plates and found seats, taking that chair only after everyone else was seated, all under the guise of being a good hostess. She is probably fussing with something in the kitchen or dining room, and now could be my chance to talk with her one on one if I don't blow it.

Luckily JoBeth and I ended up with seats on the outer edge of the circle as well, behind Marge in a large armchair. Marge wanted to make sure she could be seen and heard when it came time for her to offer her insights, so we gladly let her take the spotlight. As I slowly and quietly slip out of my chair, JoBeth immediately turns to me with panic in her eyes.

"What are you doing?" she hisses and I hold out both hands in a "steady" motion to remind her to stay quiet.

"Going to try to talk to Connie in there," I mouth back quietly, pointing discreetly to the arching doorway that Connie just dipped through.

"Okay, be careful. And bring me back another cheese straw, please," she whispers, handing me her empty paper plate and turning her attention back to the discussion. Boy, if I'm the dim witted sidekick to Cooper, I can't even imagine what JoBeth and Marge are to me.

I slip through the other doorway that opens to a foyer hallway leading down to the dining room and kitchen. I am trying not to flush Connie back into the living room, so I remain as quiet as I can without looking like a psycho stalker.

Connie is leaning against the kitchen counter furiously typing on her phone and I nonchalantly sidle up to the dining room table and start scooping cheese straws onto JoBeth's plate as an alibi.

"This is a great spread," I say quietly, trying to break the silence and not scare the bejeezus out of her. She jumps a little anyway, and instinctively slams her phone face down on the counter.

"Oh, hi, Molly. Yes, the girls do a good job bringing the food. We never starve, that's for sure." She laughs drily, and I turn my attention to all the framed photos on the wall of the dining room behind me. They are all of their family over the years–Connie and her husband, Matt, and what looks like two younger sisters.

"Are these your kids?" I say sweetly, knowing that discussing their children usually disarms people at least a little. People can't help but typically be proud to talk about their babies.

She does seem to soften a little and nods with a small smile. "Yes, that's Matthew, Melissa, and Megan. Matt owns his own roofing company here in Buffalo Creek. Melissa is a nurse at the hospital and Megan is in graduate school in Austin."

"That's great. You have a beautiful family. I was talking with Ginny Parrish the other day and she was telling me about you and her and Debbie all expecting kids at the same time when F&S closed back in the day. That must have been wild, all trying to find jobs and expecting babies." This tactic seemed to work the other day with Debbie, so my fast moving mouth and slow-to-catch-up brain decides to take it out for a spin again. Connie immediately pales, and I mentally kick myself that this looks more like it's going to bite me in the butt than work out.

"Oh, yes, Ginny and I ended up pregnant about the same

time. It was like built in friends for Matt to have Parker and Kyle. I wished I'd had something like that for the girls," she offers, looking more and more like a caged animal. I smile and nod, not wanting to press my luck as I turn back to look at the pictures, focusing on one of the five of them close up on a beach. Something huge catches my eye and I know I have the answer I need.

"This looks so nice! What beach is this?" I ask brightly, still trying to be upbeat and not interrogative.

"Uh, Rosemary Beach on 30A. About six years ago," she answers, letting out a small breath of relief that it was a question she wasn't scared to answer.

"Fun! We've never been to 30A, but I hear it's beautiful. And it looks beautiful here, for sure! Your girls have such gorgeous blue eyes! My kids both have beautiful blue eyes from my husband. Mine are green, so he beat me out!" I laugh, and she laughs with me until I turn back to the picture and look more closely at Matt. "Looks like you and your husband both have blue eyes, too. But Matt's are such a beautiful chocolate brown–I've never seen anything like them. That's so interesting."

Connie is clutching the counter with white knuckles and looks like she might pass right out. I decide to take my win and leave before I overstay my welcome and overplay my hand. "Better get these cheese straws back to JoBeth!"

I hurry back the way I came and slide into my chair next to JoBeth as I hand her a plate full of cheese straws.

"Good God, I said one, not a plate full. Are you trying to fatten me up for the winter?" JoBeth hisses and I ignore her.

"It's Connie. Matt is Langley's."

chapter
thirteen

"I NEED to speak with Coop! Where is he?" I squeal as I run through the halls of the sheriff's department a little bit later, fresh off my revelation at the "Novel Nanas" meeting. It took every single ounce of patience in my marrow to sit through the rest of the discussion of *To Kill A Mockingbird* without bursting while sitting on such gold, and I couldn't wait to share with Cooper. I rushed Marge and JoBeth out as soon as the meeting was over, and they dropped me back at the Shoppe to drive straight here.

"He's in interrogation C in a closed meeting. Wait your turn," a deputy deadpans, gesturing to the closed door of a meeting room down the hall while maintaining perfect eye contact with his computer screen. I skid to a stop in front of his desk and try to catch my breath to ask some follow up questions.

"How long has he been in there? Do you think he's almost done?" I pant, looking from him to the chair sitting next to his desk stacked high with file folders back to him. He continues staring at his computer screen, so I clear my throat a little and gesture to the chair. Still ignoring me, he closes the file open on his keyboard and sets it on the top of Mount Stackmore

I'm hinting about. I wait another few seconds before bear hugging the stack of files and plopping them down loudly on the floor next to the chair so I can sit down.

"Not much for gentlemanly manners, are you... Hawkins?" I say, peering across the desk at his name plate pinned to his uniform. "Or for taking a hint."

"Those are private state property. I can arrest you for touching those."

"Well then maybe you should have moved them yourself, sir. Where is a lady supposed to sit around here?"

"They're not. They're supposed to mind their own business and stay out of official justice department operations."

"Well, this is my business to mind. A dead body fell out of my attic, and I just figured out who the victim's secret third child is. You're welcome," I reply, triumphantly pounding his desk with my fist. I know I'm irritating this kid, but his buzzkill will not dampen my spirit. This is a huge revelation, and I won't let Deputy Der-to-Der shoot a hole in my sails. He remains unbothered, continuing to stare at his computer like a zombie and I decide to just leave it and wait for Cooper to come out to share in my excitement. Randy may be inept, but I'd take him over this kid any day.

"Do... you... mind?" he whines a few minutes later, finally breaking eye contact with the computer and giving me a dirty look as he drags out each word.

"What? I'm not even talking to you!" I snap back, annoyed that if he can't bother to be excited with me that he can't just leave me alone.

"Your leg is shaking my desk," he gripes, gesturing to my leg bouncing with nervous energy.

"Well, excuse me. I didn't realize you were doing brain surgery over there and needed precision stillness," I reply, rolling my eyes and scooting my chair six inches over so it is no longer touching his desk. I make sure it makes the loudest, most obnoxious scraping noise across the linoleum as I move, and I resist the urge to pull a JoBeth and stick out my tongue at him.

After an excruciating fifteen minutes, in which Hawkins gives up two minutes in and goes to get a cup of coffee from the kitchen and leaves me to bounce in peace, the door to Interrogation C finally opens and I hear Sheriff Cooper coming out with his guest.

"I'll keep you up to date, and if anything changes, please let me know."

"Thank you so much, Sheriff, I will. I appreciate everything you're doing for our family." I jump up from my chair and try not to run down the hall to meet him when the voice accompanying him makes me stop cold. I know that voice. I peek down the hall and see none other than Linny Fletcher Caldwell floating down the hall with Sheriff Cooper toward the bull pen where I am standing with all the pent up energy of a kenneled puppy. She is dressed head to toe in black- black leather leggings, a black oversized tank tunic, and black sneakers with her jet black hair pulled into a stylish bun at the nape of her neck. I almost laugh to myself that if she wanted to be cast as a villain, she's already dressed for the part. I can't tell completely because she's still a little way down the dark hall, but it almost looks like she's been crying, and has a wadded up tissue in her fist. What in the world is she doing here? Admitting guilt? Throwing her brother under the bus again? Trying to throw suspicion?

As I sit and mentally debate the options, they walk straight down the hall and essentially into my lap, shocked to find me waiting anxiously in the bull pen. The second she sees me, it's like Linny puts away her "sad self", and flips all her internal lightswitches to become bright and bubbly.

"Molly, isn't it? It's wonderful to see you again! How are you?" Linny beams, and I fumble to shake her outstretched hand as I am too focused on her slightly streaked mascara to notice it at first.

"Yes, hi again. I'm doing well, just busy with all the things, you know," I laugh nervously, looking to Cooper to see if he can help lob the conversation away from me. He remains silent, almost bemused, so I jump back in because, God forbid there be a silent moment in my presence. "What brings you down to Buffalo Creek?"

"Well, we've been working on memorial arrangements for Daddy, and I just had a few questions for the sheriff. How is your shop coming along? When will you be opening?" Her excitement seems slightly off, but I can't quite put a finger on why.

"Um, next Saturday. We have the grand opening during the day, and then we're hosting a community fundraiser for our daughter's cheer team in the backyard that night. We have a few soft opening days this week and next, and then it's full steam ahead on Saturday," I say, shifting my weight, and wondering why she cares. You'd think that building would be the last place she'd want to be, but clearly not. "We'd love to have you join us!" I blurt out nervously, and Sheriff Cooper shoots me a surprised look.

"Of course, I would love to stop by! So good to see you!" she chirps, as she pats me and Cooper on the shoulder and waltzes out of the bull pen to the main doors.

"What the heck is *she* doing here?" I ask the second she's out of ear shot, whipping around to face Cooper.

"What the heck are *you* doing here?" he retorts, folding his arms over his vest-constricted belly and raising an eyebrow back at me. "Why are my deputies texting me that you're being a nuisance out here?"

"I asked you first," I shoot back, following his lead and folding my arms across my chest, too.

"Come to my office."

. . .

We make our way down the back hallway and I take a seat in the plastic chair across from his desk once we enter his office. The room looks like the interior designer was going for "stacks of file folders and empty foam coffee cups meets hoarder" chic and I take a deep breath so I don't feel overwhelmed with the clutter. Mrs. Tammy must never come up here because judging by how her home looks compared to this, she absolutely would not approve.

"Alright. What is your news?" Coop asks, settling in his rolling leather desk chair and turning to face me.

"No way, I said you first," I insist, pointing back to the bull pen as a reminder. I'm absolutely brimming to share, but the self-preservation part of me feels the need to hang on to my information in the event that I share and he chooses not to for some ridiculous reason. I'm decently sure we've moved past the notion that I'm not helpful, but I'm still nervous to test it out in the wild.

He sighs and leans back in his chair. "Linny was asking when their father's estate could go to probate. They are wanting to have a memorial service for him, but would like any investigations to be over so it doesn't 'cast a pall over the memory of Daddy', and they want to move forward with estate distribution immediately following."

"Any particular reason we suddenly need 'Daddy's' money so quickly?" I ask, imitating his use of finger quotations.

He hesitates, and this confirms he in fact does have dirt. Good dirt. Or "tea" as the kids say these days. "Spill the tea," I urge, and his hesitation turns to confusion. "It means gossip; the kids call gossip 'tea'. So sharing gossip is 'spilling the tea'," I clarify, feeling a hundred years old. And if I'm a hundred, he's at least a thousand.

"You cannot share this with anyone. I'm not going down

for loose lips because of you," he warns, and I give him my most solemn and reverent nod in response. "She said she's in the middle of an adoption from South Korea and needs the remainder of her balance by next month or they're bumping her referral for another year."

I let out the breath I didn't realize I was holding. "How much?"

"Sixty five thousand."

We both sit silently for a long moment, processing this amount of money in light of the current situation.

"Coop... do you think she would have..." I ask, hoping he fills in the blanks so I don't have to accuse out loud.

"Do I think she would have killed her father to get her inheritance so she could afford to adopt this baby from Korea?" he replies bluntly. I give him a pointed look, but nod affirmatively. He shrugs and waves a dismissive hand.

"Women have done crazier for babies, that's for damn sure."

"Geez. I'm surprised she would have admitted her somewhat desperate need for such a large amount of cash outright to you. That puts an enormous spotlight of suspicion on her, doesn't it?"

"Maybe, maybe not. She might think that admitting it makes her less suspicious than keeping it a secret. Or she might not be involved in that way at all, so she's not even worried about looking suspicious."

I sit in silence for a few minutes processing. This is a significant, legitimate motive. I mean, if you're Linny, and you're staring down the barrel of an enormous financial burden for likely the one thing you're desperate for–something that only very large amounts of money can buy– you might look to your very sweet, but rapidly deteriorating father and think that speeding up the inevitable might make everything easier for everyone.

Well, that's what people who have very precarious relationships with their parents that only know Jesus on a holiday basis might think, right?

"I was mostly shocked because who wants to adopt a baby in their fifties?" Cooper jokes, snapping out of my mental deliberations.

"What?"

"Isn't she in her fifties?"

"No," I say, shaking my head and trying not to laugh. "She's in her mid forties, and would probably be *very* insulted to hear you think otherwise."

"No way. She looks way older than mid forties."

"I think it's the botox. I have a theory that women who overdo the injections look older, not younger. It's the ultimate irony that their overzealousness to not look old, in fact, makes them look older."

He nods, conceding the point. "Still kinda late to want a baby, though, right?"

I shrug. "Not necessarily. Women still have babies in their forties naturally. And if that's all you've ever wanted and still haven't gotten it, you likely don't care how old you are when it can finally happen."

"What makes you say that's all she's ever wanted?"

"Because I think it's innate in the majority of women to want kids. And what makes something more coveted? Not getting it. No one is spending tens of thousands of dollars they don't even have on something if it's not the sole focus of their existence."

"Well dadgum, we ought to just bring you on as the department psychologist or something."

"Hardly. Just observations of general human behavior."

"Alright, enough feelings mumbo jumbo. What did you rush here to tell me?"

I grin ear to ear and move to the edge of my seat for more

dramatic flair in my reveal. "Matt Wallace has brown eyes," I say, waving my hands out in a small fan for added effect. The smile drops clean off his face and he instantly looks perturbed.

"And I give a crap about Matt Wallace's eyes, why? Who the hell is Matt Wallace?"

"Connie Wallace's son!"

"Who?" he asks again, growing increasingly irritated. He's really ruining my big reveal here.

"Oh my Lord, Coop, keep up! Connie Wallace was one of the F&S secretaries when they closed, remember? Connie Wallace, Debbie Frazier, and Ginny Parrish. One of them had an affair with Langley and had his third child, we just didn't know which one because they all had boys within two months of each other. Well, Ginny seemed a little too nice and innocent for me to really believe it was her. Plus, Marge said she would never, and generally speaking Marge is always right. Then I ran into Debbie, and she said that Kyle was born then, but they adopted him from a teen mom through Baptist Family Services, so they were out. Connie was the last one I needed to talk to, and she was the winner–Matt has brown eyes."

He sighs again, and pinches the bridge of his nose like this conversation is physically hurting him. "So.. what..."

"Connie and her husband both have blue eyes," I say, waving a hand Vanna White style like he can fill in the blank himself. He gestures back with something that looks like "yeah, so?" and I relent. It really ruins the drama of the moment to have to spell everything out. "It's genetically impossible for two blue eyed people to make a brown eyed person. Which means that Connie's husband is not Matt's father. It *is* genetically possible for a brown eyed Langley and a blue eyed Connie to make a brown eyed Matt, though. Basic seventh grade Mendelian genetics."

I cross my arms and lean back in satisfaction. A few

seconds later, it's like it all clicks together for Coop and he leans back in his chair with a similar satisfied smile.

"Okay, so we have someone on the hook for Party C. You think she would have killed for that? Or him?"

"I don't know. I think Connie knows that I know, but I don't know if Matt knows or has anything to do with this. Connie was very guarded with me from the second she saw me in her home. I think it could go either way–she could be amped up to keep that from coming to light, or if there was an additional extenuating circumstance, she could be amped up to make sure Matt is included with the other two. Hard to say, and hard to prove without the Renfro version of the will."

He rubs his beard a few times while he thinks silently. "Alright, so that's our next move." He pushes himself out of his chair like he's got somewhere to be, and now it's my turn to be behind.

"What's our next move?"

"We find that version of the will."

He heads out the door and I jump up to follow him. "Hey, Coop? Can I ask one more question? Did Linny Caldwell say anything about a husband?"

He stops short in the hall and thinks for a second. "Yeah, I think she might have mentioned one. Women like that tend to be married to what I call neutered poodle men, so they don't usually talk about them like they exist. Why?"

"Was she wearing a ring?"

In the longest running saga of our lives these days, I pull back up to the house later to find feed sacks moving out of the garage again and back in the direction of the feed barn. I nod hello to Cooter and Roy as I walk across the driveway to Shep in the garage, stacking bags on an opened pallet of feed that could be picked up with the tractor.

"Did you get it?" I ask optimistically, thinking that they likely wouldn't be doing all this work if they thought there was a chance they'd get hit again.

He nods, and I am relieved that maybe this ordeal is over, giving us one less ordeal around here. "How were your open hours today? Any customers?"

"Yeah, we had several. Everyone had positive things to say. Especially positive in light of being the site of a murder."

Shep stops stacking and looks at me, a mixture of laughter and pity in his eyes. "People haven't forgotten?"

"Oh, no. I think it might be the main reason we have customers right now. Murder is a big draw, apparently."

He laughs and gives me a hug before returning to his stacking. "So where did you have to go with Marge and JoBeth this afternoon?" he asks, and I momentarily remember that I asked for an emergency school pick up without much context earlier.

"Turns out that Marge and JoBeth are in a book club with Connie Wallace. I went with them to her house to see if I could talk with her. Okay, let me run this past you to see if you can catch the clue–Connie and her husband have blue eyes. Her son Matt has brown eyes and her daughters Melissa and Megan have blue eyes."

"So, Matt is Langley's?" Shep replies, heaving a sack to the top of the stack.

"Bingo! Good grief, it took Cooper so long to get it, and I had to spell it completely out for him. It was so anticlimactic."

"It's just basic Mendelian genetics," he shrugs and I walk straight over to him and smother him in a hug.

"Thank you for being so supportive of my wild whims."

"You're welcome. Just remember this the next time I ask for help cleaning out horse stalls."

"Noted. So, are the boys glad they can move all this back, or annoyed? Like do I need a celebration dinner or a condolence dinner?"

"Eh, I think they're fine. They'll eat whatever food you put in front of them."

"Also noted." I release him from my squeeze chute hug and head to the side door into the house to start rustling up something for the aforementioned dinner.

"Hey, do you remember that old song '*Snake Farm*'?"

I stop before I get to the door and turn around so I can be fully invested in this line of questioning. "I think I do. I remember it being a little strange."

"Who sings it? The boys were asking and I said William Clark Green, but was his version just a cover?"

"Yeah, the original is Ray Wylie Hubbard. I wonder why they were asking?"

"I don't know, they were just talking through some different Texas country songs for some reason and decided they love that one. They were really honing in on ones they thought were William Clark Green, Wade Bowen, or Randy Rogers."

As soon as Shep says "Texas country", my brain snaps back to our moment on the driveway when Coach Kaci told them her favorite music is Texas country, and mentioned those three artists in particular. "Oh, no. I think they're trying to find a song for karaoke night that will impress Kaci Whitfield. Surely they wouldn't sing '*Snake Farm*' in front of everyone we know to try to woo Mia's coach, right?"

"Well, that just sounds nasty."

chapter
fourteen

"MOLLY, everything looks great! I really love the little touches on the info flyer. Well done," Kaci says as she flips through all the paperwork I've set out on the counter at the Shoppe. She's requested a progress meeting about the fundraiser since we're about a week out, so I asked her to meet me at the Shoppe an hour before our soft open hours to go over everything and so she can see the event space in person before it's time to set up in a few days.

Cooper has been sitting on the revelation of who Langley's third child is in hopes that we can track down the third will before the information gets out and makes it even harder to find. I've been hanging out at the Shoppe as much as possible, like a mother hen protecting her nest, and Coop has had constant night patrol watching just in case someone tries to break in again, but we've had a few days of near quiet. So much so that it almost makes me forget we have so much going on.

"I'm glad it all looks good to you. Do you want to walk through the back and sketch out how you'd like the tables? Our guys will get them set up, but you can decide how you think they will look the best," I say, gesturing to the back door.

Kaci's face lights up, and she follows me outside to the back yard area.

We sketch out a table map on a yellow legal pad, and plan where the stage will look the best. I've mentioned Cooter and Roy a handful of times in reference to who will set everything up and who can do any heavy lifting we need, and each time, Kaci giggles like a kindergartener. I can't really let myself think that Mia's grand plan of setting her up with one of them could actually work, but judging by her bar for intrigue, it might not be as far-fetched as I'm thinking.

"Well, do you have any questions, or any concerns?" I ask as we walk back inside.

"No, Molly, I think this is going to be great! Thank you so much for volunteering to handle all this!" she replies brightly, smothering me in a hug before grabbing her bag off the counter and heading to the door. As she exits, I am surprised to see none other than Connie Wallace tentatively coming up the front steps. The front door bell jingles as she pokes her head in the door and looks around cautiously.

"Um, hi, Molly. Are you open this morning?" she asks when she catches sight of me at the front counter. I set my coffee down and walk around the counter, gesturing for her to come in.

"Not yet, but please come in. What can I do for you?"

She stops about midway through the room and gets visibly emotional. I grab a handkerchief embroidered with a colorful llama wearing sunglasses off one of the sales tables and pass it to her, thinking I can spare one handkerchief to help her through whatever this is. She gratefully accepts it and dabs her eyes before looking down at the embroidery and frowning a little.

"Is that a llama?"

"Yeah, isn't it cute?" I reply, gesturing for her to open it up fully. "It says "No prob-llama" right there." I giggle, and she just nods. I can tell she must have a different sense of humor (if she has one at all), so I decide to just move on. She stays planted where she is standing, but continues to look around and take it all in, tears brimming in her eyes.

"I apologize for my emotions, but I haven't been in here, gosh... Thirty years? Maybe a little longer?"

"It's okay, that would probably make me emotional, too. What do you think?" I ask with a tentative smile, gesturing around to the store set up. I know we're not supposed to be prideful, but it's hard not to really love how everything turned out.

She hesitates, giving me a look that I wouldn't necessarily describe as distaste, but I wouldn't call it pleasant either. "It's... different."

I purse my lips, unsure what to say. She sees my look and quickly backtracks. "Not in a bad way; I don't mean it like that. Have you ever seen an ex boyfriend out somewhere years later? It's like that- someone you loved, and they're familiar, but just... not the same anymore. Just a Hubbell and Katie kind of thing, you know?"

I contemplate her words a little, thinking I don't really relate. My handful of ex-boyfriends very rarely cross my mind, and when they do, it's always some version of "thank you, Lord, for sparing me from that and giving me the undeserved blessing of Shep Jones instead". But I suppose that's not every-one's experience.

"Sure, time marching on is always a hard pill to swallow. So... did you come in to shop this morning? We've got lots of fun things, and I'm happy to help you pick out something if you need anything in particular," I say, trying to get the train back on track.

She hesitates again, shuffling from one foot to the other, so I point to a large maroon velvet love seat near the windows. We silently take a seat on either end of the loveseat and I wait to see if she's going to just come out with it, or if I need to jump into another round of twenty questions amateur detective style.

After several long seconds of silence, she heaves a sigh and starts spilling. "So... I think you know a secret of mine that has haunted me for a long time."

I pause, not knowing if she wants confirmation, or if me saying anything will overplay my hand. I'm not one hundred percent sure what exactly my hand is, but I'd hate to ruin it at this point. Before I can decide what to do, she forges ahead.

"I feel like I need to preface that I was not in a good place in the early nineties. I didn't have a good home life growing up. My dad went off and did whatever he wanted, and my mom retaliated whenever she could. My sisters and I were afterthoughts at the most and forgotten for the majority of the time. Unless we were misbehaving, or not living up to the fake persona our parents put out, and then we could only wish we were as invisible as we felt most of the time. I worked really hard in school to get out of that hellhole and got a full scholarship to college. My plan was to get an accounting degree and a job in a big city and never go home." She pauses to wipe tears streaming down her face and I jump up and grab another llama hanky. She dabs her cheeks and sucks in another breath to continue.

"I met Evan at college. His childhood was everything mine wasn't-stable, loving, genuine, fun. And for some reason I could never understand, he liked me. I lived on eggshells for years and years of my life just convinced that one day he would wake up and realize what a mess I was and that he should have picked a girl that wasn't so beneath him."

"You're not beneath him, Connie. You don't deserve less or worse in life because your parents weren't what they should have been. Don't sell yourself short," I encourage, thinking I am in no way, shape, or form qualified to be a therapist of any sort, but this is breaking my heart.

She looks up at me with tears still running over and I reach over and pat her shoulder. "Well, I always felt like I was. Or am. Evan never gave me one reason to doubt our relationship but I lived every day like he would walk out and leave me if I had one toe out of line and I don't know why."

I mean, it's obvious why–hello, daddy and mommy issues–but I refrain from pointing out that clear fact.

"Anyway, we graduated college and got married. I had an accounting degree and he had a history degree with plans to teach and coach. We moved here because Evan got his first job as a middle school teacher and assistant basketball coach for the high school boys. I looked everywhere for a bookkeeping job, and finally found one at F&S. Asa and Langley seemed like great guys, and working with Debbie and Ginny was like having true sisters, not the broken sister relationships I left behind."

"Then Evan's first basketball season hit. Even just being the assistant, I think I saw him for five minutes a day or less. F&S felt like even tighter of a family knowing that I essentially had no family at home. I was lonely, and going to work everyday and getting that human interaction was the highlight of my life. We made it through the first season alright, but we went another season or two and Evan was promoted to the high school, and head coach and we might as well have been strangers living in the same house. During the fall, he was focused on the lead up to the season, and then during the season he could think of nothing else but basketball, and then after playoffs in the spring and summer, it was all about what they could be doing in the off season to get back to the state tournament the next year." She suddenly looks me straight in the face with a dead calmness in her voice. "That is not an excuse, Molly. There is never an excuse to cheat on your spouse. I should have been mature enough to talk to Evan, to tell him how I was drowning. He would have been more than willing to work on anything with me. But I lived in this distorted world in my own head where I felt like I wasn't good enough for him and didn't want him to leave, but also that he completely underappreciated me and cared more about basketball than he did about me. And I can see, thirty five years later, that none of that was true—none of it. But it didn't stop me from developing feelings for Langley, seeing him trying his best to raise his kids without much help from his wife, who I told myself was an unappreciative cow and a complete nag. Maybe she was, but I doubt it. In my head, along with all my other manufactured delusions, I needed her to be the worst so I wouldn't spiral because I was the actual worst."

It is a weird space to be in to feel completely heartbroken for her, but also absolutely not condone anything she did at all. I am unsure if she's going to keep sharing, or if I even need to know anymore, but I pat her knee and give her a reassuring smile. "It's okay."

"So, just like that, about four years into working for them, Langley and I started a relationship. It wasn't romantic at first-just friends that enjoyed one another's company. It went on for a little while before anything got physical. And then it did. And then we weren't careful enough. By the time I found out I was expecting Matt, we both knew whatever that was had run its course. We never discussed anything to the alternative of going our separate ways and pretending like all of it never happened. I moved on to another job, and when Matt was little, Evan transitioned to running the YMCA instead of coaching. He still got to be around sports and mentor kids, but the hours were so much better. Our relationship honestly healed over without him ever realizing anything happened. And Matthew Evan Wallace is a good, solid man, and he is who he is because Evan Wallace raised him."

"Did Nora ever know?" I ask quietly, wondering if all of this is as cut, dried, and buried as she believes it is.

"I honestly don't know. I never really spoke to Langley after the company was dissolved. He sent us flowers to the hospital when Matt was born, and it seemed innocent enough–a peace offering from an old boss, but that was about the extent of contact." She pauses, and it feels like she is summoning the strength to say her next sentence out loud, like it's one of her deepest, most repressed thoughts. "All I want is to go my entire life without anyone I love knowing my worst mistake."

She chokes out a strangled sob, and I feel tears welling in my eyes. "Connie, we all make mistakes," I offer gently, patting her on the knee and wondering what I could even offer to try to make her feel better. I can imagine that all she wants is to keep this covered up, and what the implications of it coming out look like for her.

"We do, but some are bigger than others. It's not fair of me to expect this to all work out in my favor, but I've kept it in for so long, it just feels like that would be the best thing for every-one. At least I hope it is."

"Did you know Langley put Matt as an equal heir with the twins?"

She sighs, like this is news she isn't surprised to hear, and isn't really happy about it, either. "I've always wondered, but never knew for sure. I didn't exactly have a reason to ask to see his will, but I always knew Langley to be a stand up man."

I refrain from pointing out that this "stand up man" had an affair with her resulting in her oldest child, and try to stick to the relevant facts at hand. "I know that you'd love for all of this to stay buried, but Matt is likely due a substantial inheri-tance," I trail off, hoping I don't have to explicitly address the elephant in the room– which is more important, for your child to have significant financial stability or keep her secrets buried. I'm fully aware it's more nuanced than that, and it's easy for me to say knowing my life doesn't change in the slightest in this situation.

She sits silently for several long minutes and then cracks a small smile. "It sounds like I'm going to be outed anyway. When is the will going to probate?"

"Well.. that's the thing. We have found drafts and a partial copy naming a Party C along with Parties A and B that inherit equally, but we haven't found the full executed copy with the appendices naming all the heirs," I admit, and I can see a reprieve of relief wash over her.

"So, you're not completely sure that Matt is actually an heir," she asks, like this potentially gives her an out to keep her secret. Excitement is necessarily the right word to describe her change in emotion, but she's definitely not sad that we haven't found the evidence to incriminate her just yet.

"We haven't found the full document, but we know Party C exists. There's no other obvious answer for who it could be besides Langley's third child. Asa wasn't sure who Langley had a relationship with, just that it was one of the office ladies," I say, trying to phrase that as delicately as possible. "We were hoping to find the will to tell us who the third child is, but I kinda stumbled on it myself. Now we just need to find the actual will for it to be probated."

"Doesn't his attorney have it?"

"He has partial copies, but the closest we could find is an empty envelope in the attic here. The attorney had a series of strokes a few months ago, and his office was packed up in a hurry. He has the exhibits, but not the appendices naming who each party is."

"I'm shocked Linny and Wells don't have copies. I'd

venture to say they've been waiting for this payday all their lives."

"Well, that's the thing–they each have a copy, but they are different, and both are different from the version we're looking for."

"How so?"

"Linny's version names her as sole heir, and Wells's version names the two of them as equal heirs. Any idea why they'd be different?"

She thinks for a minute, before it looks like a lightbulb switches on. "One of the last conversations I had with Langley, he was feeling really guilty about what we were doing–we both were, obviously, but he was especially so. He said he never wanted to be the type of man that was a hypocrite, and if *they* were doing something like this, he'd disown them," she trails off, looking to me to connect the dots.

"You think Wells might be having an affair?"

"I haven't seen Wells Fletcher since he was a gangly eleven year old trying to steal money out of my purse when I went to the restroom up here. I have no idea how he turned out, but if it was anything like his childhood, I wouldn't put it past him," she bites, and then visibly softens, realizing it's probably not great for her to cast the first stone in that situation.

"Wait–he told me you used to give him pennies when they would come to visit. He said Debbie had a dish of hard candies for them, and you gave them pennies from your purse. You all were 'like second mothers' to them."

She snorts in response, giving me a snarky look. "Hardly. It's not right to hate a child, but I can tell you that none of us liked them in the slightest. Debbie's 'hard candies' were Rolaids and peppermints because they gave her terrible acid reflux when they would visit. I gave them pennies alright - Wells would help himself to my wallet when I wasn't at my desk. Only when I was missing a few hundred in cash did I finally notice. I said something to Langley at that point and he adamantly denied Wells would do such a thing, but I noticed the money returned in my wallet later that day."

I lean back into the loveseat and let this revelation sink in. How new is this development? Would Linny's new version with Wells's cut out supersede the version we're looking for?

After a few long moments of my quiet contemplation, Connie breaks the silence. "So... how long until I need to turn myself in?"

Her question catches me off guard. "Turn yourself in? For what?"

"Come clean to Matt and Evan," she replies, like it is obvious. "What did you think I was talking about?"

"Well, we're trying to find the third will, but the bigger picture is trying to find Langley's killer," I retort, throwing a vague gesture to the attic. As soon as it comes out, I slap a hand over my mouth, realizing I probably shouldn't have divulged so much.

"Wait–killer?? You think Langley was murdered?" she asks with sudden concern. I remember that the details of the investigation have been kept pretty quiet, so the general public likely believes it all to be an accident.

"Um, well... we don't know for sure, but we think it was likely not an accident."

Her eyes are wider than ever with surprise, and she wears a look of both fear and confidence. "I always knew those kids would get him."

"THIS IS hands down the coolest thing we've ever done," Mandy announces from my passenger seat, shaking a handful of Nerds gummy clusters out of a family size bag into her hand and popping one in her mouth. For reasons I cannot fully explain, following my conversation with Connie, I grabbed Mandy and Lucy and set off to find the address listed on Google for Wells Fletcher. Mandy is dialed in on this Barney Fife level stake out, and while I fully believe nothing will come from this, I just couldn't shake the innate push to at least try.

"I'm glad you're having fun," I reply, grabbing my own handful of gummy clusters. No stakeout is complete without good snacks, so after a quick pit stop for assorted candy, junk food, and caffeinated beverages, we found a discreet tree to park under in one of the swankier neighborhoods of Oak Hills to watch the comings and goings of Wells Fletcher's white two-story colonial home. We've been sitting for a long fifteen minutes, and so far we've just clocked an uncharacteristically large number of squirrels in their yard.

"So, what exactly are we looking for?" Lucy asks, pulling a pair of binoculars out of a case and pointing them in the direction of his house from the middle seat of my middle row.

There is a Land Rover and a Mercedes SUV parked on the driveway that curls to the side of the house, but we haven't seen any actual people yet. The house gives off an old money upper class vibe, with immaculate flower beds, well manicured grass, and neatly stacked trash cans next to the garage.

"I honestly have no idea. If Wells is having an affair, maybe we see something here? I don't know, I can't think people would be that reckless, but who knows?" I shrug and take a sip of my vanilla Coke from the cupholder.

"I think you'd be shocked how truly dumb people are," Mandy pops back, gesturing for Lucy to hand her the binoculars. She peers through them in the direction of the driveway for a few seconds before setting them down on the console. I can tell everyone is itching for something to happen, when it is more than likely nothing will.

"We can only hope," I agree, leaning back in my seat and trying not to doze off. The worst part about this so far has been fighting to pay attention when absolutely nothing is going on. It feels counterproductive to scroll my phone in the event that something happens so quickly I miss it. But, right now, staring at his house watching the squirrels is so boring it's about to put me to sleep.

"Look, look, look! Something's happening!" Mandy hisses about twenty minutes later, shaking me from my half-sleep. Lucy snatches the binoculars from the console and starts narrating in detail as Mandy and I watch.

"Female, late forties, workout gear, large Louis Neverfull, getting in the Mercedes." We all watch as this woman stops short on the driveway and yells something back to the house and waits for a response. After getting what looks like an unsatisfactory answer judging by the sour look on her face, she pushes large sunglasses over her eyes and gets in the Mercedes to drive away. We all slink down a little in our seats as she drives by, and then sit up with new interest once she leaves.

"So, we think that was the wife?" Lucy asks, as Mandy is quickly swiping and scrolling on her phone.

"Yes, that was Sydney Carson Fletcher," Mandy replies, flashing a Facebook profile to both of us.

"Seriously?" I ask, both disturbed and impressed at her level of commitment and expertise.

"What? We actually have thirteen mutual friends so it was way easy to find her."

"How do you have thirteen mutual friends?" Lucy asks, sounding mildly horrified.

"It looks like they were all from the time I did barre class like five days a week at this little studio when Brett and I were first married. I guess maybe she was into barre too?"

"She definitely looks like she works out. It also looks like she lives here, so if he does, too, then I wouldn't say they are separated or anything."

A few minutes later, Wells emerges from the garage with his phone wedged between his ear and shoulder in his usual uniform of golf shorts, polo, and loafers with no socks. He grabs one of their rolling trash cans and starts wheeling it down the driveway, making me think her last minute shouting was nagging him to put the cans on the curb.

"Do they have any kids?" I ask Mandy, keeping my eyes trained on him moving up and down the driveway. In between cans, he takes a break and leans against the Land Rover to give his phone chat his undivided attention. Something about his smarmy smile and casual posture tell me that isn't a business call, but who knows for certain this far away.

"If they do, they're completely ashamed of them because there are absolutely no pictures of them with children anywhere. Not even like nieces or nephews."

"WINKs," Lucy explains, and Mandy and I stare at her for more clarification. "Well-Off Income, No Kids. Like a DINK, but not Dual Income because I doubt she works."

"Actually, her profile says she's a realtor," Mandy says, flashing another Facebook profile at us, this one titled 'Sydney Fletcher, Realtor-Oak Hills Realty'. The profile picture is a high glam portrait of Sydney in all designer clothes, standing next to a marble countertop in probably one of the fanciest kitchens I've ever seen. Buffalo Creek isn't below the poverty line by any means, but it looks like Oak Hills is in a bit of a different tax bracket. "This says that Wells Fletcher is the broker and developer of Oak Hills Realty."

"They don't have nieces and nephews on his side because Linny has no kids either. But she's trying to adopt right now from South Korea," I add, keeping my eyes on Wells still farting around on the driveway.

"That sounds expensive," Mandy says, continuing to deep dive on her phone.

"It is. She was in the sheriff's department asking when the will could go to probate because she needs some of her inheritance to pay the deposit. Otherwise she's getting bumped another year."

"So, Linny needs money ASAP, helps her dad to his inevitable demise?" Lucy confirms and I nod. "And Wells gets cut out because of extracurricular activities so he helps his dad to his inevitable demise so he can have control over which version of the will comes out?"

"That's pretty much where Cooper and I have landed. Child #3 couldn't have done it because he doesn't know he's Child 3."

There is a long, pregnant pause before Mandy finally breaks the silence. "So, can we know who Child #3 is?"

I hesitate, debating if it's fair to say anything since Connie is so concerned about keeping her secret if she can. "I don't know. Child #3's mom is desperate to keep it a secret if possible."

"It's Matt Wallace, isn't it?" Mandy shoots back, the words tumbling out faster than she can help them.

"How did you know?" I ask, wondering if I'd slipped somewhere along the way.

Mandy shrugs. "I was honestly just guessing. I figured I'd guess each one and just check your reaction. I can't believe I got it on the first try!" She giggles a little, and I try to smile, but find it less amusing than she does. Something about knowing that Connie's life is poised to imminently explode makes it seem less fun than just a detached game of playing detective.

"Alright, Nancy, Bess, we've got someone incoming," Lucy says, still peering through the binoculars at Wells on the driveway. He hangs up his call as a sleek black Porsche slows at the curb just before the Fletcher's driveway and idles for a few moments before the driver cuts the engine. Lucy and I stare as the driver's door opens and long, tan legs tipped with stilettos drop out of the car. A woman with long dark hair wrapped in an intricate up-do and a slim figure dressed in business casual wear that probably costs more than a mortgage payment walks up the driveway to Wells as Mandy's fingers swipe furiously across her phone screen.

"Who is she?" Lucy mutters as we watch her sidle up to Wells next to his Land Rover and talk for a few moments before he gestures to the side door, and they walk inside together.

"That is Victoria Barnes," Mandy replies confidently a few seconds later. She flashes another Facebook profile to us and we both nod that the woman in the photo does seem to match the woman we just saw walk inside with Wells. "She is the home stager for Oak Hills Realty."

"So, she works with Wells and Sydney. Is it that unusual that they would be meeting?" Lucy asks. We are watching the front windows now to see if anything is visible, but I'd highly doubt they are dumb enough to do anything saucy in front of an open window.

"Probably not unusual to meet, but would you as a married woman meet your married boss at his house for a meeting of just the two of you?" Mandy lobs back, flicking through the pictures on Victoria's Instagram page. "She's married, too–her husband is Adam Barnes who owns the flooring company on the edge of town. He competes in CrossFit competitions on the weekends." She shows us a picture of a man crouched under a barbell filled with weights and Victoria cheering him on from the sideline in the tiniest shorts I've ever seen on an adult woman.

"I wouldn't, but from what I've seen the last few months, I'm not sure we're the norm around here," I reply, keeping a watch on the house. Just as I think it's a lost cause, Wells walks up to the front window and grabs one side of the drapes to close them. Victoria appears on the other side, her jacket gone and down to a tank top. They meet in the middle with the drapes and slip in one kiss just as the fabric closes.

"Did y'all see that?" I screech, hopping up in my seat and turning to face the other two, hoping I wasn't the only one who saw that confirmation. When I turn, I see Lucy has her phone trained on the windows with a big grin.

"Oh, I got it. That turd is going down."

We sit for another thirty minutes or so waiting to see if we can get any more evidence before we head off. Mandy gives us what feels like the entire *E! True Hollywood Story* on Wells and Sydney Fletcher and Adam and Victoria Barnes based on her social media stalking, complete with her own personal theories and commentary throughout, and Lucy and I rate the likelihood of each scenario. My personal favorite is that Wells is just one of those guys who thinks the world owes him whatever he wants, so he doesn't worry about how it affects others. From what we can see, these CrossFit competitions seem pretty time consuming, and Adam gets a lot of compliments–like more than necessary–on his appearance, at least online, so it would track for Victoria to consider going to external sources for validation about her appearance and worth.

Just as I'm about to recommend we bag it and take what we have to Sheriff Cooper, Wells and Victoria come out of the house and down the driveway. Her hair is loose from her up-do, and she's pulled her jacket back on, but hasn't buttoned it back up like her arrival. He carries a box of knick knacks behind her and places it in the trunk of her car. She drops her bag in the passenger seat and walks to the driver's side to get in. They stand beside each other chatting casually for a few moments before she reaches over and squeezes his hand. He holds it for a long minute or two, absently rubbing his thumb over her knuckles before opening the door for her. She gets in, and just before she drives off, he quickly pokes his head in the open window and gives her a kiss on the cheek. She drives off slowly, and he stands on the driveway looking a little moony before finally sauntering back into the house with a goofy grin on his face.

"Okay, am I crazy, or..." I start, and Mandy finishes my thought before I can.

"I don't think that's a hot affair–I think they're in love."

▭

"We need to see Sheriff Cooper!" I shout a little bit later as Mandy, Lucy, and I skid into the bull pen at the Sheriff's Department. Of course, my very best friend Hawkins is back manning the front desk and he gives me the sourest look when he sees it is us.

"He's busy." Hawkins maintains eye contact with his

computer and refuses to acknowledge us beyond his initial look. We stand still and impatient for a few long moments with only the sound of computer keys and us trying to catch our breath audible.

After a considerable pause, it seems we are at an impasse, waiting for additional details about when we might be able to see Cooper, and Hawkins looks like he does not plan to break whatsoever.

"When might he be available, kind sir?" Lucy asks, veering toward a bad British accent and I stifle a giggle while Hawkins rolls his eyes.

"Not anytime soon. You are welcome to leave him a message and we'll try to pass it on." Hawkins slaps a sticky note on the desk and sets a ballpoint pen on top with flourish. This kid is truly trying to get on my last ever-loving nerve, and I don't have a clue what I did to inspire it.

"Seriously? This is important information for an on-going investigation. Can we please just talk to him or have an idea when he will be available? I tried to call him and he didn't answer." I'm hoping if I just shoot him straight, he might relent. "Surely the prevailing of justice is more important than whatever personal vendetta you have against me."

"Personal vendetta? I'm not a Bond villain. Or six years old."

"Then, what the heck is your problem?" Mandy shrieks, looking like she's about to come over the desk at Hawkins. I throw out an arm to hold her back and take a breath before trying to get us back on track.

"Okay, fine. Can you please just tell him that Molly Jones came by and has something important to talk with him about?"

He nods and takes his sticky note back, making a few notes on it. "You know, it's just not protocol to allow any civilians free rein within a closed department. If he needs your help, he will contact you," he smirks to himself as he turns his attention back to his computer and I summon all the patience I have to take Mandy and Lucy by the hands and walk toward the door.

Just as we go to exit, I hear Cooper's gruff voice down the hallway. "Just make sure that the B&E report is on my desk by the end of the day, Rodriquez."

"Sheriff! We need to talk to you!" Mandy squeals as she breaks my hold and careens toward the hallway where Coop is walking up. We are one hundred percent getting kicked out of this place.

"Molly Jones, what is going on now?" Cooper's eyebrows shoot up nearly to his hairline as he approaches us at the front desk, and I die a little inside knowing we look so unprofessional. I mean, we aren't professionals, but I was trying to fake it til I make it, and that's really not tracking right now.

"We have some new evidence for you," Lucy beams, holding up her phone and dancing it around. Mandy is nodding in agreement like a small child emphatic they had nothing to do with whatever trouble is afoot and I try not to cringe.

He sighs, like he's trying to hold in both frustration and a laugh. "Well, let me just stop you right there–I'll listen to what you have to say but chances are, none of what you're going to show me is admissible in court."

He gestures for us to follow him to his office, and just as we get to the doorway, my phone starts ringing. It is a number I don't recognize, but I have a gut feeling I should answer it. I can hear Mandy and Lucy ping-ponging back and forth at ninety-miles an hour unloading on Cooper, so I step just down the hall where it is quieter.

"Hello?"

"Good afternoon, ma'am, is this the agent on record for Red Rock Cattle Company?" An official sounding male voice comes through the line, and my blood runs a little cold. I think I'm an agent on record, but I honestly have no idea.

"I think so? My husband and I own Red Rock; I'm Molly Jones, and my husband is Shep. Is something wrong?"

"You and your husband didn't do anything wrong, but I do need one or the both of you to meet with me. I'm Special Ranger Roddy McAlister with the Texas and Southwestern Cattle Raisers Association, and we've got a situation that needs your attention."

I'm a little stunned, as I knew that the TSCRA had agents that work for them, but I've never known anything to happen in real life. "Um, okay. Where should we meet you?"

"The Livingston Cattle Auction, ma'am."

"RIGHT THIS WAY, we've got them down in a holding pen over here." As soon as I hung up with Special Ranger McAlister, I called Shep and explained the situation. He picked me up at the Sheriff's office, and we took off for Rockford, about an hour away, where the Livingston Cattle Auction is located. It's one of the bigger auction barns in the area, and it typically offers a premium over smaller operations, especially for higher quality cattle that have had more invested in them. Some producers will make the trip from farther away just to get the higher premium or more advertising and exposure than local sale barns. Their bi-weekly sale is coming up tomorrow, so pen after pen is filled with different assortments of all breeds and ages of cattle, and the noise of bellowing cattle and shouting workers is enough to make my head spin.

Shep and I follow Special Ranger McAlister down a 24" metal catwalk over the dozens of 12' x 12' pens underneath us until we come to a back square holding six small black bull calves directly underneath us. "Do those look familiar to you, Mr. Jones?"

We look down into the pen and one of the calves turns up to face us. Some might say that Angus cattle all just look like the same black bovine over and over, but after nearly twenty years of raising them, those things are just about like my own four-legged kids. "That's a Rose bull calf!" I blurt before Shep can answer and he shoots me a look to calm myself. Years and years ago, we had a cow that we absolutely loved that was a stand-out star for us, so we flushed embryos and started a new line that we named "Rose". Call me crazy, but I can spot a Rose calf any day of the week. Not with my eyes closed, of course, but I know our calves, and that's one of them. They all begin milling around, occasionally looking up at us, and I know in my core that all of those calves belong to us.

"Yes, sir, that's ours."

"And how many did you think you might be missing?"

"We are missing seven on record, but there is also the possibility of a male adult mountain lion in the area, so we could have lost some to that."

"Hang on just one second, I think we had one more we were checking," McAlister replies, looking down the catwalk to another pen where a man is shining a flashlight into the ear of a calf. "Do you have tattoo or EID numbers on you by any chance?"

Shep nods and pulls out his phone to the spreadsheets he keeps of all identification numbers. "These are the ones we were missing, with their EID numbers and birthdates," he replies, handing over his phone. McAlister pulls out a list from the breast pocket of his plaid button-down and runs down it, comparing it to Shep's phone.

"Hey, Roger? You got a 5467 down there?" McAlister shouts in the direction of the last calf in question.

"Sure do, boss. Want me to send him down to that pen?"

"Yep, these are all theirs."

Roger sends the last calf down the lane and another worker opens the gate of the pen with the rest of our calves as we watch from the catwalk.

"I'm so sorry, but I'm a little lost. What is going on?" I ask, trying to get myself up to speed, but still feeling behind.

"It would appear that you had some rustlers on your hands, Mrs. Jones. This is a good looking bunch. I'd imagine they're pretty valuable calves?"

"They are embryo transfers from one of our best females and our top herd sire, all born about three months ago. They would have been the headlining sire group to sell in our 2027 sale. They went missing one or two at a time from a pasture on the edge of our property, so we assumed it was a predator. You're saying these were stolen? How did you know?"

"Your rustlers weren't patient enough to wait until these guys were a little bigger and closer to weaning. Or weren't man enough to take the mamas, too. It's a red flag to see calves come in that young on their own. They had some story about why they were by themselves but it didn't track. We checked their EIDs and those showed them as registered to y'all."

Shep lets out a long breath, like he is in disbelief. "I can't believe they're all here. I thought they were all goners. Thank y'all for catching this." He puts out a hand in gratitude and McAlister shakes it firmly.

"What happens to the rustlers?" I pipe up from behind, curious about the more juicy parts.

"They had to give an address on record for the payment, so we'll go pay them a visit. Just glad we can get them home. We can have one of the auction guys bring them back, or y'all can come back with a trailer whenever is convenient. Up to y'all," he answers, giving us a smile. "I've got to get back down to the floor, but y'all take care."

"Thank you so much, sir," I say as he slides past us on the catwalk and heads back down to the sale ring. "I can't believe someone stole our cattle right from under us. That is some 1880 kind of stuff right there."

"Yeah, and those EIDs were some 2025 kind of stuff

coming in clutch. The boys will be disappointed they don't get to keep mountain lion hunting."

"So they didn't get it that day they went out in those suits?"

"Not even close. All they came back with was a rash from the suits."

I laugh, glad that despite the rash, everyone is safe, at least. "You want to call the boys to come pick them up?"

"Yeah, that seems like a good job for them. And then you and I can ride home in peace and you can give me all the updates from this case you're working on even though you aren't supposed to be."

"Hey, Cooper has been consulting me. I'm a needed piece of this puzzle," I justify as we make our way down the catwalk toward the stairs.

"Sure, Nancy Drew. Tell me more about it in the truck."

<hr>

"Oh, darlin', I don't think I would buy that if I were you. You look more like an autumn and that's a summer color, honey," Marge scolds, taking a ruffled blouse out of some unsuspecting customer's hand and putting it back on the rack. She takes the customer by the shoulder and turns her toward a different rack of clothing and begins making suggestions from it, apparently more in her 'season'. I resist the urge not to crawl under the counter in embarrassment, wondering why I thought having Marge in here on opening day was a good idea. I think I must have thought she's only opinionated for us, and not the general public, but clearly I am wrong.

A few days later, we've arrived at our big day–the official opening day of the Red Rock Shoppe. My parents got back into town just in time, and my mom is helping man the counter with Laramie and Mia, leaving me to mill around the store and help customers as needed. And overhear all the ways Marge is asserting her opinion over selections.

"Hi, can I set anything at the counter for you? Or help you find anything?" I say, walking up to a pair of college-aged girls who have been milling for the better part of fifteen minutes so far and look like they aren't quite finding what they came for.

They catch each other's eye, and after exchanging looks with one another and a few suspicious glances up the stairs, one gives me a large smile. "No, thank you. I think we're finding everything we need."

"Okay, well, feel free to set anything up at the counter if you don't want to carry it around," I say, backing away so I don't scare them off. They are clearly up to something, but I'm going to let it ride as long as I don't have a clear reason to worry about them. Instead, I turn to the large table nearby at the base of the staircase set up with punch dispensers and platters of custom iced cookies from my dear friend Wendy. I consolidate some of the emptier platters and make sure the stacks of small paper plates and cups look neat and tidy. A few random customers stop by me to say hi, and I give out hugs and hellos to anyone and everyone. I reluctantly decide to let Marge continue to be my front of house greeter and move behind the counter as my college aged friends get within the back counter vicinity like they are ready to check out.

I see Mandy has slipped in the back and is busy making centerpieces for the fundraiser tonight at her floral counter. She has large white vases she is filling with low and wide stems to keep from obstructing any views during the show, currently sticking some fragrant lavender stems in at a perpendicular angle to her floral foam.

"Hi! Did you find everything you were looking for?" I ask as they finally set their baskets full of random selections on the counter and I start ringing everything up.

• • •

It turned out they were more so just thrill seekers looking to see where dead bodies rain from the ceiling around here, and were quite disappointed when I wouldn't oblige with a behind-the-scenes tour upstairs. Just when I thought I'd at least piqued their interest with my wares, it turned out everything they bought was for a grandmother, which was a real kick to the ego.

"That was hard to watch," Mandy quips from across the aisle when they finally exit.

"Were we that ridiculous in college?" I answer, tidying up the counter. Mom heads out to wrangle Marge to go get her hair done before the fundraiser tonight, so it's just me, Mandy, and Laramie manning the store for now, and as we get later into the afternoon, we start filling up with customers.

"Hey, Molly? Did you say you locked the upstairs door? I noticed a woman just slipped up the stairs," Laramie asks a few hours later as she brings up a few clothing items that need to be refolded behind the counter. I pause, and peer around the stairs, not really able to see anything.

"I'll go take a look. Thanks, Laramie." I pat her on the shoulder as I slip behind her and head around the corner to the stairs. Sure enough, there is a woman at the top of the stairs fiddling with the doorknob, and I can't tell if she's trying to just test it to see if it's unlocked, or if she's truly picking the lock. She has a Boston Red Sox ball cap on with her dark hair pulled into a knot at the nape of her neck, along with plain black workout leggings and a plain grey sweatshirt, but she still looks vaguely familiar. There is enough hubbub going on down the stairs that she doesn't really hear me coming, so she startles when I speak to her.

"Hi, can I help you with something?"

She clutches a hand to her heart and I hear a clink as something slim and metal falls from her hand to the floor. "Wow, you scared me! I was, um… just looking for a bathroom? I figured it might be up here?"

"Actually, it's on the first floor, near the back counter. I'd be glad to show you." I give her a bright smile, and gesture downstairs.

"Uh, yes, thanks. That would be helpful." She smiles tightly in response and follows me down the stairs and around the corner to the bathroom. As we pass by, Mandy pops her head up and gives me a wide-eyed look of panic. Once the woman is in the bathroom, she silently waves me over with wild arms.

"Do you know who that is?" she hisses, leaning over her floral counter to make sure the bathroom door is closed.

"She looks familiar, but I can't place her. Who is she?"

"That's Victoria Barnes!"

"No! For real?" I glance back at the door to make sure it's still closed, too.

"Definitely! What was she doing upstairs?"

"It looked like she was trying to pick the lock on the second floor door. Do you think Wells sent her?"

Mandy takes a few seconds of silent contemplation before nodding. "I do. There must be something still up there that he wants that he wasn't able to get when he came here before, and he thought sending her might be less suspicious."

"So, what do we do? I feel like we could use her to lead us to what he's looking for, but I don't know how."

Mandy looks around and suddenly brightens up. "Make sure she sees the fundraiser flyer! Maybe they'll come tonight and we can catch them trying again!"

"That is actually not a bad idea," I say, holding up a hand for a quiet high five just as the bathroom door opens and Victoria exits. Now that Mandy mentions it, I do recognize her, even though she isn't wearing any make-up and her hair looks different covered by the ball cap. She seems hesitant to walk by us at Mandy's floral counter, so I try to seem friendly and not like I suspect her of whatever it was she was trying to do.

"Is there anything I can help you find?" I say brightly, hoping the direct contact won't scare her off, and we have the opportunity to get her back here.

"I, um… I need a birthday gift for my mother?" An unlikely story, but I go with it just to have the chance to talk with her some more.

"Of course, we have a great selection of gifts! Does she collect anything? We have tons of unique salt and pepper shakers, if there is something in particular she might like," I answer, leading her through the display tables and pointing out random options. After selecting a set of succulent salt and pepper shakers, and another "punny" handkerchief, Victoria meets me back at the check out counter. All I can see across the way is Mandy's eyes peeking out from behind her centerpieces and I am silently willing her to just be cool as I close this out.

"Alright, that will be $42.38," I say, and she fumbles to hand me a credit card. I process her payment and slide the receipt into her bag after wrapping the breakables. "Oh, and just so you know, we're having a little fundraiser karaoke night for the local middle school cheerleaders tonight in conjunction with our grand opening. If you aren't busy, we'd love to have you." I flash my best smile, hoping I look warm and inviting enough for her to consider coming back and not like the Joker.

"It's going to be so much fun!" I hear from behind a wall of greenery adjacent to me and I struggle not to laugh at the disembodied voice among the flowers.

"Participation not required; spectators welcome." I put a small flyer with the details in her bag and slide it over to her. "Thanks so much for shopping with us today."

"It was a pleasure, really," she replies, taking her bag off the counter and giving me a genuine smile. "And karaoke night sounds fun. My husband and I were just looking for something to do tonight."

"So, you think she shows up with Wells or her real husband tonight?" Mandy asks as soon as she exits. She has finished the centerpiece in front of her and slides it down to the edge of the counter for one of the boys to come grab it and run it upstairs until it's time to decorate. Cooter, and Roy have been lurking in the shadows most of the day to help with random things here and there. Shep, Hayes, and Mia have been here most of the day as well, but I think they've gone home to start showering and getting ready for the event.

"That's a great question, and I guess we'll see when she shows up. If she shows up."

"My money is on Wells."

I hesitate, and shake my head. "I don't know. Wells and I have talked before. He may think I know who his real wife is and wouldn't want to risk it."

"Could be. I just have two more of these and then I'm going to head home to get ready. How much longer are you going to stay open?"

I check my watch and look around at the lull in the crowd. "My advertising said I'd be closed from three to six to get ready for the event, and we're already a half hour past that. I'll probably wait another few minutes just in case we have any more last minute stragglers and then shut it down for the break."

"Alright, sounds good. I'll be here if you need me!" She smiles and slides headphones over her ears to get back to work.

. . .

Over the next ten minutes, I mill around the sales floor tidying everything that's even slightly askew from shoppers. Laramie starts carting floral arrangements from the upstairs rooms out to the backyard to start table preparation, and Mandy is humming along to what sounds like a Prince song as she finishes up the last of the centerpieces. Just as I cross to the front door to flip the open/closed sign and lock the door, none other than Linny Caldwell slips inside.

"Linny! What are you doing here?" I blurt before I stop myself, and her face looks a little affronted at my blunt question.

"I told you I'd stop by on opening day, Molly!" she chastises, like we talk everyday and I'm faithless to think she would let me down. I rack my brain to even remember when I would have told her details about the opening and decide it must have been the last time I saw her at Cooper's office. She takes a small turn around the display tables at the front entry before stopping cold in front of my baby table. It is stacked high with unbelievably soft bamboo sleepers, onesies in gingham prints with ruffles, striped sets with button details, along with unique teether toys, drinkware, and an assortment of kitschy children's books. The color drains from her face for a split second before she pulls it together and shoots me a genuine imitation smile. "Everything is just darling! You are going to do so well!"

I hesitate on a reply– she's clearly going through something, and I am just not sure what to do with her, quite frankly. I honestly need her to head out so I can get changed and start the event set up, but before I can say anything, she saunters down one side of the windows continuing to shop.

"Can I help you find something in particular?" I finally ask, trying not to hover, but staying close enough to herd her out if the opportunity presents itself.

"Oh, no, I'm just enjoying looking at everything!" she

chirps back, and I die a little inside. I've never been someone who mulls things over–I like to look at my options, make a decision, and be done. But now as someone who watches people who mull things over for a living, I can tell you that it annoys me even more.

"Ok, well... we're actually hosting an event tonight and I'm needing to close up for a bit so we can get set up." She scowls slightly, and I try to pitch the fundraiser angle instead. "But the event is open to the public if you'd like to come back and join us!"

She softens a little, and nods. "Yes, of course, I won't keep you." She starts for the door, and pauses as she walks over the threshold. "It's nice to see life in this place again." Her smile seems a little ominous, and she doesn't comment about coming back before quietly shutting the door behind her and heading down the sidewalk.

chapter
seventeen

"IN THE NAAAAAAAME OF LOVE! One night! In the name of love!" A few hours later, our backyard is bumping with hustle and bustle as it feels like the majority of Buffalo Creek and the surrounding areas have descended on us for their five minutes of (local) fame. Not one person so far seems like they are in any danger of being snapped up for a recording contract, including our current performer, Patrick McGee, the high school principal, treating us to his rendition of U2's "Pride (In the Name of Love)". I am standing on the back porch overlooking the yard with everyone seated at the tables enjoying themselves when Shep sidles up next to me and hands me a cup of popcorn mixed with M&Ms from the popcorn bar.

"Having fun?"

"It actually is pretty fun. I thought Kaci was crazy when she suggested this, but it seems to be going well. People are more game than I thought."

Shep nods, and stifles a laugh as he gestures to the stage. "Are those even the correct words?"

I shrug because I am honestly not sure. "Close, but that's the edit they made for the "Elephant Love Medley" in *Moulin*

Rouge. It should be 'what more', not 'one night'," Sheriff Cooper says as he walks up behind us. He's been a bit of a ping pong ball all night, bouncing to and fro to make sure we have tight security and there isn't any funny business given our choice of venue.

"I'm sorry, what?" I ask, turning to him with a confused frown. Shep looks downright lost, as I'm sure he couldn't even explain what a Moulin Rouge is, much less know the intricate differences in the song lyrics. "What do you know about *Moulin Rouge*?"

"That would be Mrs. Tammy's favorite movie. I've seen it more times than I can count," he answers, and I detect the slightest shudder from him.

"That's pretty girly, Coop," Shep whispers, patting him on the shoulder.

"No, it's actually pretty manly to support your woman, Shep." And with that, he vanishes off behind us, presumably to patrol back upstairs or out in the front. Shep and I dissolve into laughter, and then quickly try to button it back up so Mr. McGee doesn't think we're laughing at him.

Mr. McGee wraps up his performance, and returns to his table to a hug from his wife amid thunderous applause and cheers. If anything, I've discovered that Buffalo Creek is a decently supportive little town, at least to one another's faces. No doubt every car will be brimming with discussion all the way home tonight, but at least it's all positive reactions in person.

Shep and I take a stroll down the silent auction table and bid on a few items during the next few numbers, and then head back to the back porch while the next "act" gets set up on the stage. As I walk back up the steps to check on Laramie and the Shoppe sales inside, I hear the opening horns to "The Room Where It Happens" from *Hamilton* and turn around to see my daughter and her three best friends on the stage in full Revolutionary War outfits.

"What is happening?" Shep asks, bewildered behind me. "What is this song?"

"It's from *Hamilton*. This is what happens when you refuse to raise a Swiftie," I reply, unreasonably proud of Mia, Emily, Lexie, and Lacie rapping back and forth about moving the nation's capital when I realize what's happening. Mia is grinning ear to ear singing the part of Alexander Hamilton, and I quickly whip out my phone to catch what I can on video, hoping someone else got the number in its entirety. They finish to erupting applause, and a partial standing ovation as Coach Kaci takes the stage and takes a microphone from Mia.

"How about our incoming seventh grade cheerleaders? Aren't they adorable and talented?" She gestures to the group as they take a collective bow and then prance off the stage while Kaci continues her announcements.

"We've got a lot of talent in the house tonight, folks! We are now queuing songs for the 7:00-7:30 block, so if you have a number in mind, Mrs. Lucy can get you taken care of back at the sound booth. And if you don't know what to sing, but just want to have fun up here, she can help you pick something out, too! I also want to throw out a reminder that our silent auction items have one more hour of bidding open, and then we will announce our winners in the last fifteen minutes of the night. Alright, to kick off our next block of numbers, we've got Buffalo Creek's own Coudreax "Cooter" Cogburn and Roy Blackburn singing..." She references her cue card and frowns, like it doesn't say what song they are about to sing. I instantly remember my conversation with Shep a few days ago and realize that they are probably about to humiliate us with the Ray Wylie Hubbard of it all.

"Looks like they are singing a surprise number, so give it

up for these guys!" She hands Cooter her microphone as he winks at her as he and Roy walk across the stage and take their places. Cooter looks like his usual smug and confident self, while Roy looks absolutely petrified trying to stay a few steps behind him, and my worst fears are confirmed when I hear the opening guitar and shaker of their song.

Cooter leads off by singing the whole first verse all the way to the chorus when he lets Roy take over the titular line, a touch more monotone and robotic than the original version, while he sings the harmony.

"Snake farm…"

"It just sounds nasty!"

"Snake farm…"

"Pretty much is!"

"Snake farm…"

"It's a reptile house!"

"Snake farm…"

"Uggghhhhh!" Cooter's entire body shakes in theatrics as he barrels into the second verse. He's working the stage back and forth, gyrating and dancing, and the crowd seems to be weirdly into the entire thing. Shep looks like he could absolutely crawl under the building from embarrassment, and I'm not that far behind him, despite the fact that people seem to be enjoying it.

They finish off a minute or so later with the scripted "ughhhhhs", and Roy actually cracks a smile as the music comes to a close. "Please don't say you are with us," Shep mutters, and I squeeze his hand in agreement as Cooter takes a series of bows and blows kisses off stage.

"Thank you, Buffalo Creek! That was dedicated to the biggest Texas country fan, the lovely Kaci Whitfield!" Cheers and applause erupt, and Kaci blushes on the side of the stage. "And special thank you to Shep and Molly Jones for the song suggestion! We are Cooter and Roy! Good night!" With one final bow, he and Roy head off the stage and I never thought it was possible to be this embarrassed by the song "Snake Farm".

I'm torn between being proud of them for conquering their nerves and being deeply concerned about what they consider appropriate public behavior. I'm still deciding whether to talk to them here or wait until later when the sounds of shouting float out from inside the Shoppe over the sound of the music. I jog up the steps and slip through the propped-open back door to see Deputy Randy standing with Wells Fletcher in what looks like a heated interrogation in the middle of my sales floor.

"This is an absolute outrage! You have no right to detain me; I was doing nothing wrong!" Wells is wildly gesturing amid his shouts, and Randy is standing still with his arms crossed over his belly, looking more amused than irritated by the outburst.

"Is there something I can help with, gentlemen?" I ask, trying to get the details on what's going on under the guise of looking helpful and needed.

"I was merely going to my seat on the balcony when Barney Fife here told me I wasn't allowed up there and escorted me here against my will!"

"Sir, you weren't allowed to be up there," Randy reiterates, sounding like this isn't the first time he's tried to explain it and it's getting old.

"Did he buy a ticket at the door, Randy?" I ask tentatively, wondering why Randy would say he wasn't allowed to be up there. We didn't designate certain tickets for specific places, so if he bought a general admission ticket, I don't see why he can't be on the balcony.

"He bought a ticket, and he is allowed on the balcony, but I caught him trying to pull down the stairs to the attic," Randy replies, giving both of us a self-satisfied smirk because that detail makes it a completely different discussion.

I shoot Wells a look and wait for his excuse. As he starts spinning some sort of word salad, a glint of light catches my eye–his wedding ring, snug around his finger. And now that I see them in person, his fingers look a little chubby to try to fit in the ring Cooper and I found.

I honestly wasn't listening to a word he was just saying, but I guess the look on my face said that I didn't buy any of it. Wells pauses, and looks a little contrite–almost genuine and sincere for the first time in our interactions. "I just… there are some things my dad always said he would leave me when the time came, and I can't find them. I know you've said the attic has been cleaned out, but I just wanted to check for myself if I can. I realize you never met him, but he could be a little on the eccentric side, and I have a feeling those things aren't in an obvious place."

Against all good judgement and logic, I feel like I believe him. "What kind of things?" I ask, still slightly suspicious. It very well could be a copy of the will that he is needing to destroy to not have to split his inheritance even further. Or a copy that still has him written in if he truly was written out.

He looks a little sheepish, and maintains eye contact with the floor as he mumbles, "Baseballs."

I frown, unsure if I heard him correctly over the roar of the crowd outside. Someone just finished up a loud and off-key version of "Don't Stop Believin'" and the audience has gone wild. "Did you say baseballs?"

"Yeah, Pop collected signed baseballs, and he always told me that they'd be mine when he kicked. He and I didn't have the best relationship, but we did always have a connection over baseball, and I'd like to have those if I can find them."

"So, this isn't about the missing version of the will?" Randy interjects, and Wells's face completely changes. He looks back and forth between Randy and me in confusion, and finally stops on me, apparently deciding I look more like I know what we're talking about than Randy.

"Dammit, Randy," I mutter, immediately asking God to forgive me for the salty language, but also feeling like He has to understand because, truly, *good grief, Randy, why??* I give Randy a stern look and jerk my head toward the stairs to indicate he should get lost and leave me to this.

"There is..." I start, unsure where to go with this. It's hard to know what to say because I don't want to give away any information he doesn't need to know, but at the same time, I don't know what he might already know, and what he's pretending to be in the dark about. "We have reason to believe there is an alternative version of the will out there, but we have not been able to confirm its existence and the exact contents. Your father's attorney only had a partial copy in his records, and the envelope that should have held it that we found here was empty."

"How is this version different from mine or Daughter of Satan's?"

"I beg your pardon?"

"Oh, sorry, I should have been more clear. My father was not Satan, but my sister is demon spawn. She may look all debutante and high society but she is pure evil and has been since we were kids. If you don't believe me, go ask that lap dog of an ex-husband of hers. Even he couldn't get along with her and he's basically a doorknob in a sweater vest."

"Wait—ex-husband?" I ask, letting the rest of his words sink in. I obviously knew Linny wasn't the most upstanding or trustworthy person, but this feels like a new turn.

"Yeah, I guess that's relatively new. I don't know how Jake ever did it, but seems like he finally got his fill of being controlled by my sister and let out frustrations with her pickle-ball partner or something. He didn't even have the decency to just keep quiet and wait to see if he got caught—he came clean to her. She said she kicked him out, but I'd say he was probably already packed and ready to go. No kids, pre-nup–they had the world's fastest divorce, and now Jake is probably somewhere singing *'Hallelujah, I'm free at last'.*"

"What is with this family and affairs, good Lord!" I blurt out, unable to keep my swirling thoughts from coming straight out of my mouth. Wells gives me another confused look that morphs into a bit of a smug smile.

"Have you by any chance been following me?"

"Um, no, I have not. Jesus is the only man I follow, thank you very much."

"Really? Because I thought I saw a Suburban full of middle aged white ladies the other day when I took the trash out, and the driver looked quite a bit like you..." He raises his eyebrows to emphasize his point, and I reluctantly relent.

"I had a tip from a reliable source that you might be participating in some... extra-curricular activities. So we decided to see what we could see. And it looks like we were right. You and..." I lean in, whispering the last part just to extend the undeserved courtesy of privacy. "Victoria?"

He maintains his smile, more genuine than before, and I wonder if he, too, is ready to just be caught. It has to be exhausting living a lie. I mean, I'm sure the excitement and thrill of the secret is fun to begin with, but it has to wear you down. "You love her, don't you?"

He lets out a sigh, and without a word confirms my suspicions. "It didn't start like that, okay?"

"Um, okay?" I wonder if I'm supposed to be glad that it didn't start with real feelings because that seems bonkers, but who knows?

"It started as us just being friends because Adam is a bit of an asshole and could be pretty mean to her," he starts, and I give him a disapproving look for the language. "Sorry, he can be a bit of a jerkwad, is that better?"

"Yes. There are children here, for crying out loud."

"Whatever. So, Adam would go off on her and then we'd meet to stage some houses, and she'd be all bruised up, or just mentally shot. And we started talking. And then talking turned into more than talking, if you know what I mean."

"I do, and that's gross. What about Sydney? Did you forget that you have a wife?"

"Sydney never wanted to be married to me in the first place. Our mothers made that happen. If I had a dollar for every time she's broken the 'sanctity' of our marriage, I could probably pay her tab at the country club. And it's not small."

"So why not get divorced? Why stay together if it's such a charade?"

"Because..." he starts, running a hand through his hair and looking uncomfortable. I have no idea what his reasoning is about to be if the previous topics of conversation haven't made him uncomfortable, so this should be a doozy. "Because I promised my dad."

"Promised him that you wouldn't get divorced?"

"Yeah. As long as Mom is alive, I promised we'd stay together. I know it sounds stupid, but I promised him, and I keep my word."

"Except wedding vows."

"She started it."

"Okay, whatever," I retort, pausing the volley for a minute to collect my thoughts. "So he was more comfortable with you just having an extra-marital affair than getting a mutual divorce and moving on?"

"Oh, no. I came clean about mine and Vic's relationship to him a few days before he went missing just because Mom's alive, but she's not really here anymore, you know? She has no idea who we are, so why would she care who I'm married to? He was livid. Said it was the most vile thing I could ever do to go outside my marriage and threatened to disown me in his will if I didn't end it with Vic. I told him that was fine because I knew I was doing what was right for me and I really don't need his money. Vic and I have plans. We're keeping things under wraps for now, but when the time is right, we're going to get her out and start over together. Syd's cool with it."

He seems resigned, but content in describing his circumstances. I can't even imagine what my face looks like because it feels like the dysfunction here just keeps piling up faster than a snowdrift. "So... do you think he wrote you out?" I ask, quickly zeroing in on one portion of that story that itches my brain at the end.

"I don't think so. That was just like two days before he supposedly went missing, so I don't think he would have had time."

"Your sister's version reflects that. Did you know that?"

"No, why are there so many versions, man? I have the original copy of the original version from 2022 when they went into the home. What's been going on since then? What does Linny's say? And what does this one we can't find say? Am I out of that one, too?" He looks genuinely frustrated, and this confirms my suspicions that Linny's version is in fact fraudulent. Hearing of her recent divorce, it seems her motives are stacking higher, and he's looking more and more innocent, albeit morally corrupt. But, innocent of whatever happened to Langley, nonetheless.

"Hers says she is the sole heir. The missing one says everything is split equally in thirds- you, Linny, and a Party C."

"Party C? What's a Party C?"

"The will has it broken down into Party A, Party B, and Party C. We assumed this was to differentiate between the assumption that one child's spouse would inherit and one's would not. There is an exhibit that explains who each party is, and that's the part we can't find. Party C is your..." I hesitate, unsure if it's appropriate for me to be the one to tell him this.

He raises his eyebrows to indicate I should continue, so I just say a quick prayer asking for forgiveness for whatever havoc this could end up wreaking, and rip off the metaphorical band aid. "We think Party C is your half-brother."

He physically stumbles a little, catching himself on a display table behind him. "Did you say brother?"

"Yes, half-brother. Before F&S sold and closed, your father had a relationship with one of the secretaries, and it is highly likely that her son is biologically your father's. That man has no knowledge of this, and we're trying to keep it quiet until his mother can sort it all out."

Wells starts to laugh–a dry, amused sort of laugh that has a bit of a bite to it. "Well, that's a little hypocritical of the old man, don't you think?"

"Well... judging by everything else that's gone sideways, I'd honestly say it leans more in the direction of 'learn from my mistakes', and less 'do as I say, not as I do'?" I offer, hoping that helps. I doubt it will, but it's at least something. I get another short, sharp laugh and confirm that it does not in fact help. There is an awkward silence, and neither of us really know what to say until I have an idea. "Hey, the attic is completely cleaned out, but we haven't checked the closets in the upstairs rooms. Want to check those out? Maybe the baseballs are there."

"It's worth a shot," he shrugs, gesturing for me to head up the stairs first.

Randy is posted up at the base of the stairs and I give him a nod to indicate that I am fine as we pass by. Once we get to the landing, I pull out my keys and unlock the first room on the right, one of three bedrooms up here that were later converted to offices, and are now just sitting vacant.

I take a turn through the empty room and gesture for him to check the small closet in the corner. It appears that nothing is there, so we move on to the next bedroom, and then the next. Everything is as empty as can be, and we are just about to give up when Wells ducks back into the en suite bathroom of what used to be the primary bedroom, and starts opening and closing cabinets. He gets to a tall cabinet that I assume was for linens or towels and breaks into a huge grin once he sees what is inside.

"Did you find them?" I ask giddily, wondering when I became fully invested in this rabbit trail of the mystery. He pulls out an old, worn cardboard box in reply, and sets it on the bathroom counter. "Oh, my goodness, I can't believe it! So, who is in here? Nolan Ryan? Pudge Rodriquez?" I ask, trying to think of Texas Rangers that would have been big in Wells's childhood.

"Um, yeah, I think they're in here somewhere," Wells responds absently, digging through the box and looking like he's about to cry. I grab a ball at the top and turn it over in my hand to look for the signature. It's a scribble, but I gasp audibly when I finally see who signed it.

"Is that... This is a Mickey Mantle ball!"

"Oh, yeah, I forgot he had that one," he says, still digging. I delicately place it back in the box and just watch as he rolls others to the side, clearly looking for one in particular. "Here he is–Dad's favorite." He proudly pulls a worn baseball from the bottom of the box and looks it over before handing it to me.

"Wells," I say, staring blankly at this baseball, unable to believe my eyes.

"Yeah," he answers, organizing the balls remaining in the box.

"That's a Babe Ruth ball!"

"Yeah, it is. He and I loved to watch *The Sandlot* together when I was a kid, so we made it our mission to track down a Babe Ruth ball. Pretty cool, huh?" He gingerly takes it back from me and places it in the box toward the bottom, covering it up with all the other balls.

"Do you have any idea how much all of those are worth?" I say breathlessly, thinking that if Linny knew he had a box full of sentiments worth millions, she'd be absolutely livid.

"Well, they're worth whatever someone else is willing to pay for them. But I'm not planning to sell. Hey, thanks for helping me find these. And thanks for giving me the real story about my dad. I'm interested to see if Linny lets that come to light." He pats me on the shoulder and navigates around me to get out of the bathroom and head downstairs.

"Wait! What do you mean?"

"My mother spent her entire lucid life making sure everything looked perfect on the outside when it was all a dumpster fire behind the scenes. When she started going downhill, my sister picked up that torch and carries it higher than my mother ever did. If there are skeletons hiding that we didn't know about, rest assured Linny will bury them so deep they'll never be found. There's a reason no one knows I was arrested on felony charges for smashing mailboxes in high school," he says, winking at me and heading out the bedroom door. As I stand there dumbfounded, he pops his head back in. "Quick question–was it Connie?"

"What?" I ask, trying to catch up with his train of thought moving at bullet speed.

"Did my dad have his affair with Connie?"

I hesitate, unsure if that's really my news to share. I feel some weird sense of protection for Connie, and I don't want to put her in unnecessary crosshairs, especially without giving her warning.

"I thought so," he replies, taking my silence as an answer. "My dad didn't care how we treated anyone around here–except her. Glad to know he at least cared about someone."

chapter
eighteen

"BABY! Where the hell is my husband? What is taking him so long? To find me, he, he, oh oh oh, baby!" After Wells found what he was looking for, I saw him fly off in Victoria's Porsche with her in the driver's seat as I came down the stairs to rejoin the party. Laramie is ringing up the last few customers at the back counter, and Sheriff Cooper is standing on the back porch with Shep when I walk out the back door. They are watching in disbelief as our daughter's coach—a grown adult—is gyrating around the stage belting out the viral hit "Where Is My Husband" by Raye with a few of her teeny-bopper friends singing and dancing back up for her. The crowd is eating it up, and I say a silent prayer that two ranch hands I know aren't taking this as an invitation to go put in their applications for the position she is seeking to fill.

"What is this drivel?" Cooper asks loudly as I approach, making a sour face and gesturing toward the stage. Shep stifles a laugh, and then starts gesturing to get Hayes's attention at the popcorn bar to bring him another cup.

"I think we can thank TikTok for this one, sir," I reply, holding up two fingers to Hayes to indicate I want a refill as well. Overall, I'm actually really pleased with how everything has turned out this evening, both business and fundraiser wise, and loosely sanctioned investigation wise.

"Well, it's terrible. If she wants a husband so badly, tell her to stop caterwauling and griping about it," he reasons, taking a sip of his drink and looking just completely unamused.

"It's okay, you can show Coach Kaci how it's done here in a few minutes when it's your turn," I answer casually, taking my popcorn from Hayes as he cruises by and keeps going to find the table with his friends.

"I beg your pardon?" He looks absolutely bewildered, borderline panicked as he turns to face me full on.

"I stopped by the programming table and it looks like you and Mrs. Tammy are up in three numbers. She signed y'all up for 'Islands in the Stream'." I shrug and point to his wife reapplying her lipstick and fluffing her hair in her compact mirror at a table about twenty feet from us. Something about her tight hot pink sweater and faux leather pants tell me that neither her participation nor song choice was not a game time decision, so this should be good.

"Aw, hell." I think he wanted to hope I was joking, but I think it's pretty clear Mrs. Tammy doesn't play when it comes to Kenny and Dolly.

"Break a leg, sir," Shep encourages, patting Coop on the shoulder as he trudges down the stairs to Mrs. Tammy to get the details on this change in events.

We watch the next few numbers with divided attention as I listen closely to the hushed argument between the Coopers as he argues that "he cannot embarrass himself and risk tarnishing his authority like this" while Mrs. Tammy asserts that it "strengthens his public image and shows he cares about the children". While we all know Mrs. Tammy is going to win, no questions asked, the actual show of it is decently entertaining. When it's all said and done, she drags him up on the stage to duet back and forth a la Rogers and Parton, and by the end, I would say Coop was actually enjoying himself, although he would absolutely never admit it for one second.

After the last few numbers, Kaci bounces across the stage and announces our silent auction winners and thanks everyone for a great show. "And we look forward to seeing you back here next year!" she adds with flourish, and I try not to faint thinking about doing this all over again in a year. The only consolation is that we'll at least be anticipating it, and I won't also be having a store grand opening at the same time.

People start milling around, throwing away trash and picking up silent auction wins as they prepare to leave. I smile and thank what feels like every single resident of Buffalo Creek as they file out the back gate in a steady stream, and we get to work cleaning up the urgent mess-popcorn and sound equipment, deciding to leave the table and chair clean-up for the light of day tomorrow.

"Thank you again SO much, Mrs. J! This was a huge hit! I think we've got an annual tradition on our hands!" Kaci says as she gives me an unsolicited hug on her way out. She pulls back from the hug to give me a huge grin and a shoulder squeeze before bouncing out the gate to her Matchbox car. I was desperately hoping she would get herself out before Cooter or Roy could try to make a move, and it seems like that is going to happen, although one Mr. Parker Parrish looks to be leaving with her. I am uncertain if there was any sort of prior relationship between the two of them before tonight, or if Parker felt his soul say '*here I am, send me*' when she was 'caterwauling' about the location of her future husband, but suffice it to say I'll be watching for developments there with intense interest.

Thankfully Mimi and Poppy volunteered to take the kids back to their house for the night as Shep and I stay and finish up the post party clean up. Sheriff Cooper and Randy do one last sweep of the building to make sure we don't have anyone left lurking before heading to do patrols around the block to make sure everyone gets home. Shep locks the back gate as the last of the guests leave, and I tidy the Shoppe floor for a few minutes before he joins me inside.

"Not a bad opening weekend, don't you think?" he asks, pulling me in for a squeeze chute hug. I feel my entire body relax in his arms, and hold him tightly so he won't let go too soon.

"It was good, but I am beyond tired," I reply, my words muffled against his chest.

"Well, this is just the beginning. You get to come work here every day now," he laughs, gesturing out to the sales floor despite me keeping a firm grip around him.

"Yeah, I'm starting to wonder what I was thinking."

"At least we didn't have any party crashers."

"Uh, not exactly," I say sheepishly, realizing now I don't really know where he and Coop were while Wells and I were on our baseball hunt. "Wells Fletcher did show up and got caught trying to get in the attic. He was really just looking for this box of signed baseballs his dad was supposed to leave for him. We actually found them in the cabinet of the primary bathroom."

"Signed baseballs? Anyone famous?"

"Would you believe Babe Ruth?"

Shep shoves me away from him and holds me firmly by the shoulders. "Are you telling me there has been a box in this God-forsaken ghost infested hole you convinced me to buy with a baseball signed by Babe Ruth in it?"

I laugh and nod. "And Mickey Mantle. Nolan Ryan, Pudge Rodriguez, too, but I'm not sure who else. I think there were probably fifteen or so baseballs in there."

"Do you have any idea what all of those would be worth?"

"I have an idea, but Wells said he's not selling. Apparently he and Langley didn't have a great relationship, but that's one good memory, so he's keeping them."

Shep lets out a sigh and a laugh, pulling me in for another hug before letting me go. "Things are never dull around here, that's for sure."

I nod in agreement and wander over to the base of the stairs. "Hey…" I start, unsure of what I'm even asking or wanting to do, but feeling like something is just tickling my brain about all this. "Would you come upstairs with me?"

Shep raises his eyebrows and points to me, and then himself, and then upstairs.

"Yes, but not like that!" I tease, rolling my eyes. "I want to have one more look in the attic myself, but I don't want to go up there alone."

"Sure, why not. I guess if the ghosts wanted to carry us away they already would have by now. And if it's our time to go, it's our time. I hope Mia and Hayes know we loved them." He continues teasing me up the stairs all the way to the attic pull down. I take a deep breath and pull the string to release the stairs, bracing myself as it opens. Our lives went spiraling like a tornado the last time I did this, and I can't help but have a little touch of PTSD as I do it again.

Of course, nothing happens, and we anchor the ladder before tentatively climbing up into the attic. We stand still on the small landing and look around, confirming that it is actually completely empty.

"So… what did you want to look for?" Shep asks, gesturing around to the empty landing and insulation fluff off over the rafters.

"I… don't know. I don't think there's probably anything up here, but the Fletcher twins wanted up here for something. I guess Wells found what he was looking for, but maybe there is something Linny is still looking for. The version of the Party C will is still out there somewhere."

We look closely at all the insulation, in between the rafter joints, and up at the ceiling beams, and still come up empty. "I guess there really isn't anything up here. Maybe we'll find it somewhere else. I haven't asked Augustus Renfro if his dad had any computer files, or if they were just paper. Maybe that's a lead we can check on," I say, heading back for the ladder. I climb down and dust myself off at the bottom before turning around and finding myself face to face with Linny Caldwell and her .38 special.

"Linny... What are you doing here?" I ask tentatively, backing up to the ladder and running into Shep making his way down.

"Just checking on the last of Daddy's things," she chirps, waving her pistol to the side to indicate we are in her way.

"I'm sorry?"

"There is something of my daddy's left in the attic and I need to check on it and then I'll be on my way. Just scoot on up there with me, and we can get this over with."

"Why would we go up there with you and your gun?" Shep snorts, and I pray she doesn't get sassy about his bluntness. Shep Jones has never been one to mince words, but we also aren't typically talking to someone holding us at gunpoint.

"Because I can't exactly trust you to stay down here without me, can I? You'll shut me up in there. Ask me how I know." She gives us a wicked grin, and that was the moment I started to really buy into Wells's assessment of his sister. "Now you two can go up there with me, and I'll decide up there if you get to come back down."

"Linny... did you... did you kill your father?" I take a deep breath and step away from the ladder so Shep can also get down. We stand still next to the wall, waiting to see how she is going to react. I highly doubt she'd shoot us here in the hallway because it would be impossible to get us up the attic ladder to hide, and if she's got it in her mind to kill us anyway, confessing to us won't matter. Her confession isn't my primary goal at this point–it's more to keep her talking and distract her from pushing us up into the attic in hopes that Cooper and Randy might circle back and rescue us.

"Of course I didn't kill my daddy!" she snaps ferociously, leaning forward slightly, and I jump a little at her fervor. "It was an accident! Just more mess from this family for me to have to clean up!"

"What do you mean?" I prod gently, softening my face to encourage her to continue.

"No one can just keep their word around here! Not Jacob, not Wells, not Daddy. There is no such thing as a good man, Molly. You may think this joker here loves you, but let me tell you something–every man lies. And every man cheats. Just wait," she snarls, waving the pistol as she swaps from her right hand to her left. It's at this moment that I get a clear look at her left hand and see a faint tan line where a ring used to be, but isn't any longer. She would have to try it on to confirm, but the tan line looks incredibly close to the size of the silver band Cooper and I found on the balcony.

"Linny, why were you and your dad here? Did he tell you about his affair? Because Wells didn't know."

"Of course he told me! He told me everything, always! I always had to be the one to make everything right, to set every-thing back up when it fell apart. Why do you think no one knows about Wells's felony charges?" she shrieks, and I roll my eyes.

"I did actually know about that. But why were you here?"

"Because once again, Wells can't be trusted. He tells Daddy about how he's got this mistress he can't live without and begs him to let him get divorced but stay in the trust. Daddy is livid, and calls me and says we need to get his old files to take to Cassius to change the will. I think he's probably starting to go south like Mama, so I humor him and come pick him up. He tells me to come here and he lets himself in. We go up to the attic and he starts digging through these file boxes until he gets to the one he's looking for. He tells me this is his actual real will–not the one Wells and I have had all these years. He starts explaining that part of why he's so upset with Wells is because he once made a mistake like that and it almost cost him everything. He never wants it to be known while he's alive, but wants to do right by everyone when he's gone. Shows me this copy of his will where everything is split in three ways, and we have a half-brother who's going to hit pay dirt, but I get to be the one to deal with all the shame and humiliation of my father being a philanderer."

I'm no mental health expert, but something tells me the last forty six years of this woman's life have done her dirty on healthy relationships and coping mechanisms. She has given up on holding us point blank and has begun raving up and down the hall as she weaves her tale.

"So, the real will is up there?" I venture, wondering if I should even draw her attention to us.

"In pieces," she snarls. "After I read it, I refused to give it back to him. There was no way I was going to let this get out to the public, and I told him so. We tussled over it a bit, and he fell and hit his head. There was no way to explain that accident without explaining what we were fighting over, so I said a very painful goodbye, and I left him to deal with the consequences of his actions."

"We found the empty envelope in the floor joints- but where is the will? Or the pieces, as you say?" Shep chimes in, and she rushes over to him and sticks the muzzle of her gun right in his chest. I suck in all my breath and try not to cry as she stares him down silently for a few long moments.

"Not a word from you. I don't listen to men anymore. Didn't you hear me? They're all liars." She maintains a stone cold iciness on her face and I am unsure if I should say anything or attempt to touch her for fear of her accidentally pulling the trigger. After another moment or so, she relents and backs up a few inches. "Yes, it's in pieces all over the insulation. I wasn't going to wade through and pick them all up while my daddy bled out on the floor. Chances are it's disintegrated, but I need to know for certain. I wasn't sure where the envelope had landed in all the commotion, but I knew it didn't have the documents, so I wasn't really worried about it."

"If it's in pieces, do you really need to worry? No one is going to be able to find all the pieces to put it back together and know what it said. I think his secret is safe," I fib, knowing that there are plenty of other people out there now that know, and are definitely going to be talking about it. "I've been up there a few times and never noticed anything on the insulation."

"I just need certainty that it is gone! I thought I wouldn't have to worry about evidence because this building has been abandoned for years. Then, in the worst timing, Asa sold it the next week right out from under us."

"Are you sure that's the only copy? We found a partial copy with Cassius's son a few weeks ago. It's just missing the appendices, but people still know it exists. If you're worried about that one, you should probably be worried about more, right?"

"No, I made sure someone took care of that. No one will find those copies," she answers confidently, starting to pace. "Who do you think Celia Renfro's new tennis partner at the country club is? And which member of the hospital Board of Directors nominated her to take over the neurology wing at Buffalo Creek Medical Center instead of the hole she's been working nights in? Who is she currently indebted to in Crawford County?"

"I'm guessing you, since you're talking about yourself in a sinister third person?" Shep quips and I automatically smack him in the ribs. "I mean, *you*?" he answers, putting an extra upward inflection on the word "you" to indicate an abundance of fake surprise. It's a wild ride to be scared witless that the love of my life is about to die, and then ten seconds later, hope he'll just be quiet to keep you both from getting killed.

"Yes, me, you twat. Me, the only one who ever gets anything done around here. The only one who realized Mama was declining and needed help. The only one who adheres to any type of moral standard. The only one who does what she says she's going to do. Which reminds me–I believe I said you two were coming up into the attic with me. So, let's get to it." She trains the gun back on us and motions for us to head up the ladder.

"One last question, please?" I squeak, just because my curiosity can't stand it. She relents, motioning with her free hand for me to just ask. "How did you pull off the will with just you?"

"Well, that's the one upside to Jake's mistakes–his little cupcake happens to be an attorney. It was quite easy to buy my silence about what happened between the two of them with a simple estate edit. And she was more than happy to oblige since she's up for partner in the fall and a moral lapse on her end would look terrible to the board."

"Is the adoption real?"

"That's two questions."

"Geez, fine, can I ask one more 'one more' question?"

"Yes, the adoption is real. I need all this matter settled so I can get my money and get my baby. I can't depend on anyone else, but this baby will know she is loved, cared for, and adored and we'll only ever need each other. You two are going to unfortunately be locked in your attic and unable to get out, and they'll decide all three of you were just victims of a tragic accident–a faulty attic ladder… Now, move!" she barks, lunging toward us with the gun. We glance back at her with a bit of trepidation and start for the ladder. I take a deep breath and start climbing as Shep puts a reassuring hand on my back. A few silent tears slip down my cheeks as I think that if we are somehow spared this time, I will absolutely find a better hobby because these near death experiences are the absolute worst.

I reach the top of the ladder and look down the hole to see Shep right behind me and Linny at the base of the ladder. "Linny, there aren't any pieces left. You really don't have to worry about it, honestly. Just let us down, please!" I plead, as Shep makes it back on the landing with me.

"Oh, well, that makes much less work for me, but I don't think soooooo!" she shouts just before a shot rings out and deafens us all for several moments. Shep and I look down through the hole and see Cooter and Roy lying flat on Linny, pinning her body to the ground as they use piggin string to tie her ankles and wrists. I'm assuming she misfired upon being tackled, and I'm terrified to see what ended up being the unlucky target. Before I can say anything, Shep pulls his phone out of the zippered breast pocket of his light blue Poncho pearl snap shirt and pushes a button before holding it near his mouth.

"Coop? Did you get all that?"

"Sure did, Shep. Hold her there; we're coming in!" He answers through the speaker, and I can hear the front door bang open downstairs.

"When did you do that?" I ask, in grateful shock.

"I hit him on my speed dial when I heard you say she was down there. I didn't know what she had planned, but I figured he would want to know. I didn't think she would realize I had it going in my shirt pocket."

A few seconds later, officers swarm up the stairs in all black tactical gear and surround Linny on the ground. Cooter and Roy jump up to let them through, and they quickly stand her up and move her toward the door to the stairs.

"Ah, just who I was looking for," Cooper says as he slips in the door. He looks her straight in the face and gives her a warm smile. "Madeline Fletcher Caldwell, you are under arrest for attempted murder, abuse of the elderly, and estate fraud. You have the right to remain silent and anything you say can and will be held against you..." As he launches into her Miranda rights with joy and gusto, Shep and I descend the attic ladder and start folding it up to close it. Coop finishes up and gestures for them to move her downstairs and out to a squad car when something suddenly hits me.

"Wait! Linny– one more question. Please?" The officers turn her to face me and she looks like she could spit fire and burn down villages. "Why did you have your mom in here that first day I met you?"

She pauses, and as she formulates her answer, it's like we all see the smallest glimpse of humanity peek through. "She deserved to know what happened. I brought her here and confessed the truth. And she told me to tell the servant girl downstairs to bring her a cup of tea and make sure her car was ready to go to her bridge game that afternoon. My mother, the woman who raised me, was not a warm person, but I know she loved me, my brother, and my father, and only ever wanted to protect our legacy. But, she died seventeen months ago when that disease took her memory. She may not know that she knows the truth, but she deserved to know the truth."

I nod in understanding, and contemplate an answer, but they move her out before I get a chance. Once we are alone, I turn back to Cooter, Roy, and Shep all standing behind me and gesture for them all to bring it in for a group hug. "We gotta stop doing these elite level trust falls, guys," I laugh, holding back tears. Shep just pulls me close and kisses me on the top of the head as the guys move back and Cooter clears his throat to ask a question.

"Hey, Boss? You can shoot me down, but uh, Dairy Queen closes in thirty minutes. Any chance y'all want to go hit them up real quick?"

"I CAN GET you right here, sugar, come on up," Marge says, motioning to the line formed in front of the check-out counter at the Shoppe. For some unknown reason, over the last several weeks, Marge and JoBeth have decided they are my newest employees, and show up every weekday afternoon for two hour stints to do whatever job they decide they want to do– not necessarily what is most needed, but just what sounds like fun for the day. I have let those two run amuck because it's the last week of school when parents are expected to be at the school for all manner of assemblies, concerts, projects, and hang-outs at all hours of the day, and well, the extra help hasn't hurt, even if it is really picky about its assignment. It's been a quiet five or so weeks since all the commotion of the fundraiser night, and I'd say the community has more ques-tions than answers at this point, but thankfully, people have left us alone for the most part. Business has been steady, and despite my moody help, we've settled into a pretty good groove.

I've just let myself in the back door, after attending Hayes's academic awards ceremony, to see Marge ringing up customers, and JoBeth out tidying up the sales floor. I slip past

Marge and set my bag on the back counter before sidling up behind her to check on things.

"How's it going?"

"Just fine, just fine. How was the assembly?"

"Fine. Has it been busy?"

"Busy enough. The Thursday ladies prayer group came in to get gifts for their secret sisters."

"That's nice. How did that go?" I ask tentatively, wondering if the most tenuous member of the Thursday prayer group was in attendance.

"It was fine. JoBeth had to remove Geraldine Farwell for inappropriate behavior. But it was just fine." A small, self-satisfied smirk crosses her face and I audibly groan.

"What inappropriate behavior? Am I going to read a bunch of negative reviews of us on the community Facebook page because of this?"

"Oh, no, everyone in here was in complete agreement that she was out of line."

"Are you going to share what her egregious behavior was with me?"

"No, darlin, I think it's better for you to be in the dark about it. But, don't worry, we took complete care of it. And now JoBeth is reorganizing your denim," she says brightly, putting a printed receipt in the bag in front of her and sliding it across the counter to the customer. "Thank you for shopping with us, sugar. Come back to see us!"

"I don't even have denim, what are you talking about?" I ask, moving out from behind the counter and walking toward JoBeth. Before I get to her to investigate, the front door swings wide open, and Cheerleader Barbie bounces through.

"Hi, Mrs. J! It's wonderful to see you! How are things going?" She's clad in a gray Buffalo Creek Warriors tank top and tiny red bike shorts with her hair piled on top of her head like she's either been working out or running errands. I've never been able to confirm if they've actually made her teach at all this semester, or if she's just on deposit until the next school year, but it doesn't look like she's been working at the school.

"Pretty good, Kaci, how about you?"

"I have been amazing! I actually met someone at karaoke night," she divulges, leaning in closer and giggling.

"I thought I saw that. I hope it's been going well. Parker is a really good kid. His mom plays mahjong with my grandmother," I explain, gesturing to Marge behind the counter.

"Oh, it's going so well! That's actually why I'm here. I wanted to see if you have any cute dresses because we're going on a really fancy date tomorrow night and I can't find anything to wear. I think he's going to propose!" she squeals, jumping up and down a little. I stifle a laugh, thinking she cannot be serious, but her continued excitement tells me she is most definitely not kidding.

"Uh, wow, okay. Yes, we have a few racks of dresses over by the front windows. If you need to try anything on, you can use a room upstairs. Let me know if you need anything," I say, giving her a smile and gesturing toward the windows. That would sure be a trip if Ginny Parrish ended up with a future daughter in law in a matter of five weeks, but I guess when you know, you know, right?

Kaci bounces off to find the perfect dress to possibly become the next future Mrs. Parrish, and I turn back to Marge at the counter. She makes eye contact with me and points discreetly to JoBeth a few tables away speaking to a woman with her back turned to me. The back of her hair looks familiar, and I slowly walk up behind and confirm my suspicion that she is Connie Wallace.

"Hey, Connie, how's it going?" I ask quietly as I put a hand on her shoulder so I don't scare her.

"Hi, Molly! You are actually the one I came to see. Can we talk?" She smiles, and it seems genuine, but also a little weathered, and I wonder if she's been through quite the ringer over the last several weeks. Given the nature of how things played out with Linny's arrest and the rest of the situation, I'm certain more of her personal details are more public than she would prefer, but she seems to be handling it well.

I lead her to the backyard and we have a seat at the patio table on the porch. She looks a little nervous, but not half as nervous as she did the first time she visited me here.

"Well, I... I just wanted to tell you thank you," she says, nodding confidently and keeping it succinct, like she has prepared ahead of time and plans to keep it very simple.

"Um, you're welcome? But what did I do?"

"You respected our privacy and let us deal with this in our own way without blasting it all over town. And you fought for Matt to get his share when you didn't have to."

I smile, trying to find the words to say something. "I mean, of course. Has he met with an attorney about the estate yet?"

"He did a few days ago. It's going to be enough for him to franchise his business and have offices in a few different places, which is his dream. He and his wife can get into a bigger house and start having babies because they've put that on the back burner to build the business. It's going to be a really good thing for him," she asserts, giving me another slightly sad smile.

"That's great. He's going to be my first call here in a few months when we need a new roof on this old gal." I wink, and nod toward the Shoppe building. I wait to see if she is going to say anything else, and when she doesn't, I venture to the next topic tentatively. "How are you and Evan?"

"We're okay," she says, letting out a large sigh. "He was really mad for a little bit, and he had every right to be. We are not living together right now, but we are going to counseling and it's going pretty well. I... I have hope." Her voice chokes, and I see tears welling in her eyes. Luckily for her, I grabbed a handkerchief embroidered with a black Angus cow and the phrase "Udderly Fabulous" on my way out here for just such a time as this.

"Do you not sell any handkerchiefs that are just normal?" she asks, holding it out when I hand it to her, and I stifle a laugh amid my own tearing eyes.

"Nope, nothing here is normal. Normal is just a setting on the dryer."

She laughs. "I like that. I'll admit, normal is pretty relative."

"Not my relatives, but sure," I say with a wink, earning another laugh.

"Well, again, I just wanted to say thank you. I appreciate you being someone who is willing to help others even when you have nothing to gain. That's a little rare these days, you know?"

"That's very sweet, thanks, Connie. Hey, maybe we can grab lunch sometime?" I say as we stand and I give her a hug. We've come a long way from me ambushing an old lady book club to get to meet her, and I'd like to think despite some of the heartache, it's been for the better.

"Yes, I'd like that. And you'll have to come to the big opening in a couple months," she tosses out as I walk her to the back gate.

"Opening?"

"Yes, Wells and Matt have actually become sort of... friends? It's a little bizarre to see, if I'm honest, because Wells was always an entitled brat to me. But they have gotten to know one another and like spending time together. Once all the legal dust settles and they know what they have to work with, they want to pool together some of the inheritance to start a shelter for domestic violence survivors in Crawford County. I'm not sure the exact ties to the cause—something about Wells and a close friend of his–but they are pretty excited about it. They want to keep adult and child psychiatrists on staff so clients can get additional resources beyond the standard food, shelter, and clothing. The Fletcher Foundation will hopefully open in six months or so, and I'm certain they will want your attendance," she explains, squeezing my shoulder and giving me another hug.

"That sounds amazing, and I would be honored to attend."

▭

A few days later, a little eaten up with curiosity, I find myself in Oak Hills parking my Suburban in front of a "Visitor" sign at Magnolia Blossom Retirement Community. I've heard through the grapevine (Connie) that Wells has taken over the weekly visits to his mother, and I'm hoping to run into both of them at the same time here, just to get an update on the whole situation.

"Hi, I'm not sure if she's taking visitors, but I'm here to see Nora Fletcher? And possibly her son, if he's here?" I tell the receptionist as I check in. She gives me a visitor badge and has me wait by the desk while she calls Nora's nurse to check to see where she is.

"Molly? Hey! Good to see you! What are you doing here?" Before the receptionist can report back to me, Wells walks by the front desk with two dishes of vanilla soft serve headed in the other direction. Weirdly enough, he looks actually pleasantly surprised to see me, and it catches me a little off guard to see a man that is genuine and joyful in front of me, versus the pompous jerk I first met.

"Hey! I am actually here to see your mom. And you, if you happened to be here. How's it going?"

"It's uh... it's actually going really well. You want some ice cream?" he asks, looking down at his two soft serve dishes that are rapidly melting in his hands. "Mom likes a little afternoon treat."

"No, thank you, but that's really sweet. Can I come with you to see her?" I ask, tentatively gesturing in the direction he is headed.

"Yeah, of course. I'd say she'll love to see you, but she'll have no idea who you are. She thinks I'm a neighbor boy from her college days," he laughs, leading me down the hallway.

We stop at a locked checkpoint, and are buzzed through by a desk attendant into the memory care wing. After navigating a few more hallways, he leads me through an open door into apartment 223, where Nora Fletcher, looking ghostly as ever, is perched on a high back armchair near her window, staring at a bluebird on a branch outside.

Wells hands her the dish of ice cream, and she silently takes it and starts to eat it. I sit in a dining chair about twenty feet away, and Wells pulls another chair right between us so he and I can talk, but he's nearby if his mother needs anything.

"So... how often do you come here?" I quietly gesture toward his mom, who is fixated on the bluebird and her soft serve to the point that I'm not sure she realizes we're here.

"About once or twice a week. Like I said, she doesn't know who I am, but at least she's not always sitting alone. I probably should have been doing this before, but..." He trails off and heaves a little bit of a sigh before continuing. "I don't know if you could tell, but my sister is a bit of a control freak. She has her way of doing things, and I could never get it just right, so it was easier for everyone for me to just go with the inept narrative and save myself the trouble, you know?"

"Well, I'm glad you're getting this time with your mom now."

"Me too. And I'm glad Lin can maybe get some help. No

one should feel like they are that essential to the general function of everything. It's not healthy."

The last I heard, Linny was awaiting trial in a women's prison for her various charges. Luckily, August Renfro was able to recover an old electronic copy of the new version of the will on desktop computer from Cassius's office that looked like 2002 was its prime. As for now, Linny will likely forfeit her share of the inheritance under "slayer statues", meaning she had direct involvement in the death of the decedent, but it could change depending on what she ends up convicted of. I agree with Wells that more than anything, she needs to relax and get some help.

"How has it been to get to know your brother?" I ask delicately, not wanting to overstep, but genuinely curious how it's all melding together.

"Actually... It's been great. It's a little weird to think that my dad just had another son we didn't know about, but Matt's a great guy, and we've got some big plans. Did Connie tell you what we're doing?"

"She shared a little. She didn't really know what the personal tie to the cause of domestic violence was though," I say, trailing off and hoping he fills in the blank. I know the tie is Victoria, but I'm curious what this means for them and their relationship, and his relationship with Sydney.

He gives me a sheepish smile, and nods his head. "Yeah, Syd and I called it quits the night Linny got busted. It didn't have anything to do with that–I just felt like it was time. We're still friends and she's going to stay on as an agent with the group for a little bit until she decides what she wants to do next. Getting Vic out was a little more complicated. She filed a restraining order and got a temporary protection order put in place while serving him the divorce papers so she could get out safely. Her attorney has had a few meetings with his and has made it clear that as long as he stays away from her, she won't say anything to anyone about the real reason they're splitting. She's staying with me for now, and we're planning to get married once both of our divorces are finalized, which shouldn't take too long since they're both uncontested with no kids."

"And she's in support of the Fletcher Foundation?"

"She is going to be our executive director when we're up and running. She actually has a background in non-profits, and I think between that and her personal connection, she'll be perfect. She'll help a lot of people," he says proudly, and I take a second to marvel at what a change it makes in someone to see them living with joy and contentment instead of turmoil and chaos.

"Miss?" Nora Fletcher's tinny voice floats across the room and catches my attention. I look up and see her staring right at me, so I point to myself and she nods to confirm. "Miss, do you know how long my husband is going to stay?"

I look around and point to Wells, wondering if she is mistaking him for his father. She shakes her head vehemently, and points to the bluebird on the branch outside. "My husband has come to visit me, but I'm afraid he's going to leave before I'm ready to say goodbye."

I'm equal parts touched and creeped out, so I'm uncertain how to respond. I vaguely remember Marge sharing one time that there is an old wives tale that bluebirds represent loved ones sending comfort and joy, so it's honestly a little too coincidental that there's one here visiting now, and that adamantly believes it's her husband.

"I'm not sure, Mrs. Fletcher. Maybe just spend all the time with him you can, and he might come back tomorrow," I offer, shrugging my shoulders and hoping that satisfies her curiosity because if it doesn't, I've got nothing.

This seems to appease her, and she goes back to giving her full attention to the window. "You know what's weird," Wells starts, pointing to the bird. "That thing is here every single time I come to visit. What are the odds?"

⬚

"Wait... where are y'all going with those? Do you think you finally got it?" A few days later, I pull down the driveway with a load of groceries in the back because it is officially summer break and my children's stomachs have grown three sizes since school let out. It's like the Grinch, but appetites, and they are less nice as they grow, rather than more.

As I roll by slowly, Cooter and Roy are once again hauling feed sacks down from the garage to the barn. Since our initial traps, we've caught more rats than we can count, but somehow the feed continued to get ransacked every time they moved it back to the feed barn. Now that summer is in full swing, I casually mentioned to Shep that I'd love to have the garage back to park in so my car wouldn't be as hot, and it seems like they've taken initiative to solve this rat problem once and for all. As I creep by them, I roll down my passenger window to get an update on the situation.

"Oh, we got him, Boss. He's been a slippery sum-buck all spring, but we finally got 'im," Cooter replies, hoisting his bag a little higher on his shoulder.

I know I'm going to regret asking, but I can't help myself. "So... how big did he end up being?"

Roy balances his bag across his shoulder and holds his hands about 24" inches apart without saying a word. I let out an involuntary yelp. "We had a rat THAT big around here?"

"Oh, no, Boss, it turned out to be not a rat," Cooter clarifies, and I should be less scared, but I somehow don't feel that way.

"Okay... what was it then?"

"It was nature's masked bandit," Cooter replies poetically, and I try not to roll my eyes.

"Which is?"

"It was a raccoon, ma'am," Roy answers bluntly, and it suddenly all makes sense. Of course it's been a raccoon this entire time.

"I see. Well, should I ask what you did with it?"

"Let's just say I'm going to have a really legit Davy Crockett costume this year, Boss." Cooter grins and I nod, now knowing exactly what they did with it. At least it can live on in infamy, I suppose.

"Okay, well, y'all be careful carrying those back down. Dinner's at 5:30." They both nod affirmatively and I roll up the window to get back to the house. Just as I park and start hyping myself up to carry in all these groceries, Mia comes running out of the house and up to the driver's side window.

"Mom! Guess what!!"

"You came to help me carry in groceries?" I say with a hopeful smile, knowing that is absolutely not why she came out here, but might inspire her to help now that she's out here anyway.

"Ew, no. This is great news!" she clarifies, thrusting her phone in my face. I'm looking at someone's skinny fingers on the left hand with a large diamond on the ring finger, tipped with long, almond shaped nails in an obnoxiously bright shade of Pepto pink.

"Whose hand am I looking at here?" I ask, already tired of this guessing game I'm certain I won't care about.

"It's Coach Whitfield! She and Parker are getting married!" Mia squeals again, and runs back into the house after turning a small donut on the driveway. So much for the help, I guess. And kudos to Kaci for actually having a very good temperature gauge on her relationship–I never would have guessed 6 weeks of dating would lead to a rock that big, but I'm clearly old-fashioned.

Before I can get myself out and actually start on the groceries, my phone starts to ring, flashing a number I don't recognize. Against my better judgement, I go ahead and answer it.

"Hello?"

"Hi!" A loud voice, possibly a little too deep for a woman's voice, but higher than you'd expect for a man's, booms through the speaker. "Is this Molly Jones?"

"Um, yes?"

"The Molly Jones, amateur ranch wife/ mom detective?"

"Yes? I'm sorry, who is this?"

"We haven't met, and that's why I'm calling. I've been reading up on you and studying what you've had going on. I want you to be the featured guest for the next season of my podcast."

"Is this a prank? What are you talking about?"

"My name is Trudy Grimes and I host and produce a podcast about strange but true crimes in Texas, and it sounds like you are exactly who I need on my show. I'm sure you've had your five minutes of local fame, but it's time to take you national, girl."

epilogue

"RED ROCK CATTLE COMPANY, this is Shep," Shep says as he pushes the speakerphone button to answer the ranch landline in between sips of coffee. It's been a relatively quiet summer, and we've been in bull sale preparations for the last few weeks to get ready for our fall sale. We typically have some interest from buyers to look at bulls far out in advance, but it seems like it's been busier than usual. Luckily, I don't know as much about that side, so Shep is on the hook to answer the phone every time and we don't have to waste time with the charade of rock, paper, scissors for who has to answer it.

"Shepherd! This is Bill Bullock. How are you, son?" I spin around in my desk chair adjacent to Shep at his desk to face him and shoot him a look. It's an innocent enough greeting, but it curls my toes, and I don't like it. We are not friends with Bill Bullock, or even acquaintances, and for him to act like we're so buddy-buddy really rubs me the wrong way.

"Oh, hey, Mr. Bullock. What can I help you with?"

"Well, I just wanted to give you a call to make sure you were joining us next week for our summer Bull-nanza sale. You should have gotten a flyer in the mail. My old buddy Pat is gonna come play for us, and we'll bring out the good whisky and prime rib. I'm expecting to see you there, son." His tone isn't threatening, but it's not exactly friendly, either. As far as I'm aware, we actually aren't planning to be at his sale, so I'm curious to hear Shep's answer.

"Uh, yes, we got the flyer. That's a pretty big get, having Pat Green," he starts, flashing me a nervous look. Clearly an expert at these situations, I give him nothing but wide eyes and a series of helpless shrugs. I have no idea why Bill Bullock is calling us like some Angus-bull mafioso. But it feels like a shakedown, and unfortunately I have zero experience and no answers for that. "We are probably not going to be able to make it. Our fall sale is in the middle of September, and we're pretty covered up getting ready for that."

Shep returns my shrugs with a series of his own shrugs, and we wait for Bill's response. There is a long pause on the line before he finally simply replies, "I see."

We sit for a few long minutes, unsure if Shep should elaborate more, or if it's better to say less. I am the absolute queen of rambling to fill a silent void, and I've never been more thankful that Shep is in charge of a conversation.

"Is there anything else I can do for you, Mr. Bullock?" Shep finally asks, looking ready to wrap this up.

"Well, here's the thing, Shepherd," he drawls, and I resist the urge to punch him through the phone. One of my biggest pet peeves is when people who don't know us very well call Shep "Shepherd", especially when he's introduced himself as Shep, and *especially* when it sounds as condescending as Bill Bullock does. "I do believe I was in attendance at your spring bull sale, was I not?"

Shep sighs, leaning back in his desk chair. "Yes, I believe we saw you there. We appreciate you coming down."

"Yes, and I don't believe I was just in attendance. I do

believe I was also a customer, was I not? At a more than generous rate?"

And there it is—he doesn't care about giving us prime rib, Pat Green, or a new herd sire. He wants quid pro quo for the bull he bought from us.

"Yes, I do remember you buying one of our yearling bulls. I hope he's working well for you, sir."

"He's fine. But I'm a little worried that you aren't going to be. You see, we have a bit of a tradition in this business of supporting one another. You want to be supportive of other producers, don't you?"

"With my business?"

"Of course with your business. I don't know if you're aware, but that is how you really succeed in this facet of the industry—help others help you."

"I see," Shep bites back, using Bill's own words and clenching his teeth. "And exactly how much am I supposed to support you to have you support me?"

"I think an equal relationship is more than fair. Mutually beneficial, if you will."

I lean forward in my chair and put my forehead in my palm. Bill Bullock spent high enough in the five-figure range to make me choke on my coffee at the time, for no discernible reason. Now the reason is crystal clear.

"Here's the thing, Mr. Bullock, I appreciate you reaching out but we are pretty closed on our genetics at this time, and aren't really in the market for any new animals. If we end up needing something in the future, we know where to find you."

Shep Jones has always been able to bluntly slice through intimidation and get on with his life, and thankfully, today is no exception. Bullock lets out a small snort on the other end before responding in his own blunt way.

"You sure about that, Jones?"

"Absolutely positive."

"Well, I hope you decide to change your mind. Because you're surely going to regret it if you don't."

acknowledgments

First and foremost, thank you to my readers. Without you, this is just an unrealized dream, and I'm so grateful you would spend your time and money to read words I've written.

A special thank you to...

My Pilates gals- Dayna, Sandy, Susan, Rhonda, Mary Ann and Denise (plus your book clubs!)— it means the world to me that you've been such wonderful cheerleaders and believed in me so wholeheartedly.

Dr. Sandip Mathur for generously sharing your expertise and experience. You were right— Google Docs was a game changer!

The endoscopy unit staff, who have been the most encouraging and supportive, plus always being willing to be a guinea pig for my cooking. Feed the People Fridays are one of my favorite things.

The staff at Discount Tire TXW09 for never batting an eye when I set up shop to write like your store was my office away from home. We had 2 flat repairs, 2 slow leaks, 3 rotations, and an install of a new set of tires during the making of this book and y'all gave me a great place to get work done but were also the most efficient.

My family (with a special shout out to my Aunt Jean)- thank you for always being supportive. Aunt Jean, I hope you loved this one, too!

My kids— I am so unbelievably proud of the two of you and the tiny humans you are becoming. You are caring, compassionate, helpful, and hilarious, and I am so grateful God chose me to be your mom. Thank you for telling your friends that your mom is an author with pride and not embarrassment, and I hope I always make you half as proud as I am of the two of you.

Steven— saved the best for last. Just when I thought you couldn't get any more supportive, you just keep raising the bar. What a joy and privilege it is to do life with you. I would have never pictured our life to be this 13 years ago, but gracious, God gives more than we can ask or imagine, and He's done the best job writing our story. Our story will always be my favorite story to tell.

Now I better wrap this up because we've probably got cows to feed... ;)

about the author

Morie Smith lives in west Texas with her husband, two children, six dogs, one horse, and herd of Angus cattle. As a family, they own and operate Red Bank Cattle Company, a registered Angus seed stock operation. Morie graduated from Texas Tech University with a BS in Speech, Language, and Hearing Sciences, and a Doctorate of Audiology (AuD), but is currently focused on ranching, writing, and raising kids.

also by morie smith

Molly Jones and The Homeplace